ONLY MONSTERS IN THE BUILDING

A CANADIAN WEREWOLF NOVEL

MARK LESLIE

Stark Publishing

Stark Publishing
Waterloo, ON
www.markleslie.ca

Only Monsters in the Building / Mark Leslie -- 1st ed.
Hardcover ISBN: 978-1-989351-90-1
Trade Paperback ISBN: 978-1-989351-92-5
eBook ISBN: 978-1-989351-89-5
Audiobook ISBN: 978-1-989351-91-8

First paper printing April 2024

DEDICATION

For mom and dad, and mom and dad
Jean and Gene & Lorraine and Eddy
with the deepest love and appreciation
for making me who I am

NOTE FOR READERS

All the books in the *Canadian Werewolf* series following Michael Andrews—an ex-pat Canadian trying to make his way in the Big Apple while living with the side-effects of lycanthropy—are meant to be read as stand-alone novels.

However, they do follow a sequential timeline.

If this is your first exposure to the series and you'd like to "get caught up" there is a brief "the story so far" landing page for your convenience.

Please note that this summary page contains spoilers.

markleslie.ca/canadianwerewolfthestorysofar/

Table of Contents

ONLY MONSTERS IN THE BUILDING

Prologue: Betcha Never Thought This Would Happen to You

Upstate New York

Thursday, Sept 7, 2017
5:56 a.m.

I stared at the dead body on the floor in front of me, still not able to believe what I was seeing.

How could my therapist be dead?

And was I responsible for what had happened to him?

Never in my wildest dreams did I imagine I would find myself in this situation. After all, no boy dreams about growing up and turning into a monster. Nor becoming a suspect in such a tangled murder mystery.

But here I was, caught up in the middle of both.

I looked up from the man's lifeless body, slowly panning the faces of my companions. They looked as shocked as I likely also appeared to them. I normally had the benefit of being able to smell the emotions that others gave off, could usually hear the beat of their hearts. But my senses were mostly dulled, and what little I was able to pick up offered none of the usual indicators I relied on to be able to effectively read people.

I stood in complete disbelief wondering how these two things I never imagined I'd be in the middle of came crashing together. Neither therapy nor being a prime suspect in a convoluted murder had been on my own personal bingo card.

As I've said, neither of those are the type of aspirational things a young man dreams about.

Being a policeman, a firefighter, or perhaps even a cowboy. Sure, these are the things the average boy from my era would often fantasize about and share with the people around him.

But no, not this.

'You know what I'd like to be when I grow up, Mom?'

'No, son, what's that?'

'I'd like to be a frustrated, angry, and confused ex-pat Canadian who spills his guts to an overpaid shrink at a secret resort in upstate New York.'

'Oh, isn't that nice.'

'But there's more, Mom, so much more.'

'Really?'

'Yeah. Well, you see, it would be great if what would lead me there would be the fact I'd been bitten by a wolf—and not just a regular wolf, but a werewolf. Who even knew those things were real? —and then spend the rest of my life cursed to morph into a six-foot long grey wolf for about ten days every single month. And when I'm in wolf form, I'd have no connection to my human consciousness. Except, maybe, for fleeting snippets of occasional moments, it would be like a complete blackout to me. I'd be waking up naked, cold, and

scared somewhere, with no idea of where I was, or what I'd done during my time as a wolf.'

'Oh my. That sounds like it could have quite the impact on you.'

'Yeah, and if that's not enough, I wouldn't just turn into a wolf; when walking around in human form I'd still maintain some of my enhanced wolf senses, not to mention extraordinary strength. And I'd live in New York City. Yeah, the place where my favorite superhero, Spider-Man is from. And I'd fight bad guys the way Spidey does.

'Aren't you glad that every two weeks when you got paid from your job at the Mini Mart you'd buy comics that you brought home. And that the Spider-Man comics were the ones I loved the best?'

'You always loved it when I read to you from the time you could barely even sit up on your own. And you took to reading so quickly. You always liked writing, too.'

'I also want to become a writer. A writer living in New York.'

'Oh dear. No, Mikey. Writers don't earn enough money to live. And New York is expensive. No, no, no. If you want to be a writer, you're going to need to make sure you have a **good** job in order to earn a living. Because neither writing nor being a superhero are ways to earn a living.'

'You're right about the fact that fighting bad guys as a vigilante doesn't bring in money. If anything, it'll introduce trouble and hardship. But I'll be one of those rare writers who strikes it rich, Mom. With movie deals, and every book I write becoming a **New York Times** bestseller.'

'That's nice, dear.'

'And I'll meet someone special while researching for one of those books who I fall madly in love with. She'll fall madly in love with me, too. Only, I'll have to lie to her about my wolf curse; because, really, it's a far worse condition than snoring, or suffering from uncontrollable flatulence. But she'll figure it out anyway and be so mad that I deceived her and didn't trust her with my secret that she'll dump me.

'Oh, that's terrible.'

'Yeah. It will be. But she'll come back into my life again later and I'll pine for her for years, because I'll never stop loving her After a few ups and downs, and a mutual trauma we experience we will eventually get together again; but it won't even last a day before we learn that this special woman, I'll be head-over-heels in love with comes from a long line of witches.

'Witches?'

'Oh yeah. I'll learn that not only are werewolves real, but so too are so many other paranormal beings. Including witches. This woman that I practically worship will turn out to be a witch who never really knew her family legacy. The other thing she won't be aware of is a long-time feud from centuries earlier that placed a curse on their clan that prevents the two of us from being together.

'And that, when we should have been fighting this thing together, she'll leave without a single word to me.'

'Oh my.'

'Yeah, and it'll be the final straw that'll drive me to finally seek therapy.'

'But it's good that you go to seek help.'

'Maybe. But that's what'll lead me to be in this cabin in the middle of nowhere with a half dozen other Paranormals, as we're all being treated in group therapy sessions. And that is what will lead me to being a main suspect in our therapist's brutal murder.'

No. Not this.

I shook my head. Of course, I'd launch into a much deeper dive into some made-up memory of chatting with my mother in that imagined fashion at a time like this. Ironic that Dr. Laurier, my therapist, isn't around to appreciate me engaging with one of the fundamental exercises he'd tried to teach me this past week.

But this was definitely *not* the time for such naval-gazing introspection.

I shouldn't be regressing to talking to my mother from the child persona that's buried deep within me.

What I should be doing, instead, is trying to figure out what went down here, and whether I am actually the one responsible for this man's death.

Frustratingly enough—and I know this sounds extremely selfish—but, though it was an excruciating experience, it had started to feel like it was working; that these types of regressive internal discussions were starting to make a positive difference.

Though my senses were muted, I was still able to pick up the most intense of emotions. But there was no such scent of guilt coming from any of the others who stood in a circle around the dead body.

The main emotive smell I was picking up, which layered the air around us, was shock, tinged with a layer of confusion.

But one of us had to be the guilty one.

The question was: which one of us?

I couldn't even be certain whether I was responsible. Last night was a full moon, and it was normal for me to have no memory or knowledge of what the heck I'm up to when I morph into a grey wolf.

That was, after all, one of the reasons I was here.

All the other were-creatures I knew were able to not only control the change between man and beast, but they also retained full consciousness, control, and memory of their time in animal form.

But not me. I've always blacked out. I only remember fleeting glimpses, smells, sounds, tastes, and touch, that linger, as if behind thick cloud cover, in the back of my mind.

Did I do this when I'd blacked out last night?

But I suppose I'm getting ahead of myself here.

To properly examine the situation, what I should really do is go back to the beginning. To how I ended up here among a group of other paranormal creatures in this remote retreat in Upstate New York.

I looked around the room one-by-one at the other patients as we stood in a circle around the dead body of Dr. Brendon Laurier.

At Ellie, whose brow was scrunched up as she, too seemed to be deeply analyzing this situation.

At Shian, whose eyes were wide with shock and fear, reminding me of the first time we'd met.

At Linnaeus, whose hands kept gesturing in the air in front of him, as if he were trying to keep the entire group calm, but without knowing exactly how to do that.

At Chester, whose own body subconsciously followed Linnaeus's every move while absently reaching out to touch the fabric of his sweater, as if wanting to be picked up by the giant of a man.

And finally, at the thin and emaciated face of Vlastislav whose silent tears were thick and cloudy.

One of us had to be guilty of whatever lead to the death of the therapist who was supposed to help us learn to become better functioning Paranormals.

Chapter One: There Are More Things in Heaven, Earth, and Diner Conversations Than Are Dreamt of In Our Philosophy

New York City

Monday, August 28, 2017
11:52 a.m.

"Therapy!"

Buddy J. Samuels blurted this word around a huge mouthful of the sandwich he'd just bitten into. He was the sort of fellow who was never able to hold back on sharing a thought. If an idea, or even some seemingly random strip of trivial tidbits came into his mind, he let it out, regardless of the situation. Also, apparently, regardless of the amount of food in his mouth—or, in this case, the amount of food he was spraying across the table at me.

I'd been used to that by now, of course. Buddy was a little rough around the edges, and he loved the sound of his own voice, but he had been my one reliable and consistent friend ever since I'd moved to New York nearly a decade and a half ago.

And over the years he had developed the uncanny habit of showing up at just the right time.

Like today, for instance.

I'd been moping around my apartment, frustrated with my situation, and unable to get anything productive done. It had been a week since I'd received news from Gail's brother Ben that she'd already left town. And it had been three weeks since the last time I'd seen her.

The hardest thing about my last encounter with her is that I hadn't even been in human form when we'd last locked eyes. Most of what I know from what went down that fateful day was shared with me by Ben, Gail's twin brother.

All I have of those final moments with her are vague, hazy, memories. Elusive snippets at best, of a fight. I don't even remember how Gail's mother died while saving my life. I'm not only responsible for the most traumatic thing to happen to the woman I love, but I have no conscious memory of that moment.

Prior to that fateful day, the only times Gail and I had been together—apart from those twelve hours of re-embracing the special intimacy we'd initially discovered back in 2011—had been in the height of tense drama, and often surrounded by a bunch of evil humans and hordes of demons and other nasty creatures intent on killing us.

In addition to not having Gail around, I also had to deal with the fact that her brother Ben—whom I'd only recently been able to see eye to eye with—was also leaving town.

Ben and I had been planning on continuing to collaborate to find and destroy more of the Baloreye artifacts that carried the curse preventing Gail and I from being together. But he had been called away, back to New Orleans, to the coven of his family.

So, there I was, alone.

Again.

More alone than I'd felt even when I'd first arrived in this city from that small town in mid-Northern Ontario all those years ago.

When the phone rang, I should have known it was Buddy who was calling. Buddy, the traveling salesman who accidentally saved my life from that wolf attack in Upstate New York—his car seeming to magically burst around the corner of the highway just as the wolf had begun to sink its teeth into my forearm.

Buddy, who gave me, a complete stranger who was hitchhiking a ride, trusting me implicitly, and with the openness and kindness of a young child that had not yet been spurned nor corrupted by society. Sure, I was a naïve small-town Canadian, but how would he know that?

Buddy, who'd been there for me; helping me to learn the ropes as this country bumpkin struggled with gaining my city legs.

Buddy, who, from time to time, popped back into my life at the most oddly convenient moments, blathering on about something that seemed, in a tangential way, to be related to whatever issue I was facing.

Buddy, who waltzed right in to distract a small group of thugs who'd taken me as their prisoner.

Buddy, who saved my life after I'd been wandering the streets of Los Angeles in the middle of the night drunk out of my head and, attempting to stop a vicious mugging, ended up becoming their pinch-hitter victim instead.

And Buddy who, until just a few weeks ago, I had no idea actually knew my secret; the werewolf curse that had infected me on that night when we'd first met.

He'd known all along but pretended not to.

It made me wonder if he'd been "playing" at his naïveté and innocence all these years.

I stared across the table at him, then swung my head to glance around at the other inhabitants of the diner.

A man in an expensive and perfectly fitted business suit sat on one of the stools at the counter, engaging in a serious business conversation on the Bluetooth headset tucked around his ear. He was obviously a regular as, earlier, I'd heard the waitress behind the counter greeting him by his name: Paul.

The guy in the orange coveralls sitting directly across from us was plowing into a giant platter of scrambled eggs, bacon, sausage with an intensity and focus as if he were engaging in one of those timed food challenges where, consuming the entire plate in a given time gets a free meal, a nifty not-available-for-retail-sale t-shirt, and your photo on the wall between the restroom doors.

A young woman two tables down from the focused feaster was nursing a bowl of oatmeal and a piece of toast while keeping her nose buried in one of three large textbooks she had stacked on the table in front of her. The sound of her heartbeat and breathing suggested to me she was strung out on caffeine and a lack of sleep; very likely a medical student from the college down the street who was on the tail end of an all-nighter just before a major practical exam.

None of them seemed to be paying any attention to our conversation. At least not that I could tell from the scents and noises I was picking up from them. They were all engaged in their own stories, their own worlds—not at all interested in what was going down between me and Buddy.

"Therapy?" I finally replied.

"Yeah. That's just what you need."

Buddy finished chewing, took a sip of his coffee and then carefully set his cup back down and slowly twisted it so that the handle was perfectly parallel to the edge of the table. Only after he completed this gently orchestrated cup manipulation did he lean forward to return my intent stare.

"It's time to face the fact, Michael," he said, his voice low and serious, "that you're not like other werewolves. It's time to get to the root of your issues. It's time to get some therapy."

"Therapy?" I repeated.

He nodded. "Yes. Therapy. And stop repeating what I'm saying, or you'll turn this conversation into a sad adaptation of an old Abbott and Costello routine."

"Therapy is for the weak," I sighed and looked away.

Oh, who was I kidding? I'd always been weak. In high school I'd been the epitome of the 90-pound weakling. My entire childhood and early adult life I'd been a thoroughbred book-nerd. A bully's prime target. Even after being bitten by that wolf and discovering the incredible strength and enhanced powers I was endowed with, I was never, very consciously, good at confrontation. And I still saw myself as that meek, mild-mannered, and polite Canadian. Many of the battles I'd found myself in the middle of these past few years were more likely due to the alpha wolf blood that coursed through my body than anything else. It seemed like I was benefiting from a newly christened instinct that took over as I launched myself into nefarious situations.

Regardless of all those powers and abilities, I still identified with what it was to be weak.

And Buddy knew that about me.

He had, after all, been playing the role of a fairy Godmother since we had first met. Neither Buddy nor I completely understood the nuances behind this role, other than the fact he was driven by some unseen force and was often acting on some sort of supernatural instinct that drove him to be in specific places and to funnel bits of seemingly random trivia that resulted in helping resolve some of the situations of the charges under his care.

Ultimately, as was his role, he was looking out for me, and he had my best interests at heart; even if he didn't fully understand some of the things he was compelled to say and do.

I knew that what Buddy was suggesting might make sense, that it was likely the right thing to do. But where would I find a therapist I could share my lycanthropic affliction with?

"Besides," I finally said aloud, "where the hell am I going to get the type of therapy someone like me needs? Who can I trust with my secret . . ." I glanced around the room one more time to confirm that none of the other patrons were listening ". . . affliction?"

"That's the thing," Buddy said, and the infectious grin he often sported sprouted on his face. "I know just the right place."

"You do?"

"Yes. Up north, in a spot outside Phoenicia, about a hundred and twenty-five miles north of the city."

Though I'd lived in the United States for a long time, I still thought in terms of kilometers, not miles, and I'd grown up measuring distances by discussing the time it took to get to a place.

"I don't know what a hundred and twenty miles means, Buddy. How long would it take to drive there?"

He pursed his lips for a moment and considered the question before answering. "It's about two and a half hours away. Maybe two hours and forty-five minutes, or even three hours, depending on traffic."

"Okay, so what is it about that spot?"

"It's a retreat, located in a secluded area of Panther Mountain in the Catskills. Nobody is really sure why they have the name that they do. It's possible that panthers might have once inhabited this region, but they are no longer residents of that area. Maybe it was climate change, maybe something else. Did you know that some geologists believe that the mountain is on the site of some ancient meteorite impact crater? In the 1970s a geologist by the name of Isachsen of the New York State Geological Survey at the New York State Museum in Albany spent much of his personal research time and noted a significant sandstone and shale fracture pattern that—"

I interrupted him. "A retreat?"

"What?"

"You said this place is a retreat?"

"Yes, a secret retreat. For Paranormals."

"How can such a place exist?" I stammered. A few months ago, I hadn't even been properly aware that other Paranormal humans existed. And a few weeks ago, I had no idea that my best friend, and the only woman I'd ever truly loved, was one of them. That she'd descended from a long line of witches.

Now, suddenly, it seemed every second person out there was a Paranormal. I felt like I'd suddenly been transplanted into the middle of some sort of comic-book universe.

"As Hamlet said to his dear friend, *there are more things in heaven and earth, Horatio, than are dreamt of in your philosophy.*"

I stared at him. "Yes, Buddy, I'm familiar with the play, and that line. And over these past few years I'm beginning to truly understand what Shakespeare meant."

"Ah, but did you know that, though the later versions of the text read 'in your philosophy' as if Hamlet is critiquing his friend's closed mind about the possibility that the ghost of Hamlet's father is actually walking about, that's not how it originally appeared? In the First Folio edition, and, in The Arden Shakespeare **Hamlet: Revised Edition** published just last year, the text reads 'in *our* philosophy.' This lends more to the idea that Hamlet is not making a personal attack on his friend's limited beliefs about the world than he is acknowledging the limits of human knowledge and science."

"No, I didn't know that."

Buddy often liked to ramble on about seemingly trivial tidbits, interjecting them into conversations, turning what should be a short back and forth exchange to more of a one-sided lengthy monologue.

Ever since, just a few weeks ago, I'd come to understand that some of those things he spouted off were designed by some unknown paranormal force to influence me and help me learn something, or make the right decision when I faced a challenge, I could never be sure if I was listening to the ramblings of a buffoon running off at the mouth, or some wizened advice that carried some hidden message.

As part of my studying English Language and Literature in university I'd dug into many of Shakespeare's plays and knew the concept of sanity and insanity were a major element in this one.

Was Buddy's bringing up Hamlet suggesting that my own sanity was slipping?

"This place in the Catskills," I said. "How do you know about it?"

Buddy shook his head. "It all just came to me this morning when I woke up. Where it was, what it was about, even the number to call to make arrangements for you. So I called. And the plans have already been set in motion. A car will be coming to pick you up outside The Algonquin Hotel this Saturday morning to take you there."

I shook my head. "You made these arrangements without even asking me?"

"Would you go if I had asked?"

"No. Of course not."

"But don't you want to know more about who and what you are? Wouldn't it be good, for the first time, to be able to spend some time learning more about the paranormal world you've been living with one foot in all these years?"

I thought about how, since the early 2000s when I arrived in New York, I'd first turned into a wolf and, confused, and terrified about what was happening to me,

I felt I had nobody to talk to about it. I mean, who would understand? And if anyone found out, wouldn't they just try to lock me up in some cage in a lab somewhere so they could examine me, perform experiments on me, dissect me?

For years I'd bumbled through life, trying my best to live with this curse; and these abilities, keeping it a closely guarded secret, never letting anyone in. It's the reason I'd initially lost Gail all those years ago. And it had truly only been in the last several months that it felt like I wasn't alone in this; that others knew about my secret.

Heck, most of those others—Gail's brother Ben, her best friend Isabeau, her entire family—understood so much about the Paranormal world, while I was only beginning to learn about it.

Maybe it would be best for me to have someone to talk to about it; to meet some other Paranormals without it being in some life-or-death situation.

Buddy reached across the table and grabbed my arm, squeezing it gently. "Look at me," he said. "You know I'm right. This is for the best, Michael."

"I know," I stared down into my own coffee cup. "I need to do something. And why not this? I mean, I've done everything to try to live a normal life ever since this has happened to me."

Buddy laughed. "That *normal life* hasn't been working out all that well for you, has it?"

"No," I grinned. "Especially not this summer, at least. "I've likely seen more of you since June this year than I normally see you in any given year."

"And I've seen more of *you* than a heterosexual man raised in a world of Archie Bunker sensibilities is comfortable with," Buddy said with a bemused sound in his voice. I knew he'd been referring to how he'd nursed me back to health when I was beaten half-to-death by a bunch of thugs in Los Angeles, which required him removing my soiled and bloody clothes, and, just a few weeks ago when he'd met me at sunrise in Central Park with my cell phone and other personal effects where I'd awoken from a night as a wolf, as I do, entirely naked.

"You've still never explained much about your own special abilities. Or why you're constantly showing up and saving my ass, or offering tidbits of wisdom like some sort of—"

"Hairy Wolf Mother?"

I laughed. When we'd last met, I'd said it felt like he was as a type of Fairy Godmother, but Buddy had come up with that more apropos adaptation of the term.

"Yeah. That. You never did explain it."

"That's because I don't understand it myself. We've been through this, Michael. Things just come to me." He tapped a stubby finger on the side of his head. "I do read a lot; constantly. It's one of my passions. I listen to a ton of non-fiction audiobooks, podcasts, and programs on NPR when I'm in the car alone. And I spend endless hours traveling across the US. When I'm alone at restaurants or coffee shops, I'm listening to conversations. I'm constantly consuming things about the world. I take things in, absorb them. I've always been thirsty for information, for news, for historical details, for gossip. All of it.

"And sometimes, in that swirling mess of things I've absorbed, an inspiration comes to me. I'm compelled to spew one of those nuggets of information to a particular person at a specific time.

"Take, for instance, when I approached you back in July in front of Rockefeller Center and offered you a slew of insights into the underground of New York City. I was in town for an underground construction worker conference and was compelled to relay a bunch of information I'd picked up from working at that event. I had no idea why; I just felt something in me driving me to get to Rockefeller and when I got there to share that information with you. The burning desire left once I relayed that information, and so when you took off, not having time to have lunch with me it was all good."

I remembered it clearly. When Buddy and I had been chatting that day Gail had texted me that the thing we'd all been staked out and waiting for was going down. So I took off.

"But not long after, without knowing how or why, I figured out a way to hack my way into your group cell phone chat." He paused and winced, as if he'd just heard a particularly nasty noise like nails scratching down a chalkboard. "And to share the lyrics from that Simon and Garfunkel song with you."

I nodded. "And that led us to the spot where we really needed to be to intercept Marco and the other PFA members."

"But that was it. I had nothing else. And I had no idea why I was doing it. It's like this dominant voice; no, not a voice, but a feeling—an all-consuming feeling—compels me to be somewhere, to share some sort of information with a specific person. And then, once it's done, it all fades back to normal."

"Yes," I said. "But you never told me that. You never explained it."

Buddy closed his eyelids tight together and his face tightened as if he'd just bitten into an extremely bitter lemon. He was breathing in short shallow breaths and his heart started beating rapidly, like he was in an extreme amount of pain.

"Are you okay?"

"Uh, yeah," he said in a low voice. "I just. Ahh, I'm getting this shooting pain. Migraine-like. Hits me right behind the eyes. I think it's because we're talking about this. It's like something's telling me to *not* talk about this with you."

I reached out and put a hand over top of his. "Okay. Got it. We don't need to get into it. I understand that, just like I don't know why I can't control my changes, nor maintain my consciousness when in wolf form, you don't know why you have these insights and compulsions."

He nodded, and his breathing and heartbeat began to return to normal.

"Let's just roll with it, shall we?" he said. "Let's just take a lesson from Del Griffith and *go with the flow.*"

I grinned at Buddy. He often reminded me of the character John Candy played opposite Steve Martin in that 1980s film *Planes, Trains and Automobiles.* Of course, the fact that Buddy had quoted from the movie numerous times over the years kept that comparison of him to the Canadian actor always top of mind. Buddy looked like an interesting combination of John Candy meets Buddy Hacket with a sprinkling of Lou Costello. But much of his character was like the one Candy played as Del Griffith, the gregarious traveling salesman in that classic John Hughes film. Buddy could have been the lovechild of Del Griffith and Cliff Clavin, the know-it-all trivia-spouting mailman on the television sitcom *Cheers.*

Because Buddy had quoted from that John Candy/Steve Martin film so many times over the years, I knew the line, and scene, he was speaking about.

"*Go with the flow,*" I said, "*Like a twig on the shoulders of a mighty stream.*"

Buddy nodded and then put on his best impression of actor Pat Morita as Mr. Miyagi from another 1980s film, *The Karate Kid.* "I've trained you well, Michaelsan." That character was also apropos for our relationship. The advice, and the random trivia he spewed at me was like the "wax on/wax off" type tasks the karate master had his young student engage in. They seemed to have nothing to do with the martial art, but the movements were later used as a type of muscle memory skill in young Daniel's fights.

Over the years, Buddy had never steered me wrong; even if he himself had no idea why he was telling me the things he shared.

And perhaps this retreat was one of them.

"So . . . this retreat," I said, slowly nodding my head. "You never knew about it before today, did you?"

"No. It just came to me. I mean, the information about the Catskills and Panther Mountain are among the many things I'd read about years ago. But this secret location, and what it is, that came out of nowhere."

"As it does."

"You really should go do this, Michael."

"I know. And I will. But this all seems like so much."

"You are hurt. You have lost. Lost battles. Lost love. You blame yourself for the death of Darina. You also blame yourself for having killed a terrorist. You are angry. And alone. And scared."

I nodded.

"In *Karate Kid III* when Daniel was flailing out of control, when he was angry, and reacting with unadulterated violence against his aggressors, and uncertain if he could ever heal from it, Mr. Miyagi compared his student to a Bonsai tree that had been snapped in half. He said '*Inside you have strong root. No need nothing except what inside you to grow.*' Do you know what that means?"

I shrugged my shoulders.

"It means that if your root, the center of your being, your spirit, is strong, then you could heal, you could mend, you could grow, again. But I don't think you can do that without going back to those roots, back to things that might even be underlying elements of your life well prior to your encounter with the wolf. If you're able to dig down, find that part of yourself, you can restore the balance and find the equilibrium to keep going.

"It's not going to be easy for you to do this. It's going to get a lot harder before it becomes better. There's much to overcome that has nothing to do with you and Gail and has everything to do with the man inside the beast. You've denied the beast. But prior to that, you've also denied the man."

"Yeah. I'm starting to see that."

"It won't be easy. But it's something you must do in order to grow back up. And you will."

I nodded and grinned.

"Yes. I will."

And for the first time in several weeks, I felt a bit of a spark of hope.

Interlude: Therapy Session
There Must Be 50 Words That Mean Obsession

Excerpt from therapy session recordings of Dr. Brendon Laurier

Sunday, September 3, 2017
10:04 p.m.

DR. LAURIER: *Tell me about your obsession with Gail Sommers, Michael.*

MICHAEL ANDREWS: *I don't have an obsession with Gail.*

LAURIER: *You don't?*

ANDREWS: *No. I mean, I'm in love with her. I have always been deeply in love with her. From the first minute I laid eyes on her I knew there was something extraordinary between us. I knew we were destined to be together. I'd never felt like that with anyone before. From the moment I saw her, I felt myself* *sinking so willingly into something that was life changing. I felt myself falling madly in love with her from almost the very beginning. And I never stopped loving her. Not once in the half-dozen years between that special 'us' we'd discovered.*

LAURIER: And that doesn't strike you as a little fixated?

ANDREWS: [Mutters something indecipherable]

LAURIER: What was that? I didn't quite hear.

ANDREWS: Okay, maybe it was a little obsessive. But what's the point of talking about it. I mean, the woman I loved more than anything in this world left me. Even though I know she loves me as much as I love her. But she's done it twice now.

LAURIER: That must be devastating.

ANDREWS: It is.

LAURIER: What happened the first time she left?

ANDREWS: I was a mess, of course. But I suppose it was inevitable. I mean, how could I expect to have any serious long-term relationship with a woman when living with the curse that I have?

LAURIER: You pined for her?

ANDREWS: Yes.

LAURIER: You longed for her?

ANDREWS: Of course. Who wouldn't? You've seen pictures of her. She's an absolute knock-out. But she's also clever, witty, brilliant, and so incredibly observant. No, not just observant, but intuitive. And resourceful. Gail is such a remarkable woman, and yet she's not cocky nor too self-assured. She's incredibly humble. It's like she isn't even aware of her own magnificence; just how impressive and captivating she can be. Just how spectacular a person she is.

LAURIER: Yes, she is a very attractive woman. And from what you've shared about her, a genuinely unique and decent person.

ANDREWS: Gail is the best. I loved her at first glance. I never stopped loving her. Not even when I found myself falling head over heels in love with Lex.

LAURIER: Hmm. [Long pause, the sound of a pen scratching noise in the background] *I'm just making a note, so we don't forget to explore this other aspect of duality; that you claim to have been in love with two different women at the same time. I think that's something worth exploring in more depth.*

ANDREWS: I don't really understand it, but yeah, I fell for Lex even though I was still in love with Gail. Ever since Gail had come back, I realized the huge mistake I had made letting her walk out of my life. She knew how I felt. I shared it with her again and again.

LAURIER: *Was she ready to return to a romantic relationship?*

ANDREWS: *No, she wasn't. And every time I tried to bring it up, she kept saying that's not what she wanted. But I could tell that she still loved me, that she still wanted me as intensely as I still wanted her. You know, it's one thing to love someone and to know that they don't love you. That's painful, but it's something you can move on from. How do you move on from knowing that the person you're madly in love with, that you know you are destined to be with, feels as deeply as you do, bears the richness of the same love, and yet denies that longing, represses those feelings, and refuses to act upon them? When you understand what Gail and I had discovered in one another, how could a person throw that away?*

LAURIER: *It must have been painful to remain platonic friends with her despite those intense feelings.*

ANDREWS: *Yeah. Of course. Like I said, Gail is a remarkable woman. It crushed my heart to have her that close, to know how she felt about me, but to not be able to act upon that mutual love. But I'd rather have her there, at arm's length. I might not be able to hold her, or love her in the way I wanted, but I could still have her in my life.*

LAURIER: You embraced the pain. The self-torture. That's rather interesting.

ANDREWS: What do you mean?

LAURIER: I was just observing.

ANDREWS: Do you think I enjoyed doing that to myself? That I enjoyed the agony I lived with every day?

LAURIER: Could it have been a distraction from an underlying pain that you hadn't yet come to terms with?

ANDREWS: [Laughs] What is it, Doc? Are you going to tell me I did that to myself because of my belief that my mommy never truly loved me?

LAURIER: Is that what YOU are saying, Michael?

ANDREWS: I don't know.

LAURIER: Would you rather talk about your mother right now?

ANDREWS: No. I want to talk about Gail.

LAURIER: Okay. Tell me more about Gail.

ANDREWS: I love Gail more than I'd ever loved anyone in my life. I need her. I want her. Gail and I are soulmates. And the fact is, we both knew that. Except, I was the only one who was willing to act upon it.

LAURIER: And yet, you acted upon feelings for someone else, didn't you?

ANDREWS: You mean Lex?

LAURIER: Yes. Alexandria Jones. If you were so fixated on Gail, why is it that you fell for the first woman who showed an interest in you?

ANDREWS: That's not true. That's not true at all. Lex wasn't the first woman to show an interest in me. I'd had plenty of women interested in me. And, c'mon, I'm not just being overly confident when I say this. I can tell, Doc. I can read a woman's sexual desire in her heartbeat; from the emotive scents she gives off. Heck, just a couple of days before I met Lex in Los Angeles, I struck up a wonderful conversation with a beautiful and charming woman at the airport. And she was really into me. But I managed to keep my own response to that in check. So no, I didn't fall for the first woman who showed an interest in me.

LAURIER: So why Alexandria?

ANDREWS: Lex was something else. We just clicked. There was something intriguing between us. It was so similar to the way that Gail and I clicked, you know.

LAURIER: Naturally.

ANDREWS: What do you mean, naturally?

LAURIER: Alexandria had paranormal abilities. You had that in common with her.

ANDREWS: She did. But I didn't know that at the time. I just knew that when I was with her, I felt . . .

LAURIER: Yes?

ANDREWS: I felt something truly unique. Something . . . I don't know. Powerful.

LAURIER: Something you hadn't felt since you first met Gail?

ANDREWS: Yes. [Long pause]. It's the same way I was smitten with Gail immediately upon meeting her. Gail was great. So, of course I was smitten. She was stunning, fun-loving, and charming, and smart. She was compassionate, and genuine. All the things I love in a person.

LAURIER: You forgot to mention Paranormal.

ANDREWS: Yes. She was. But, like I said, I didn't know that.

LAURIER: No, you didn't know that, but would you say you felt it?

ANDREWS: What do you mean?

LAURIER: You mentioned in a previous session that Alexandria had a very specific effect on you, something besides mere attraction.

ANDREWS: When I was hanging out with Lex, even though I didn't realize it until much later, I was a normal human again. My werewolf curse was gone. Lex had the power to nullify the paranormal, just based on her proximity to people.

LAURIER: [Pen scratching]. Perhaps the love you felt for Lex was how she returned you to a state of innocence. When you were with Lex you were no longer Michael Andrews, the man cursed with turning into a wolf based on the phases of the moon. You were Michael Andrews, the writer. Michael Andrews the Mundane.

ANDREWS: I was.

LAURIER: What was it like?

ANDREWS: Did you know that prior to Lex coming into my life, I'd never once witnessed a full moon over the city of New York? It was incredible. I could be myself with Lex. Just me. Not that other being that I turned into and had no control of. Not the other aspect of myself that terrified me.

LAURIER: [Pause. Pen scratching] *So Alexandria had you feeling good about the real you. The 'old' Michael. That pre-New York City Michael. What happened in Los Angeles?*

ANDREWS: *Los Angeles was more like some sort of fantasy. An adventure away from home. It was almost like one of those 'what happens in Vegas stays in Vegas' type of escapes from reality. I mean, c'mon, this was Hollywood, after all. The land of make-believe.*

LAURIER: *What happened when it was time to leave that fantasy realm?*

ANDREWS: *I was back in New York. The city, and the reality that I shared with Gail. And everything came crashing down. Gail was there at the airport from the moment we landed. Apparently, she'd snapped out of whatever it was that was preventing her from acting upon her love for me. At the time I thought it might have been a case of 'absence makes the heart grow fonder.'*

LAURIER: *But it wasn't that, was it?*

ANDREWS: *No. I later learned it was the effect of a spell placed on a talisman that Gail's friend Isabeau had planted. It was preventing Gail from acting upon her love for me.*

LAURIER: *So you found yourself back in New York. Gail still loved you. And she was ready to act upon it. But you'd already fallen for Alexandria.*

ANDREWS: Yeah. Like I said, I found myself madly in love with two different women at the same time.

LAURIER: How did you handle that conundrum?

ANDREWS: You mean apart from wishing I could go back and tell my seventeen-year-old loser self that one day he'd have two beautiful and sexy women interested in him at the same time? That for a short time he'd feel like Jack Tripper.

[Long silence on the tape.]

ANDREWS: You know, Jack Tripper was the character John Ritter played in that sitcom. Three's Company. *Where he was roommates with two beautiful women. Janet and Chrissy.* [Singing] *"Come and knock on our door . . . we've been waiting for you."*

[Long silence.]

ANDREWS: [Singing] *"Where the kisses are hers and hers . . ."* [Speaking] *". . . and his."*

[Long silence.]

ANDREWS: Because Jack Tripper was a bit of a lady's man. And . . . when I was young I always . . .

[Long silence. Sound of throat clearing.]

ANDREWS: Okay, I get it. I've gotten off track. What was the question?

LAURIER: How did you handle that situation?

ANDREWS: One day I went to see Gail at her store.

LAURER: Did Alexandria know you did that?

ANDREWS: I don't understand the question.

[Long silence.]

ANDREWS: I did not share that information with Lex.

LAURIER: You lied to Alexandria. As you once lied to Gail.

ANDREWS: [Mumbles something under his breath]

LAURIER: Did you want Alexandria to be angry with you? Maybe even break things off with you?

ANDREWS: Why the hell would I want that? I'd just discovered something truly remarkable with Lex. Not to mention, when Lex was around, I could be a normal human again.

LAURIER: Is there something inside you that seeks out excitement? Does part of you enjoy causing some trouble?

ANDREWS: I already told you: I'm Canadian. Responsibility is very important to me. I've always believed that—

LAURIER: 'With great power comes great responsibility.' Yes, yes, I know. You've mentioned Spider-Man. [Sound of flipping pages] Several times. But for someone who takes on so much, who works so hard to always be responsible, isn't it a bit of a relief when you can push that burden on to someone else?

ANDREWS: I'm not sure what you're getting at.

LAURIER: Earlier you called Gail observant.

ANDREWS: Yeah. Gail has this way of just knowing, you know. Like she has a sixth sense about her. I'm pretty good at being able to read people based on their scents, their heartbeats, those little things the average person can't tell. But it seems to come natural to Gail.

LAURIER: Of course it does. That's part of her special abilities. She's a Seer. Even before she became aware of her heritage, that power was present in her.

ANDREWS: Yeah. It was one of the things I always found fascinating about her. Gail just knew things; she knew people. There was no point in lying to her because she could always see through it, you know.

LAURIER: And yet you lied to her. You deceived her.

ANDREWS: [Unintelligible murmur]

LAURIER: What was that?

ANDREWS: I didn't want to lie to her.

LAURIER: So why did *you lie to her, Michael? Why did you attempt to deceive her when you knew that she was able to see through your deception?*

ANDREWS: Why are we talking about Gail and Lex? I thought we were here to talk about my werewolf curse. Aren't we trying to figure out why I don't maintain my consciousness when in wolf form?

LAURIER: Do I go into your writing space and tell you how to do your job?

ANDREWS: [Unintelligible murmur]

[Long silence]

LAURIER: Michael, sometimes therapy is like trying to stare at the sun. The light can be too bright if we stare right into it, and we're blinded to what's there. Sometimes, we're best to take glances at it. Or to ease into it. When you first wake up in complete darkness, and you turn on a bright light, you have to shield your eyes from the brightness and allow your pupils to have their adjustment period as you eventually acclimatize yourself. Understanding ourselves can work the same way. Often, we can only get to the root of something by traversing a careful path around it, slowly working our way inwards, until our eyes and our minds adjust to the concept at hand.

ANDREWS: I suppose that makes sense.

LAURIER: So, tell me, Michael. Why did you lie to Gail? You called her [sound of page turning] clever. Resourceful. Intuitive. Why did you keep your werewolf nature a secret from her, particularly when you knew that she would be able to see right through your deception?

ANDREWS: I don't know.

LAURIER: You don't know?

ANDREWS: No.

LAURIER: I think you do know.

ANDREWS: You do?

LAURIER: Yeah. I think you know but you're not ready to admit it. Not to me. And perhaps not to yourself.

ANDREWS: I had my reasons for lying to Gail.

LAURIER: I know you did.

ANDREWS: I never told Gail about my werewolf curse in order to protect her.

LAURIER: To protect her?

ANDREWS: Yeah. From me. I mean, what kind of relationship could we truly have when I turned into a monster with no control over who I am or what I do? What if being with me would put Gail into some sort of jeopardy?

LAURIER: That's a good point. You lied to her in order to protect her from your werewolf nature?

ANDREWS: Yeah.

LAURIER: Then why do you continue to lie to yourself about your werewolf nature?

Chapter Two: What Is It with Me, and Women, and Mayhem?

Upstate New York

Saturday, September 2, 2017
11:49 a.m.

I spent most of the first two hours of the ride in the back of the dark gray 2016 RAV4 stuck in my own head, whirling around with endless loops of anxiousness over the fact I was about to be thrust into the middle of a group of other people who would suddenly know my secret.

But as the vehicle passed over a bridge that crossed a narrow part of what appeared to be a wide river, it was one of only three times that the driver of my vehicle spoke.

"This body of water is the Ashokan Reservoir," he said in a classical New Jersey accent, where the word *water* became *wattah* and in his version also rhymed with *rez-eh-vwah*. "It's one of several reservoirs that feeds into New York City. Beautiful, ain't it?"

He kept talking, but his mention of reservoirs reminded me of the last two clashes I'd had in July and August; two of the biggest battles of my life. And both of them ending with the loss of a woman I loved.

I mulled over memories of that as I stared across the large expanse of glass-like water to the mountains in the west that rose high enough to kiss the low-lying clouds.

"What the hell?" Buddy had shared that this was supposed to be a retreat. That term usually suggested a place to get away from it all, to withdraw from the stress of the world, to think, to study, to even pray perhaps, far from the daily duties and responsibilities of the world.

But if passing over this body of water, and its reminder of what I was attempting to retreat from was any indication, I'd be forced to dive headfirst into the entire reason I needed to come here in the first place.

And a good part of it had to do with Gail, and with Lex.

With losing them both.

The other part, of course, had to do with this werewolf blood coursing through my body. And the fact that I had no control over that other part of my being. Why was I the only werewolf who didn't have control over both halves of myself?

What the hell was wrong with me?

This retreat—and of course, the irony that I was doing the exact opposite of retreating from reality by coming here—would, hopefully sort it all out.

And to start with, I was going to have to face the fact that I couldn't take the default position of keeping my werewolf curse a secret from the entire world.

For nearly the first dozen years after I was bitten, I hadn't told a soul about my affliction. I didn't know that Buddy had always known. So, I hadn't told him, even though it would have made sense for me to do so.

Gail was the first person to learn my secret. But she had figured it out entirely on her own.

Not long after that, I found myself sharing my secret with four other people. Now, this driver was taking me to a secret resort in Upstate New York where I'd not only meet a therapist who'd already been provided a file with a background on me, but also a half dozen other patients who were also going to know that thing I'd held close to my chest for fourteen years.

I mean, at this point, why wouldn't I want to just take out an ad in the *New York Times* and publicly announce it, or stage a major press release in the middle of Times Square?

I could see the headlines now.

New York Times Bestselling Mystery Author Revealed to Be A Monster.

No, there'd likely be something a little cheekier in the headlines, particularly given the click-bait style of head-lines for online article sharing.

Bestselling Mystery Author Bites Off More Than Even a Big Bad Wolf Can Chew.

Hmm, maybe something funnier?

Big Bad Wolf Blows Down Fragile House of Cards for Mystery Writer.

Or maybe I should consider an article that might fit in a paper like *The National Enquirer*. Yeah, some over-the-top exploitative type of—

I stopped myself.

What was I doing?

I was doing what I usually did in such a situation. Skirting the issue at hand while letting myself go down some inane and self-indulgent rabbit-hole that really led me nowhere except right back where I'd been in the first place.

It was something I did in my writing too. And it was something that the very first editor I'd worked with—and every single one since—constantly chided me about and tried to coach out of my writing. One of my editors, who initially went into detail explaining a sentence or two; or perhaps even an entire string of paragraphs, could be cut, because I had already explained the details a line or a page or two earlier. After a while, likely getting writer's cramp from doing it so often, he just wrote the words COULD CUT THIS with an arrow pointing back up to where that exact same thing had already been shared, expressed, explained, or revealed.

I still have many of those printed drafts of my novels. I haven't been able to get rid of them. Perhaps I'm not just a hoarder when it comes to words on a page, but I do a bit of hoarding in the physical world too. And many of the hoarded pages have the aforementioned COULD

CUT THIS and those huge, curved arrows riddled throughout the pages. If one added up the miles of those arrows pointing back to repeated elements on the entirety of the novels he edited for me, one might be able to circumnavigate the island of Manhattan with that distance.

I'd circle the drain for far too long, believing I was creating suspense, or tension, or some other effect. But it was clear to my editors, to the readers, to virtually everyone but me, the direction of where that scene was going. It was painfully obvious. But I had the habit of taking that proverbial pen on yet another lap, another tour of duty, another circular jaunt. I was like a pilot who, upon efficiently getting the plane to the destination city, didn't just go in for a landing, but circled overhead for a while, as if to perhaps savor the view.

That type of constant pause for pontification in my thinking—and, naturally, in my writing—was something I remember speaking with a fellow Canadian author about. Terry Fallis, who had a knack for writing deliciously clever novels, many of them involving a fish out of water situation—which was a well of great material for humor and satire—had shared something about that when the two of us were on a panel together at Book Expo America a couple of years back. Terry said that he was from the school of writers who believed the following: *Why use five or six words to describe something when twenty-five or thirty would do?*

But perhaps this was something I did for a reason.

Heck, maybe being here for this group therapy session would help me better understand that, and so many other things about myself that have simply eluded me over the years.

And, hopefully, whoever the person they have treating us here—all I know is the name that Buddy gave me, Brendon Laurier, plus an assurance that he's not only discrete, but the best at what he does—will be able to offer me some sort of tool I can use to deal with the overwhelming sense of grief I'd been walking around with lately.

Sitting in this vehicle for these past two hours has reminded me of just how ultimately powerful the loss of Lex and Gail within the space of about a single month has impacted me.

And I haven't really stopped; not since I first met and fell in love with Lex in Los Angeles back in June. This past summer was a runaway train sort of a time, involving all kinds of evil I didn't even realize existed, not to mention a mountain of confusion related to those two women I loved.

What *was* it with me and women, and mayhem?

Perhaps this was something I would be able to unpack once I started this therapy with Dr. Laurier.

A few miles after we had crossed that massive expanse of water, we left the main highway for a side road that ran through the outskirts of a small town, then meandered beside a river for a while as it went deeper and deeper into a heavily wooded area. Though we had passed several minor side roads, many of them unpaved, we hadn't seen any sort of service station nor evidence of civilization for a while. But now, as the car slowed down even more, he had taken us down a much narrower dirt road that twisted and turned as we made our way to a higher elevation. Then we decelerated at one curve, more the way one might do when turning off a road and into a driveway, rather than navigating a turn, and he aimed the car directly into the thick brush on the side of the road along a steep drop as he appeared to consult a small flatscreen device.

For a moment I worried that he was going to run us right off the road, into those bushes, and what would most certainly be a suicidal plunge down an impossible incline, but my nostrils didn't pick up any sort of heartbeat change or emotive sense that would indicate the heightened emotions that would go along with that.

Still, my eyes told a different story.

"What the—" I began to say, but he held the back of his hand up as if to tell me to settle back, and that all was okay.

As the car lurched forward, the front of the vehicle nosing into the thick and thorny underbrush, the leaves, branches, and prickly thorns wavered slightly like some flickering mirage. And we drove straight through them. Despite the minor ripples of the visual effect, I still winced as we passed through the ghostly underbrush. The car tilted down, but not as dramatically as the landscape had suggested, and after about thirty seconds of moving through the dense foliage—the light around us dissolving away in a way that was not dissimilar to the way it gets dark when a plane flies through a thick expanse of clouds—we emerged on the other side, descending down a road that, while steep, was nowhere near as precarious as it had appeared from the other side.

The driver didn't say anything, and I was still shocked at what had just happened as I looked back up the dirt road that disappeared into the thick wooded area we had impossibly driven through.

Sure, I'd seen magic recently; more magic than I had ever even known was possible. But this was something quite unique.

I know, Buddy had assured me that this secret location was in a secure spot that no normal human would ever be able to discover. And I'd be here with a very intimate group of other Paranormals as we each unpacked our individual trauma.

But, knowing what I knew—only recently, of course—is that not every Paranormal out there was a peace-loving and apologetic Canadian, or at least on the side that would rather do no harm. Some of them had nefarious intent. And how was I to know where exactly everyone in this group stood on the spectrum of good versus evil?

I'm normally an optimistic type of person; one who sees the goodness in people, and in situations. I tend to not dwell on the darkness, or, when faced with it, I enjoy—like Mr. Rogers—looking for the helpers, or the positive in a situation.

But as I watched the thick bushes recede behind us and we drove deeper down that steep road and into the dense cover of the woods, I couldn't help but succumb to the overwhelming sense of dread that came over me.

Chapter Three: The Cabin at the End of the Long and Winding Road

Upstate New York

Saturday, September 2, 2017
12:23 p.m.

After traversing another couple of miles that meandered up and down hills and around turns like some backwoods roller coaster, the dirt road forked into a large open area. About one hundred yards straight ahead was a massive two-story cabin on the other side of what looked like a large man-made pond that stood before it. On the second floor was a wide expanse of balcony with a railing made from logs underneath the peaked roof overhang of the building. The balcony looked out over the pond and the manicured lawn that led all the way to the road on either side.

The driver moved our vehicle along the right fork of the road that maintained a wide distance of perhaps the width of a football field away from what appeared to be the back of the huge building. The pond connected to a narrow strip of water that ran along the back of the structure. Six windows of various sizes spotted the flat back of the building on the ground floor at random intervals, and on the second floor were another half dozen much smaller matching windows evenly spaced across the expanse.

Not a single person was visible anywhere on the expanse of grounds at either the side or the back of the building as our vehicle slowly crunched along the single-lane gravel road. And as our vehicle continued along, the huge log-framed building disappeared behind a thick copse of mostly red maple trees so quickly that I wondered if the building itself might have been a mirage.

The vehicle slowly moved through the thick wooded area for several hundred feet before it began a gradual turn left, where there was another opening on either side with two buildings that were much smaller than the log cabin. The larger one, which was about twenty-five feet wide and a single story, was built from what appeared to be smaller logs, and had an A frame wood-slat roof. The other smaller one—which was less than half the width of the other—was perhaps only ten feet high with a flat roof and reddish-brown painted wooden walls and no windows. Beside it was an even smaller ten-by-ten-foot shed painted a lighter shade of brown.

Those buildings also disappeared behind foliage as we continued to curve to the left. The narrow road was again surrounded by trees on both sides as we moved along, and then returned to a large opening that revealed the other side of the stately building we had passed on the other side.

To the left of this building was a large inground pool, tennis and volleyball courts, and a series of benches along a meandering pathway that led under and around oak, elm and maple trees that grew out of the beautifully manicured grass and up to the main entrance to the cabin. The front of the cabin had a far more regal and grander look to it. The entire front featured a deck about a foot and a half off the ground that ran the entire front of it with a log wood constructed railing. In the middle of the building was a set of three stairs that led to a beautiful wooden double doorway with a pair of arched stained glass transom windows that formed a half circle above them. The second floor of this side of the building featured four small upper-level balconies with similar log railings.

"And here we are," the driver announced—like it wasn't already obvious—as our vehicle pulled to a stop parallel to the main entrance. The back door locks clicked off, and I took the opportunity to slide out of the back seat and to stretch.

From a set of bushes about thirty feet or so off to our left, out stepped a man who could have been the older brother of actor Jason Sudeikis from Saturday Night Live. This had to be Dr. Brendon Laurier, our retreat host.

The warmth in his smile struck me from even this distance—he radiated an aura of comfort. As this fresh feeling of calm washed over me, I realized that, apart from that momentary spark of hope I felt when Buddy mentioned this retreat at breakfast the other day, I'd actually been dreading what this experience might be like.

"You must be Michael Andrews," Dr. Laurier said as he approached me with a beaming smile on his face. One of the first things I noticed is that it was difficult to get a bead on his heartbeat or emotions. The sound and smells were there, but they kept shifting like some sort of auditory and olfactory kaleidoscope.

Prior to the past couple of months, had something like that happened before, I would have chalked it up to there being something wrong with me. Whenever I caught some sort of nasty bug—which never lasted long due to my enhanced constitution—or I had too much to drink, my senses and enhanced abilities went out of whack. Most often, though, they were muted. But because of my recent experiences, and learning of the possibilities of spells being cast and associated with a location that could affect a person, I wondered if there was some sort of enchantment placed upon these grounds that interfered with my ability to leverage those powers.

What I experienced was more like those times when I'd been unable to read Buddy. It would make sense, after all. The entrance to the road leading up to here was enchanted by some sort of illusory spell. Why wouldn't this place have some sort of magical enhancement that might work to protect the personal privacy of the clientele? We did, after all, exist in a world that would likely not do well to know that us Paranormals not only existed, but walked among them.

As I was adjusting to the dizziness of not having those senses, Dr. Laurier reached me.

"Welcome, Michael, to Mandrake Falls Retreat." He reached out and took my right hand in his own, clasping his left overtop of mine. His hands were soft, uncalloused, and warm. His touch, like his voice, and his smile, were a complimentary composition of comfort that calmed me.

"Thank you," I said. "And you must be Dr. Laurier."

"Y—" Dr. Laurier started to say and then seemed to choke on something. His eyes bulged out as he released my hand with his right and brought it up to his chest. "I mean," he said, and his voice waivered slightly, a lot less deep than it had been a moment ago. "Welcome to Mandrake Falls Retreat. I am . . ."

His voice faded off again and he took an unsteady step back.

"I am . . .

"I . . . uh . . . that is to say . . .

"Iyam . . ."

With every new thing he said, Dr. Laurier's voice became far softer and had the hint of a lyrical Celtic lilt to it.

"Oh, feck," He said. "Damn, damn, damn." And by this time, his voice was distinctly female with a slight Irish accent.

Suddenly, Dr. Laurier was no longer a middle aged, bearded white man. He was a petite, and very cute twenty-something Black woman with a pixie haircut and a grin that made me think of a young Halle Berry.

"I'm sorry," the young woman said to me, with a bit of an Irish lilt that almost rhymed with *airy,* scrunching up her face as she blushed, now even more adorable. "I was just having a laugh on ya."

I stood looking at her, still confused. Was Dr. Laurier some sort of shape-shifter himself? He was an attractive man for sure, but I much preferred this cute female form he was now in.

And I simultaneously felt an unexplainable force radiating from her that seemed to pull at something deep inside me. I closed my eyes and took a deep breath as I tried to shake that feeling off.

"Yes," I finally said. "I'm Michael Andrews."

I offered my hand again, and the woman reached out to take it. "Pleased to meet you, Michael, I'm—"

"Ellie!" a familiar male voice called out, interrupting her. It was the same voice I'd just heard coming from the person I was shaking hands with. I looked over to the front entrance and saw the exact same man who'd been standing in front of me a few seconds earlier. That middle-aged Jason Sudeikis man I'd intuited to be Dr. Laurier.

I looked back at the woman who was still grasping my hand.

"I'm Ellie," she said, and she grinned again. Despite my confusion, I couldn't help but be entranced by her smile and her warmth. "Ellie Emerson. I'm a faerie. But apparently a bit of a shite one still. You see, I was doing a bit of the practicin' that Dr. Laurier has prescribed for me."

Dr. Laurier had descended the front steps of the building and was now standing beside us.

"Ellie," Dr. Laurier said in a far gentler voice than I'd heard him utter from the doorway. "That's not the best way to welcome a fellow guest, now, is it?"

"But I thought the illusion would be easier, since he didn't already know me. And I was doing quite well until it came to trying to lie to him. That's where I failed."

I found it so charming how she sometimes pronounced certain words that started with the soft 'th' sound with a harsh 't.' But not always. When she spoke quickly, she said *taught* instead of *thought*. But most other words, like 'the' and 'that' she produced the softer vocalization.

"She did have me convinced," I said to Dr. Laurier. "I thought she was indeed you. And not even my . . ." I paused, stumbling upon the words—I was simply not used to people knowing about my paranormal abilities, ". . . extra sensory abilities picked up on anything amiss."

I realized that, while Ellie had been in the guise of Dr. Laurier my sense of smell hadn't picked up much. But even now, like I'd noticed when I stepped out of the car, my senses were significantly dulled. Not quite regular human senses, but dramatically less than I'd gotten used to. I could now pick up on the now slightly cinnamon-like scent that Ellie was giving off. Dr. Laurier himself had more of a musky Old Spice style natural odor to him. Those were both coming through, at least a little. But moments ago, when it had just been Ellie and me, I was picking up on no real distinct scent, nor a heartbeat. It had been like the illusion she was projecting had been affecting my senses.

"Ah yes," Dr. Laurier said. "Ellie, you are more powerful than you realize. Just look at how far you've come since you first arrived. And yes, that's because you worked very hard at it. But you also work too hard at it. You need to give yourself a break, take some down time."

He then turned to me.

"And now, to officially welcome our new guest. Welcome, Michael, to Mandrake Falls Retreat." Dr. Laurier reached out and took my right hand in his own, clasping his left overtop of mine.

I couldn't help but grin at Ellie as he did this. She had mimicked his handclasp and tone of voice perfectly. Right down to the comforting effect his voice and handshake had on me.

Ellie blushed again, then averted her eyes and slowly backed away as Dr. Laurier placed one hand on my shoulder and with the other gestured toward the main lodge building.

"Allow me to show you up to your room inside Mandrake Lodge."

Interlude: Therapy Session
Truly, Madly, Deeply

Excerpt from therapy session recordings of Dr. Brendon Laurier

Wednesday, September 6, 2017
10:09 a.m.

LAURIER: Today I would like to return to something, to a phrase that you used several times in more than one of our previous sessions. [Sound of pages flipping] *You described your feelings for Gail, as well as your feelings for Lex, as "madly in love."*

ANDREWS: Yes, I believe I used that phrase.

LAURIER: You used that phrase more than half a dozen times in two different sessions. Did you realize that?

ANDREWS: No, I didn't. And I didn't realize that you had a second career as an editor.

LAURIER: *How do you mean?*

ANDREWS: *Oh, you see, one of my editors highlights when I use a word or a phrase repeatedly on the same page. It really helps to smooth out and buff my writing flow. You know, those pesky and annoying little bumps that aren't visible to me when I'm writing but can be jarring to a reader.*

[Silence.]

ANDREWS: *I do it all the time. There are phrases that I lean on, sort of as a crutch. You know how people say things like 'you know' or 'like' a handful of times in the space of two or three sentences? Or some other people who use the word 'fuck' like they just bought a tub of them from a bargain bin and are so stinking rich with them that they throw the word around as a noun, a verb—both transitive and intransitive—but also as an adjective, an adverb, a pronoun, a conjunction, an interjection, and a preposition. [Laughs] Not to mention as a proposition too. I mean it's a word with such linguistic versatility. But all I'm saying here is that we all have our habits; things that we do or say without consciously being aware of them. And that also comes in the guise of words or phrases that we regularly sprinkle into the things we say; or in the case of writers, the things we write. Like I said, it's a habit. Something we subconsciously fall back upon.*

LAURIER: *Are you familiar with the concept of 'avoidance' Michael?*

ANDREWS: Yeah, sure. It's something that a lot of writers must deal with. I know I've suffered from it. The procrastination I regularly struggle with can sometimes be seen as a type of avoidance. I mean, when it's time to get some solid writing down, it always seems to be the perfect time for me to look up a new recipe I want to try, or to do the laundry, or wash the dishes, or maybe even scroll Instagram for hours. At times, even with a deadline approaching, I have this habit of painting myself into corners. And yet, most of the time, I manage to pull that rabbit out of the hat at the last moment. But every time I do it, I think 'This is the one. This is the time that everyone else will realize I'm just a hack who is making it up as he goes along.' But so far, I haven't yet been caught with my pants down. I've managed to keep everyone fooled.

LAURIER: Especially yourself, right?

ANDREWS: What do you mean?

LAURIER: Do you remember the question I first asked you?

ANDREWS: Sure. It was something about a phrase that I used a lot.

LAURIER: Do you remember what that phrase was?

ANDREWS: 'Madly in love.'

LAURIER: *You used that phrase to describe your feelings for Gail.*

ANDREWS: *Yes. That's how I feel about her.*

LAURIER: *But you also used that same phrase to describe your feelings for Lex.*

ANDREWS: *I guess I did, didn't I?*

LAURIER: *Why do you think you use that specific phrase?*

ANDREWS: *I don't know. I suppose it's the best way for me to describe that feeling of what happens when I find myself falling in love with someone.*

LAURIER: *The term 'falling' is an interesting word to use for that feeling, isn't it?*

ANDREWS: *Yeah. But I think it captures what it's like so well. Because falling is something that happens to you. It's like you can't help it. You give in to it, the way you give in to gravity. You have no control over it. It's just there. It happens naturally.*

LAURIER: *Gravity is one of those inevitable forces that control us, right?*

ANDREWS: Yeah. Short of leaving the bounds of the earth, we're all prisoners of gravity. We can't escape its effect on us. Like I said, we have no choice. It's there. We can climb, we can jump, we can even create devices that temporarily allow us to fly through the air. But it's always there, always pulling us back to earth. We don't control it. It controls us.

LAURIER: So, falling in love is akin to losing control.

ANDREWS: Sure, it can certainly feel that way. You just give in to those intense feelings. You let yourself go.

LAURIER: You abandon responsibility?

ANDREWS: Yes.

LAURIER: It's liberating to allow something else, or someone else to be in control, isn't it?

ANDREWS: Oh yeah. It's ecstasy.

LAURIER: That's interesting, isn't it?

ANDREWS: What do you mean?

LAURIER: The other day we talked about your passion for Spider-Man's mantra. That with great power comes great responsibility.

ANDREWS: *Sure. It's the thing that drives me. It's why I feel I need to use these powers I have to help others.*

LAURIER: *You take responsibility very seriously, right?*

ANDREWS: *I do. I always have.*

LAURIER: *That's quite a burden to take on, isn't it?*

ANDREWS: *Yes, but someone's got to do it. Someone must step up. Somebody has to make a difference.*

LAURIER: *Even if that leads to risking one's own ability for a long-term relationship?*

ANDREWS: *If a person is responsible for something big, like helping others, like saving the city, like preventing monsters from destroying the world that we know, doesn't that take precedence over a personal and selfish need?*

LAURIER: *Do you think that having a partner, a girlfriend, a love in your life is selfish?*

ANDREWS: *No. I didn't say that.*

LAURIER: *What were you saying, then?*

ANDREWS: *I just mean that when you're with someone, you need to give everything to them. You dedicate yourselves to them. They're everything to you. They come first. They're the first thing you think about when you wake up in the morning, and the last thing you think about when you close your eyes to sleep at the end of the day. They're your everything.*

LAURIER: *That's rather intense.*

ANDREWS: *Love is intense. It's all-consuming. The person you love is someone you give your entire heart to, your entire world to. They have to be the focus. They must be the most important thing. And that's why, as I said earlier, if you have a responsibility to some other calling, for some other purpose, then, yes, there can be a conflict of priorities.*

LAURIER: *Do you think that it's not possible to hold multiple priorities?*

ANDREWS: *No, of course I do. It's just that something had to take the highest priority. And when you're in love with someone, then* they *must be that priority.*

LAURIER: *That single person must be the priority?*

ANDREWS: *Yes. They're the one. They're the light in your day. They're the thing you pour most of your time, energy, and passion into.*

LAURIER: *Would you say that you pour a lot of yourself into the aspects of control, responsibility, and love?*

ANDREWS: *When you put it that way, it's like the holy trinity of my life.* [Laughs]

[Long pause.]

ANDREWS: *I know, I know, I'm deflecting. I'm avoiding. But I feel very deeply about those things. I don't take responsibility lightly. And I'm an intense and compassionate lover. I put all of myself into those things.*

LAURIER: *Do you ever wonder if you might put too much of yourself into them?*

ANDREWS: *No. I don't think you can put too much of yourself into something. If you believe in something, then you own it. You commit to it. And if you love someone, you commit to them, fully, completely.*

LAURIER: *Can you be fully, and completely, in love with two women at the same time?*

ANDREWS: *Uhhh. I . . . That is, I'm not sure . . . I . . . uh . . . don't know . . .*

LAURIER: *Are you sure you don't know?*

ANDREWS: *How do I know what I don't know?*

LAURIER: I'm asking the questions. Michael, you take pride in your focus on responsibility, right?

ANDREWS: Yes. Responsibility. That's my wheelhouse.

LAURIER: And you take responsibility very seriously, correct?

ANDREWS: One hundred percent. Yes.

LAURIER: Do you think that loving a person involves a sense of responsibility?

ANDREWS: Yes. For sure.

LAURIER: What sorts of responsibility?

ANDREWS: Well, you care for them, for their well-being. You consider and respect their perspective. Their feelings. You're there for them, for their needs.

LAURIER: Anything else?

ANDREWS: You look out for them. You protect them. You nurture them. You support them. You comfort them.

LAURIER: Is that it?

ANDREWS: No. There's more. So much more. Uh . . . you also do things with them. You spend time together. You talk. You share. You share feelings. Passions. Likes. Dislikes. You engage in activities together. You experience things together. You grow together. You dream together. You're a team. Or, more accurately, a couple. You face the world together. You make decisions together. But you also have to recognize and respect your differences and leave room for change. There's a beautiful Rush song called "Entre Nous" that explores this concept. That phrase is French and it means "Between Us." The idea is that we're together and yet slightly apart. But those differences, those spaces that are in between us must be nurtured and respected, because they are what leave room for both people to grow. Love is so enriching, so powerful. And you want to do everything, be everything with that other person. But you also need to allow them to also be themselves, be who they truly are. Because that's the person you respect, admire, and desire. They are a part of you, but also their own person. It's a beautiful and intricate dance where neither person leads, but both lead.

LAURIER: That sounds like a lot.

ANDREWS: It is a lot. It's an all-consuming thing. But it is so incredibly magical when you can find someone to love and make it last.

LAURIER: So, based on all that you've said love is, would you say that being in love requires a lot of responsibility?

ANDREWS: Yes. I would say that. One hundred percent.

LAURIER: Then why is it that when it comes to something as powerful and important as love, you abandon responsibility?

ANDREWS: I didn't say that.

LAURIER: You talked about what's it like to give in, to allow love, like gravity, to take over.

ANDREWS: Yes, but that's part of the thrill, the joy, the excitement. Allowing yourself to fall under the spell of love.

LAURIER: Doesn't that sound like you're giving up your own control, your own responsibility?

ANDREWS: I never thought of it that way. I always thought of it in the most romantic sense.

LAURIER: Do you suppose that, by allowing yourself to give up control, you give up responsibility, and therefore someone else, or something else can take the blame?

Chapter Four: The Grass Is Always Greener on the Other Side of the Troll's Bridge

Saturday, September 2, 2017
1:40 p.m.

I was startled by a loud roar while crossing the footbridge spanning a part of the mountain river that had to be at least two hundred feet across. It was so loud it made the wooden boards underfoot vibrate. Taking an immediate defensive position, I twisted around to try to see where the guttural noise had come from.

It hadn't been more than an hour since I'd arrived. After Dr. Laurier showed me where my room was, he told me to make myself comfortable and to explore the grounds. That's what I'd been doing when that howl surprised me. I still hadn't gotten used to the fact that, here at this resort, my senses were so dulled that it was easy for someone—or something— to be able to sneak up on me. I wouldn't be able to hear the footsteps, the tell-tale heartbeat, the emotive scent of them up to mischief as they approached.

I was less than halfway across, but there was nobody in sight on the path behind me. Nor on the path ahead. The forested area I was walking through was as tranquil and lovely as it had been prior to the roar I'd just heard. Birdsong, the sound of the leaves blowing through the trees, and the trickling of the river under the bridge I was standing upon were all I could hear.

Had I somehow imagined the roar?

"Hello?" I called out hesitantly. "Is anybody there?"

"Who's that trip-trapping over my bridge?" The gruff male voice came from below, from underneath the bridge.

What the heck? Was I *really* trip-trapping?

"Uh . . . I'm Michael. Michael Andrews."

There was a long pause. "Michael Andrews. What is . . . your quest?"

For a brief and bizarre moment, I flashed upon that scene from *Monty Python and the Holy Grail*, and I almost responded with: 'To seek the Holy Grail!' But instead, I said, "I'm just taking a walk to check out the majesty of this beautiful location."

"There is a price for crossing my bridge, and if you don't pay, I will gobble . . . "

The voice faded and there was a long pause before the voice started up again.

"I will g—" A choking sound cut off the word. Then there was a snort. "Gobble you . . ." Another choking sound was then followed by a series of giggles.

Then outright laughter. His voice was coming from the far side of the bridge, so I continued to cross it.

Half-laughing, the voice, still deep in tone, was now far less gruff than it had been before. "I'm sorry, I keep trying to say, 'I will gobble you up,' but it just sounds so incredibly juvenile."

Getting to the end of the bridge, I navigated my way down the dirt and grass slope that led to the walkway underneath.

He continued speaking. "But what are the alternatives? 'I'll eat you?' Nope. That one has too much of a sexual connotation to it. 'I'll bite your head off' does have a nice ring to it. But that's also a phrase someone says when they snap back in an angry fashion. I thought about 'I'll grind your bones' but that's just too derivative of the giant in *Jack and the Beanstalk*.

"So, you see, I just can't see myself enacting this charade. I don't care what my ancestral forefathers may think of me, or what my legacy is supposed to be."

The stranger came into my view just as he was finishing, and as my eyes adjusted to the dim shadows from beneath the bridge, I was startled at the sight of him. He didn't look at all how this current voice sounded. But he did match that terrifying roar I'd previously heard.

He stood over eight feet tall with bluish-green skin, a bald head, huge jug-like ears and a bulbous nose. His chest, shoulders and arms were a mountainous landscape of explosive rippling muscles upon muscles that would have made Arnold Schwarzenegger's physique seem more like Olive Oyl.

"I'm Linnaeus. Linnaeus Kristiansen," he said, taking a step forward and out of the shadows. "I'm a troll." He was wearing only a fur loincloth, and one of his brawny legs was as thick around as my entire torso.

I instinctively took a half-step back. No, I couldn't pick up on his heartbeat, nor any scent that might give away a surprise attack, and he was speaking courteously, but that didn't mean the giant didn't frighten me a little.

The beast noticed my reaction, and looked up at the bright sky, grinning, his razor-sharp teeth that had previously been hidden in shadow gleaming in the sun. They could, indeed, bite my head off, likely in a single chomp.

"I know, I'm quite the sight to behold, and far from the stereotypical Adonis, one might say. But give it a moment for the light to take effect. I only look this unprepossessing when I have been basking in the shadows. The light will rectify that in short order."

We stood facing one another and as I looked at him, I noticed that his height was reducing, and his color was beginning to soften and to take on a lighter fleshy tone. His muscles shrank in size, as did his over-pronounced nose, and ears. Within a couple of minutes, the man who was standing before me was still close to seven feet tall and looked more like wrestler and actor Dave Bautista than the grotesque monster he had been just moments before. His facial features were still, however—when it came to human standards at least—rather monstrous and ugly. And even the enormous muscles on his body weren't fine toned like the aforementioned wrestler, but bulbous and lumpy. He looked like a man, but still maintained a lot of the aesthetics of his more natural form.

He reached out his hand. "You introduced yourself earlier as Michael?"

I shook his hand, noting how the grip of his massive hand could likely crush my own like a pile of dry leaves.

"Yes, Michael Andrews. I just got here."

"And what is the nature of your anecdotal chronicle, Michael Andrews?"

"Pardon?"

Linnaeus shook his head, and an expression crossed his face that suggested he was disappointed in me not understanding what he was asking. But the grimace ran away from his face quickly, replaced by a fresh bright smile. "What's your story, Michael?"

"Well, I'm a writer, initially from Ontario, Canada. And I have a series of books that follow an Antiquarian by the name of . . ." I paused, remembering that I wasn't in Mundane society any longer. I was at Mandrake Falls, a retreat for Paranormals. That's what he was asking. I began again. "I'm a lycanthrope. A werewolf. I'm not one naturally. Meaning, I wasn't born one, but I turned back in 2003. The reason I'm here is that, unlike the other werewolves that I've met, or learned about, I have no control over the change. I turn into a wolf on the sunset on the night of a full moon."

Linnaeus nodded his head sympathetically.

"I get that. Oh, I get that, indeed. You saw how I met-amorphosized when I stepped forth out of the umbrage from this immense waterway's overpass. How I trans-formed back into my normal human guise? Well, I don't have any government over that, I'm afraid. Whenever I'm in the dark for a prolonged period I begin to involuntarily take on my more natural troll form."

I couldn't help grinning. Finally, I'd met someone like me, who had no ability to control his body's transitions. "Then we both struggle with our inability to prevent the change into our other forms?"

"Oh, on the contrary," Linnaeus said. "That's not why I'm here. I have arrived at this particular establishment because I'm supposed to frighten people away. My role, my legacy, my very lineage, requires me to be a terrifying troll like one might read in the literature of time imme-morial. To terrorize people enough to unnerve them in such a way that they take leave from my bridge forever, or to face the dire consequences of me . . ." he paused, and chuckled as he uttered the final words of that sentence, " . . . gobbling them up.

"I'm sorry, I still can't say it without laughing."

"What? The word *gobble* is where you get hung up?"

"Partially. I mean, it's the utterance of a turkey after all. How can anyone take that with any grain of serious-ness? No, the real issue at hand is that I don't *wish* to frighten people away. I desire to meet them, to converse with them, engage in cerebral or philosophical commun-ion to investigate who they are in their core, and what makes them tick. I adore other people. I'm at my best and truest self when I'm engaged in dynamic oral intercourse with folks from all walks of life. I don't want to be a misanthrope who hides under a causeway and throws folks into a panic. I want to affectionately welcome them in with open arms. I want to invite them to accompany me for a most delightful chinwag. To offer them a beverage and bountiful nourishment; to break bread with them, not break their bones."

I remembered the thunderous roar he had let out when I was crossing the bridge.

"But that rumbling roar you let out. You scared the crap out of me."

"Absolutely; I am quite aware of the formidable effect I instill in others when I release a cacophonous bellow from deep within. But were you conscious of what I did immediately after? I frivolously mimicked a line from a Monty Python picture."

I laughed. "Yeah, I recognized that."

"Because even before I got to the time-worn trope about gobbling you up, I knew the idea was ludicrous. I'm inadequate for this line of work. I am too sociable by nature. I have no desire to frighten people off, never mind inflicting harm if their response is to not be frightened away.

"I've been trying to rehearse the role to which fate had cast me in, to become a master of this heritage assignment, but I just can't embrace it with any seriousness. And if I don't wise up, I destroy not only my birthright, but the legacy of my entire lineage of people. There are very few of us in existence. By the rules of my people, I not only need to live in complete solitude, but I have to sustain the legends. I need to instill actual terror, not momentary surprise, in my bridge victims. That timeless trepidation in a locale is what inspires the word-of-mouth tales that keep those narratives alive.

"I inherited a bridge in Maine that has been in my family for generations. There used to be local lore about it being haunted by some ghoulish creature who hides underneath it and is a threat to animals, small children, and any person who dares to transverse across it alone in the dark of night.

"Except these legends have faded over time. And if I'm not able to, in my own lifetime, resurrect those tales, then I have completely abandoned my legacy and my heritage, and I've brought great shame and disrepute upon my kind.

"But I can't do that if I start to quote from parodies involving bridges. I can't do that if I start to laugh when I talk about gobbling someone up. And to be honest with you, Michael, I'm not sure that I'm ever going to be able to measure up to what I'm required by the fates for me to be."

He started to cry at that point.

"Hey," I said, stepping forward and wrapping my arms around him; at least as much as I could. "I get it. I know what it's like to not measure up. Give yourself some time. You're here among people who understand you. You're here among friends."

He lowered his head onto the top of my shoulder and sobbed.

"But that's just the issue at hand!" he wailed. "I treasure the experience of having friends and being surrounded by people. But I'm not supposed to have friends. My kin are condemned to live a hermetic life."

Interlude: Therapy Session
Have We Talked About the Lonesome Loser?

Excerpt from therapy session recordings of Dr. Brendon Laurier

Monday, September 4, 2017
3:14 p.m.

LAURIER: Do you think a hero should have friends?

ANDREWS: What?

LAURIER: You're a hero, right. A superhero. Like Spider-Man.

ANDREWS: I never called myself a hero.

LAURIER: That's right, you never did. But what you do on a regular basis is heroic. And you regularly bring up Spider-Man, particularly when you talk about responsibility.

ANDREWS: Yes. Part of my love of reading came from Spider-Man comics. My mom used to buy them for me every week in her job at the Mini-Mart. I couldn't get enough of those stories.

LAURIER: What was it about Spider-Man that appealed to you?

ANDREWS: Ah, that's easy. Peter Parker. He was a nerd. A bookworm. Like me. Meek, shy, studious. He preferred to have his nose in a book than stick his nose into other people's business. I saw a lot of myself in him.

LAURIER: And yet, as I understand it, after he got bitten by that radioactive spider, when he put on the mask, he became something else.

ANDREWS: Yeah. The mask gave him a freedom he didn't otherwise have. Anonymity. He could be something else. He could be anything else. He could be someone else. I remember reading an interview with Stan Lee when he said one of the reasons he liked the fact that Spider-Man's entire face, and entire body was completely covered is he could be anyone. Anyone. Which meant that no matter what a kid looked like, when they were watching Spider-Man in action, they could more easily see themselves in the role. They could see themselves as that hero.

LAURIER: Anonymity has its perks, doesn't it?

ANDREWS: Oh yeah. You can get away with things. You can take chances. You can . . . I don't know . . . be anything. Do anything. And get away with it.

LAURIER: Spider-Man could do anything and get away with it. So why, do you think, he chose to use his powers for good?

ANDREWS: Well, that's because he learned a lesson. When he first got his powers, he used them selfishly. To break free from the constraints that society had placed on him. His social pecking order as a nerd with no friends. The lower middle-class home where he was raised. His role as an orphan. His parents had died, and he was being raised by his aunt and uncle.

LAURIER: You were adopted, weren't you?

ANDREWS: Yes, I was.

LAURIER: That's yet another similarity to Peter Parker. Were you also aware of that?

ANDREWS: Yes, very much so. It's one of the other things I really identified closely with. I mean, Peter's aunt and uncle doted on him. They loved him so much, and they raised him like he was their own. Well, he was their own family. But you know what I mean. They coddled and protected him. And maybe part of the reason he was so soft, so meek, was because of that coddling.

LAURIER: *Did your adopted parents coddle you in a similar way?*

ANDREWS: *I have to correct you there. I've never called them my adoptive parents. They are, simply, my parents.*

[Sound of pen scratching on a note book]

LAURIER: *So, like Peter Parker, you were raised by loving people who weren't your birth parents, you stumbled upon supernatural powers, and you leveraged those powers to become a hero.*

ANDREWS: *Yes. Although I never used the word hero. I just used my special abilities to help people.*

LAURIER: *Why did you move to New York? Was it yet another parallel to Peter's life?*

ANDREWS: *Oh yeah. For sure. I mean, I grew up reading about him and his adventures. New York City had such an appeal to me. I felt like I knew the city. It was as much a character in those stories as anything else.*

LAURIER: *So, you've modeled major elements of your life after Peter Parker?*

ANDREWS: *I suppose I have. And before you ask, no, it wasn't always subconsciously. I mean, it's not like I was aware of every parallel detail. But a lot of it was purposeful. I did move to the city specifically because of my admiration for it via those comic books and the stories I read. When I realized I had enhanced superhuman abilities, I couldn't help but get all WWPPD.*

LAURIER: WWPPD?

ANDREWS: What Would Peter Parker Do? [laughs]

LAURIER: We've talked about many similarities about Peter Parker's life. But do you realize there's one element that we haven't discussed?

ANDREWS: Let's see. He was an orphan. Like me. He was a nerd, a loner, and a loser. He lived in New York. He used his superpowers for good. What else.

LAURIER: You just said that Parker was a loner and a loser. We didn't really get into that part though. Why do you describe him that way?

ANDREWS: Well, when he was in high school, he didn't have any friends. He was a loner. An outcast. A nerd. The jocks and all the popular kids took no notice of him. And when they weren't ignoring him, they were teasing him, mocking him. That pretty much makes him a loser.

LAURIER: Is that how you also felt in high school?

ANDREWS: Yes, somewhat. Like Parker, I was awkward. Tall, skinny, big jug ears. Not all that athletic. I definitely didn't think of myself as a winner.

LAURIER: When Parker put on his mask, the anonymity of that was liberating for him, wasn't it?

ANDREWS: Yeah. When he was Peter, he was pushed around, mocked. But when he put on the mask, that freed him to be a bit of a wise ass. To say things he would never have otherwise said. To do things he never would have done without it.

LAURIER: But you never had the luxury of a mask to hide behind?

ANDREWS: No. Not even when I came upon my newly acquired powers.

LAURIER: Do you think that moving to New York was one way of replicating wearing a mask?

ANDREWS: What do you mean?

LAURIER: Well, you grew up in a very small town, right?

ANDREWS: Yes. Just a few thousand people. Pretty much everyone knew everyone else.

LAURIER: So, moving from a small town with a few thousand people to a city of more than eight million people certainly provides that anonymity, right?

ANDREWS: Exactly. In that town I was trapped, forced to be who everyone thought I was. But in New York, I could be who I wanted to be. I could be outgoing, adventurous, not the pushover nerd loser I was back in my home town.

LAURIER: You could start over, right?

ANDREWS: Yes.

LAURIER: And yet, you didn't. You kept mostly to yourself. Why did you hang on to that role of loser and loner?

ANDREWS: I didn't hang on to those roles. They just came with the territory.

LAURIER: How so?

ANDREWS: Okay, early on in my arrival to the city, I discovered the wolf bite had affected me. I was terrified of the changes that had come over me; of the fact I blacked out and turned into a wolf. I mean, without any forewarning, there I was dealing with this unbelievable situation. I was a monster. Some disturbing beast. Who could I trust with this information? I mean, if the authorities ever found out, they'd likely want to either kill me, or lock me in a cage to study me. Neither of those appeals to me. So I kept it to myself.

LAURIER: *And yet, despite this apprehension of getting caught, you started to leverage your super-powers, your enhanced abilities, to help others.*

ANDREWS: *Yes. I was inspired by Peter Parker, like we discussed. But also by someone I dated briefly, years before I met Gail. Rachel Jean. I learned that there are some things we have no control over. The way we look—which was what she was dealing with—or the abilities we possess. We could ignore them. Or try to work against those things. Or, we could embrace them. And use them to our advantage. So I took a cue from Rachel, and my comic-book hero, and made a vow to leverage my gifts to make a difference.*

LAURIER: *Making a difference by taking on a huge responsibility?*

ANDREWS: *Yes.*

LAURIER: *Does that responsibility ever involve sacrifice?*

ANDREWS: *It does. All the time. You have to put the needs of others ahead of your own needs, your own desires.*

LAURIER: *Does it ever get hard?*

ANDREWS: *Of course. It's constantly hard. Especially when there's nobody, really, to talk to about it.*

LAURIER: *That sounds lonely.*

ANDREWS: *Yes. It is lonely. And very isolating. You know, I was thinking about that on the drive up to this retreat, actually. How for the first dozen years or so in New York, after I gained my powers, as a side-effect of this curse, that I hadn't told anyone. It has only been in recent years that I've trusted others with my secret. And now, being here, this is pretty unreal to me. I mean, I'm not used to so many people knowing my most intimate secrets. And yet, here we are.*

LAURIER: *Yes. Here we are. Your first ten years or so in New York, you didn't make any friends, did you?*

ANDREWS: *No, that's not true. I had friends. I mean, I showed up in the city with Buddy.*

LAURIER: *Sure. But he doesn't live here. He lives mostly on the road. You only see him for short times as he's traveling through.*

ANDREWS: *I've got my agent, Mack. And his assistant, Anne.*

LAURIER: *Yes, but they're work colleagues, aren't they?*

ANDREWS: *And I'm friends with several of the staff at The Algonquin Hotel. I mean, Paul, the doorman, and I talk about writing all the time.*

LAURIER: Do you ever spend time with these folks outside of seeing them at their jobs?

ANDREWS: [Mumbles incoherently.]

LAURIER: Pardon?

[Long silence]

ANDREWS: No. No, I never really thought of that. I suppose I don't really have any friends. At least not any that live in this city. Apart from Gail.

LAURIER: But hasn't Gail left the city?

[Long silence]

ANDREWS: Yes. [Long pause.] *She's gone. She has . . . left me. Again.*

[Sound of sobbing. Followed by silence. Then the sound of a nose being blown.]

ANDREWS: Okay. Sorry. I just needed to . . . get that under control again.

LAURIER: That's quite all right. Speaking of control, do think that you might have put up barriers to making friends when you moved to New York?

ANDREWS: How does not making friends connect with control?

LAURIER: When you get close to someone, whether it's a lover or a friend, that requires vulnerability, right?

ANDREWS: Sure.

LAURIER: But when you're that vulnerable you can be hurt.

ANDREWS: Yes.

LAURIER: Does it hurt when someone you care about leaves you?

ANDREWS: Of course. It's devastating. Being left, being abandoned is one of the most terrifying things.

LAURIER: Do you ever feel like you were abandoned by your mother?

ANDREWS: Of course not. I mean, she died. But she didn't abandon me. She was loving, nurturing, caring. She gave me everything I ever needed—perhaps too much, even—right up until her last moments.

LAURIER: My apologies. I don't mean the woman who raised you, the one you know as your mother. I'm talking about the woman who gave birth to you. Do you ever feel abandoned by her?

Chapter Five: It's My Bridge and I Can Cry If I Want To

Saturday, September 2, 2017
1:53 p.m.

"It's shamefully unjust," Linnaeus muttered as he flicked his wrist, launching a small flat stone that skipped nine times across the surface of the river before landing on the far side of the opposite shore. "I wasn't raised with the nurturing guidance for becoming illuminated of my predestination."

His voice cracked as he uttered the last few words, and he dropped his head onto the arms resting on his propped-up knees and started to wail. I couldn't help but try to trace the numerous deep indents on his head that had reminded me of actor Dave Bautista when I first saw him. I couldn't help myself, because this had been the fifth time he'd broken down into wails and tears in the past hour and a half. I had to distract myself from the discomfort of it somehow.

We were sitting on the shore partially underneath the bridge—I sat in the shadow while Linnaeus was in the sun—and had been chatting and sharing each other's back stories. Both of us had taken turns crying when talking about the things that we felt were wrong with us.

I had broken up when I talked about how devastated I was to have lost Gail again after all those years of pining for her. And I'd always felt I was too much of a softy; that I could barely start talking about intense emotions—whether sad, or even happy—without feeling the waterworks start coming on. Heck, I can break down and sob when watching an impactful television commercial. I couldn't watch tear-jerker movies in a theatre because I was afraid of getting kicked out for disturbing the rest of the patrons. My parents had to haul me—kicking and screaming and blubbering uncontrollably—out of a theatre during the local showing of *ET* in that classic scene where, on the examination table adjacent Elliot his new friend appears to die.

It's obvious I've never been accused of displaying blatant toxic masculinity, but Linnaeus made me feel like, in comparison, I could be cast as Butch "Top Dog" Badass of the Manly Macho Club.

"I was raised by my mother until I was eight years old," Linnaeus continued. My father was long-gone to parts unknown because of the independent nature of trolls. You see, we mate to propagate our kind, but it's against our inherent make up to be anything but solitary.

"Like so many animal species, trolls are ensconced in the maternal safety and protection in our fledgling years until we're able to stand on our own and depend upon ourselves."

I nodded. Humans, unlike other animals, are dependent upon their parental units for a much longer period of time.

"Usually, in a troll's life, the parent begins to have that revelatory discussion with their offspring when they're about to hit puberty. But my mother perished in a house fire when I was eight years old. Alas, she never had the opportunity to have that important discourse with me. I was whisked off to a local orphanage without getting any of this hereditary knowledge, or training on how to keep my true nature hidden from Mundanes.

"During puberty is when our troll bodies begin to react to the shadows. It's the dark, the deep shadows that cause the reaction for us to physiologically adapt into our proper selves. As you can see, we're human in the light of day. Light and sun has no ill effect on us. But it's when our skin basks in darkness where our kind flourishes.

"I was thirteen years old and living in a Catholic orphanage when my natural form first began to manifest. It happened while I was in the midst of a deep slumber. One of the nuns was doing her rounds to authenticate all the boys were reposing in their appointed stations. When Sister Agatha came upon me, I had already morphed into the troll body of my ancestral heritage. Similar to the way you saw me when I was standing within the shadows of this bridge.

"I woke to the sound of screeching. Sister Agatha stood at the foot of my bed, her breath hitching as she let out scream after gut-wrenching scream.

"Perplexed, I glanced from her and down at my feet, which were protruding more than a foot out from the end of my bed and out of the covers. They were enormous, and a dark blue-green hue rather than the normal fleshy color. And they were hairy. *They can't be my feet!* I thought. But then I wiggled them, and the hairy toes on the end of the feet I was staring at moved in response.

"The bed seemed insufficiently sized for me now, and it buckled beneath my terrific weight. My face and lips felt bloated, and I reached a hand up to touch it. I noticed that my hand—like my feet—was swollen and much larger than it had been when I'd fallen asleep, and the backs of my fingers were covered in thick hair.

"Instead of touching my lips, my fingers brushed against something rigid and sharp. I struggled to understand what it was in that moment; later I realized it was one of my over-grown and extended bottom teeth that protruded up past my lips.

"Sister Agatha was still rooted in her spot, and caterwauling her own befuddlement and trepidation. Gandering across the room I noticed my roommates all sitting up in their own beds, staring at me with the same look of horror that inhabited the nun's face. Her screams had woken me, my three roommates, and likely half of the rest of the floor. She'd been so loud I suspect she might have woken a few of the people who were laid to rest in the cemetery that lined the side of the *Sisters of Mercy School for Boys*.

"Brian, the boy in the bed immediately close to mine had been my best friend since the day I first arrived at that orphanage. We had set foot upon those grounds on the very same day, and that immediately bonded us. We were tight. Really close. We did everything together. Lunches, homework, chores. I'd never had a brother, but Brian was the closest thing to that I'd experienced. And I was so alarmed, not to mention bewildered. I had no idea what was happening to me. Brian was the person I turned to in that moment. If anyone could help me through it, he could.

"Or at least, that's what I had assumed.

"I stared pleadingly at him as he was perched in his bunk, clutching his blankets up as if they were some sort of shield that could protect him from the impossible monstrosity before him.

"'Brian,' I said. 'It's me. It's Linus. What's happening to me? I'm scared.'

"He said nothing in response. But the repugnant look in his eyes told me all I needed. He hadn't even heard me. You see, Brian wasn't looking at his best friend. He might as well have been staring into the darkest pits of hell.

"Then he reached to the table that sat between our two beds, opened the top drawer, pulled out a silver cross, and held it in a shaking hand between the two of us.

"The next thing I knew, something wet struck me in the side of the face. I turned to look back at Sister Agatha. She was lobbing something at me. Holy water. She must have thought I was some sort of demon.

"Mortified, I lept from the bed, crashed through the dorm window, plummeting to the ground two stories below. But neither the shards of glass from the window nor the tumble itself brought pain; only a mild and temporary discomfort. I realized that my skin was thicker, tougher, and I was powerful and strong.

"I didn't stop to pay much heed to any of that. I simply sprang to my feet and scurried through the graveyard and into the night."

Linnaeus shook his head, pausing to pick up another flat stone and begin to turn it over and over between his large fingers.

"I'm not sure how long I ran. But I absconded as far away as I could from that place. I didn't want to see Sister Agatha or any of my roommates or so-called friends again. And that hurt; because of that special bond I'd had with Brian. But I knew it was over. I could never look him in the eyes again. Not after the way he'd gaped at me with such revulsion. So I just kept running.

"When I roused from sleep the next morning, prostrate in the middle of a cornfield in the stringy mess of my torn pajamas, my body was human again; though I was quite a bit larger and more muscular than I had been before. I had also shot up more than a foot in height sometime in the middle of the night.

"I came to learn, over time, that whenever I was ensconced in thick darkness, I took on my true and natural form. During the day I maintained a form that more resembled humanity. And if I managed to stay in lighted areas at night, I didn't morph into a giant, hideous creature.

"I stumbled around for the next several years, not understanding who or what I was, or what had happened to me. Instinct, combined with the brute natural form allowed me to survive on the meat of wild animals in the thick of night. I managed to stay hidden, and mostly out of sight whenever the darkness took hold as I emigrated from town to town, from orphanage to homeless shelter. If I slept with a bright enough night-light on, I wouldn't change into the monstrous form. And when in human form, I relished in the company of others, and enjoyed pretending I was normal, just like they were.

"It wasn't until my late teens, as I was living a mostly nomadic lifestyle, constantly moving, when my father finally found me and relayed to me the ways of our people. Or, at least, the ways of *his* people. You see, I learned something about myself that I'd never known. My mother wasn't a troll. She was an ogre. Or, ogress, as is the proper term for a female. She lived separately from her own kind. Her intellect was far superior to the rest of her people, and so she distanced herself from them. She met my father, who was a troll, and was enamored, I suppose, by his superior cognitive skills. I inherited a combination of traits from them both.

"That's about all I know, as he relayed it to me. We didn't end up in discourse about it for very long. I've had longer conversations at the drive-thru window than my interactions with him. You see, real trolls, proper trolls—

of which I'm not—don't bond with others; they don't forge relationships. They are authentically independent creatures who thrive on solitude.

"But by the time I became fully cognizant about who and what I really was, it was too late. For years I'd been nurtured in a way unlike the upbringing I was supposed to have received; one that should have started when I was roughly ten years old. All I'd known was the kind and caring love of my mother. And then, after that, the friends I'd made along the way. And because I was a stranger relocating myself so often, I'd become exceptionally skilled at striking up conversations with others, at making friends promptly and deftly.

"What I never knew is that my kind were taught and conditioned to fear and never trust other people, no matter who they were. We're not meant to maintain companionship, even with other trolls. The only exceptions were the limited time one spent on the act of procreation, and the pre-puberty years of maternal care. All the rest of a troll's life is meant to be done in complete and utter solitude.

"I particularly marvel at spending time with others, listening to them, and making new friends. And it fractures my enormous heart every time I try to live up to what my kind were meant to be."

I placed a hand on his back and rubbed it.

"I get it," I said. "I've long struggled with the fact that when I transform, I'm an alpha wolf; but when it comes to who I am in human form, at my most natural and comfortable, I'm the furthest thing from that."

I didn't mention that Linnaeus was likely much further away from that than I'd ever felt. Sure, I was sensitive and could cry at the drop of a hat. But I was nowhere near as outgoing and gregarious as he was.

"But at least you're more in line with your Paranormal nature," he said, his sobs beginning to subside. "You're a lone wolf."

"You think so?"

"Absolutely. You've been unaccompanied since you got to New York, right?"

I nodded. "I suppose so."

"You enjoy your solitude, right?"

"Of course. I've always felt more comfortable with my hands resting on a keyboard and making up stories than I ever did going out and interacting with people."

I thought about that inclination. It didn't mean that I wasn't able to enjoy a good conversation or be comfortable in a relationship. Not that any relationship I'd been in had lasted that long. I think my friendship with Buddy might have been one of the longest ongoing relationships I had. But he also lived outside the city, and I saw him maybe half a dozen times each year we'd met one another.

Perhaps I truly was a lone wolf.

But what did that mean when it came to my feelings for Gail? I loved being with her. But I also did cherish my alone time. Well, given the curse that stood between us, not to mention the fact I had no idea where in the world she was, I'd be getting more than my fair share of alone time.

Current situation excepted, of course. These almost two hours that I'd been sitting with Linnaeus had been the most time I'd spent with anyone—yeah, okay, apart from my time with the driver who'd brought me up to this retreat—in weeks.

"So at least you have that," Linnaeus said. "Do you know what my automatic response was to when I heard you traversing across the bridge above me?

"It was to find out who you were. To know your name. To introduce myself. To see what the two of us might have in common. That's what comes naturally to me. Or at least, that's the way I feel and automatically react. It's supposed to come naturally to me to want to scare off anyone who comes near me; especially the ones who dare to invade my special little part of the world.

"According to my troll nature I'm supposed to try to terrify you from the moment you first started to walk across the bridge. And I exerted that effort. It took so much energy to push back my desire to call out and welcome you to my bridge, to ask if you could stay. To run out from the shadows and embrace you.

"But did you notice that I didn't say anything until you were more than halfway across?"

"Yeah,"

"That's because it took me that long to fight against that desire to be friendly and welcoming. I mean I'm here to overcome that nurturing part of me; to uncover the brutish part of me. And since we'd never met, that would have been the optimal time for me to instill dread into your heart. To make you so scared of the experience that you'd never again walk across a bridge without feeling a sense of raw trepidation.

"But what did I do? I muffed it up. I started to giggle, then laugh uncontrollably. I've been here three days now, and had five therapy sessions with Dr. Laurier. But I'm nowhere closer to becoming the monster I'm supposed to be than I was before I arrived at this establishment."

He threw his head down and again started to weep, this time with less slobber and snot than the previous sessions. Perhaps he was becoming a bit dehydrated.

"Stop being so hard on yourself," I said, purposely avoiding looking at the deep creases on the top of his bald head, and instead, casting my eyes to the far side of the river. "We just got here. And, as I understand it, therapy isn't something that solves your problem overnight. It's a process that can take y—"

I stopped.

From out of the wooded area on the far side of the river stepped a woman. She appeared out of the foliage almost like a mirage. And not just any mirage, but the type of mirage fantasies my sixteen-year-old self was prone to have.

Because she was as naked as the day she'd been born.

Her skin was tanned perfectly, an even light golden shade as she strode from the trees and to the shore. Her long, silky black hair cascaded down her torso, playfully hiding the nipples but not all the areolas of her voluptuous and firm breasts. The dark hair shimmered in the sunlight as she strode like some sexy runway model towards the water. Her hair was the same black as the tiny triangle of hair that dotted her pelvic region. And as she moved forward, a mischievous grin lit up her face in a way that seemed to cast its own light.

Simply, she was one of the most incredibly gorgeous women I'd ever laid my eyes upon.

As she continued to step forward, her eyes locked on mine, I shifted uncomfortably in the sand to make room for the blood-rushing effect she instantly had upon me.

Wordlessly—I suspect my bottom jaw might have been resting on the ground somewhere between my feet—I nudged Linnaeus's shoulder.

"Wha—?"

He too was instantly smitten by the visual delight that had suddenly been presented to us.

We watched, both of us still speechless and unable to take our eyes off her as she stepped up to the water's edge and then slowed and seemed to offer the river the exquisite taste of the toes of her right foot. As she stood there, on the precipice of the flowing waters, I felt a desire unlike anything I had ever felt; an almost animal sense of lust stirred hard and strong in my entire body.

The woman, now stepping into the water, conjured up the iconic image of Honey Ryder in *Dr. No* as she emerged from the water and onto the beach towards

James Bond. Unlike Ursula Andress, the actress from that film, this woman wasn't in a white swimsuit, and she was walking into the water, rather than out of it. My mind quickly flashed to another Bond movie, this one featuring Halle Berry emerging from the water in an orange swimsuit in a much later bond film, *Die Another Day*. For a moment, the gorgeous woman's features seemed to take on those Halle Berry features I'd seen in Ellie's face when I first met her a few hours ago. Then they shifted, and she looked like Lex, particularly the night I first met her at that bar in Los Angeles and felt so smitten with her. And then, finally, she appeared to me as Gail.

Gail? I couldn't believe it. She was here. She was back. I was as captivated as I had been that day in the coffee shop when I'd first laid eyes on her.

I heard myself let out a guttural groan of pleasure.

Then, as this magnificent and alluring woman was knee-deep in the river, her legs suddenly molded together into a single thick torso-like mass of flesh. Suddenly off balance, she threw her arms up in alarm and collapsed forward, bellyflopping into the water with a painful sounding fleshy smack that echoed under the bridge.

Linnaeus and I simultaneously jumped to our feet, partially snapping out of whatever spell had kept us fixated on her. She had disappeared beneath the surface of the water so quickly I wondered if she had been some sort of illusion. But the ripples from where she had flopped into the water assured me what we had seen was real.

But before we could do anything more, a dozen feet closer to us, her gorgeous face broke the water as she swam towards us.

She moved much faster than seemed possible, and that's when I noticed the massive fish-like tail and fin that swished in the water behind her, propelling her forward at an incredible speed.

As she gracefully cut through the water, I felt that same erotic captivation re-taking my entire being, and I stepped up to the water, my shirt already off, and beginning to pull off my pants.

Reaching the half-way mark, the mermaid suddenly stopped, and her sensual glare instantly disappeared as her eyes became large and saucer-like.

"Aw nuts," she said in a squeaky high-pitched voice. "It's too—!"

But whatever she'd said was cut off by her own scream as she started to flail madly in the water, splashing like some sort of giant human Mixmaster.

Chapter Six: Are You Some Sort of Sharpie? Because Your Pick-up Lines are Fiiiine!

Saturday, September 2, 2017
2:11 p.m.

Linnaeus and I moved faster than the babysitter's boyfriend when a car pulls into the driveway, diving into the river and swimming out to the flailing woman.

It took mere seconds before we reached her, but her arms were thrashing, and she was spinning in the tornado-like style that the Tasmanian Devil ran in that *Looney Tunes* show.

Fortunately, there were two of us, and we were both exceptionally strong. Whatever it was that had been blocking my enhanced senses did not seem to have any effect on my superhuman strength.

But speaking of strong, this panicking woman packed a pretty solid punch. I've been struck by several different tough guys over the years, but her blows were intense. By the time Linnaeus and I finally managed to drag her back to the shore I had been struck at least half a dozen times by an elbow, forearm, fist, and back of the hand. I'd also been scratched numerous times in the face, arms, and chest.

With Linnaeus and I on either side of her, elbows hooked around her armpits, we managed to pull her, and ourselves, exhausted, back to where the two of us had been sitting and talking.

We collapsed onto the sand and rocks beside my discarded shirt and pants and spent a few moments catching our breath before any of the three of us said anything.

"Thank you," the woman finally said in that same squeaky voice she'd called out in just prior to her panic seizure in the water.

She placed her arms behind her on the ground and adeptly pulled the bottom half of her body, which was a magnificent, glistening aqua-green texture of fishy scales that ended in a massive fin, completely out of the water.

"Are you okay?" I asked, still winded.

"Yes," she said. "I am. Sorry, I panicked. I'm . . ." she paused, cleared her throat, and then began again. "I didn't realize how deep that river got. I'm . . . er . . . afraid . . . of . . ." There was another pause, this one longer. "I have a fear of depths."

Linnaeus let out a surprised burst of laughter.

That startled me, and the woman.

She looked at me, surprised and her big wide eyes and the perfect roundness of her mouth just then reminded me of the hilarious bellyflop she'd done.

I grinned at her. She smiled back.

And the two of us joined Linnaeus in his laughter.

"A mermaid," he said, still breathless, both from the laughter and the rescue effort. "Afraid of water."

We all laughed more.

"I'm not afraid of water," she squeaked, breathlessly. "Just of depths."

That set us off again, and all three of us flailed on the ground in hitching fits of laughter that was likely just as much relief that we'd all survived the ordeal.

By the time we finished laughing, I noticed that, now that it had been completely out of the water, her lower body had transformed back into human parts. I couldn't help but notice her long, sexy legs, and as my eyes wandered up her beautiful naked body and up to her face, I was feeling that similar intense desire that had taken over when I first saw her across the river.

My eyes finally met hers, and I found myself falling into their aqua-blue depths. These eyes were suddenly Gail's eyes. Oh, how I missed and yearned for them. I struggled to remind myself that this woman wasn't Gail, and it took almost everything in me to not reach out and touch the side of her face.

She pursed her lips, then licked them, before speaking.

"Do you work at Dick's?" she whispered, gesturing towards the visible bulge in my underwear. "Because you're definitely sporting the goods!"

I looked over at Linnaeus whose face was sporting the same incredulous look I imagined I wore. We both started to giggle.

That cheesy pick-up line broke the spell her look had had on me.

"W-What?" I said.

"S-sorry," she muttered. "I just can't help it. It's in my nature to seduce." Flustered, she turned her head away, and then brought one arm across her breasts and the other over her crotch.

"Oh, I'm so stupid," I said, reaching on the other side of me to grab at the dry clothes I'd previously shed. "Here, take these, put them on. Cover yourself up."

"I'd offer you my own attire," Linnaeus said, gesturing at the flimsy wet loincloth around his waist. "But I couldn't bear the thought of how much the sight of my entire naked body would turn both of you on."

We all laughed again as the woman quickly slipped my grey t-shirt over her head, and then reached for the pants "Thank you," she said. Still sitting in the sand, she hitched herself up and pulled on my jeans. They were too big for her, but they did the job of covering her up.

She looked up at me and reached a hand to the side of my face.

"You're bleeding," she said. "You're all scratched."

My eyes met hers. Like before, I felt myself being pulled in.

"I'm . . . fine," I said. I could barely string the words together. "I'll be . . . fine."

Her fingers gently caressed my cheek, and she leaned forward, pursing her lips like before.

I couldn't take my eyes off hers. She was stunning and desirable beyond belief. She narrowed her eyes at me, and the deep, dark swells of desire she'd stirred in me several times already were back full force.

But then she spoke again.

"My lust for you is like diarrhea," she breathed. "I just can't hold it in."

The hypnotic spell she'd had on me instantly shattered.

"Wow!" I laughed. "Thank you. That was exactly the splash of ice-cold water I needed."

She started to laugh nervously. "Oh my god. I'm so sorry. So sorry. I just can't help it. It's in my nature to seduce men. Or at least to try to. But I'm just not . . . not all that good at it. Not when I open my mouth. The stupidest things come out."

"Tell me about it!" Linnaeus laughed. "I engaged in quite a similar farcical endeavor when Michael was walking across the bridge before you arrived. I'm a troll who likes to make friends instead of chasing people away. And Michael is . . ." he looked at me to see if it was okay for him to share something about me and I nodded my consent, "an alpha wolf, beta male. So, trust me, we get you."

The woman grinned.

Linnaeus continued. "It's like I'd rather have them laughing with me as their subject of ridicule than fearing me. But I have to express something to you that I have observed. You weren't even *looking* at me when you were attempting to seduce Michael, but despite that I was still picking up on some intense vibes from you. The very same essence you'd projected from across this tributary. I mean, wow, that was something else. If it weren't for the hackneyed pick-up artist lines that seemed to break the spell, both of us would be in deep right now."

"You think so?" the woman asked.

"I *know* so," he said.

"By the way," the large man continued, "I'm Linnaeus.

"You see, both Michael and I were raised without knowing that we were actually Paranormals. We were conditioned not by our own kind, but by the Mundanes. So we're a little maladapted in that way."

I realized what he was doing. Extravert that he was, Linnaeus realized what it was that this woman needed. Not sympathy, but empathy. We were all screw-ups in our own way. She was among peers who understood her.

"I'm Shian," the woman said. "Shian Pedersen."

"I might just call you Ann," Linnaeus said.

A confused look crossed Shian's face. Even with a wrinkled brow and twisted grimace, she was captivating. I realized there was likely some sort of magnetic siren dog whistle thing always radiating off her. "Why is that?" she asked.

"Because the way you appeared to us across the river naked as a jaybird, makes me think that the first part of your name is unintentionally misleading. So, instead of 'Shy Ann' maybe we should just refer to you as 'Ann.'"

Shian giggled. It was such an endearing gesture I had to concentrate hard not to visually swoon. Without even trying, there was an automatic element about her that kept pulling me in. I had to remind myself that she was a mermaid. This was clearly part of who she was.

She reached out to touch the side of Linnaeus's face. "Well, baby," she said in a slightly deeper voice, but one that still carried the mousey and squeaky overtones of her regular speech. "You can call me anything you like. Just so long as I can call you my big hunk-a-burning-stud-muffin-lover-boy.'"

Linnaeus and I erupted into a fit of giggles.

Shian sighed loudly. "That's just it. You both laughed. But I wasn't trying to be funny. It was a blatant attempt to seduce you. And a serious attempt, too. The problem is, that, unlike the way I might physically appear; unlike the constant subliminal magnetic draw I know I exude, because it's just part of the type of Paranormal I am, I am not good with people. I'm actually quite shy. And, in case you haven't noticed, I'm awkward as all get-out."

"Awkward?" Linnaeus said. "Sure, I'll give you that. But I'm not sure you're all that shy, Ann." A goofy grin crossed his face as the pun sank in, making Shian laugh. "I think you have the opposite problem that I do."

"Which is?"

"I'm a troll who is a massive extravert. I love being with people; with drawing them in. But I'm not supposed to. As a troll I'm supposed to repel and frighten them. And, as a mermaid your lot in life is to seduce and compel people to you; to lure them in. But you're introverted. Which makes you awkward and unsure what to do when interacting with others. Now, something that I've noticed about people with a tendency towards introversion is that they really don't do 'small talk' all that well. That's the most uncomfortable thing. I've learned that they really enjoy going deep into a subject; having personal and insightful connections. They find those stimulating and their natural introversion falls away. I mean, look at us three, having a meaningful conversation. And I suspect that makes you more relaxed and comfortable."

It's interesting just how much thought Linnaeus had already put into this for someone he'd just met. His concern always seemed to be about what he could do to bring comfort to the people he was interacting with. No wonder I liked him, despite having seen his grotesque natural surface appearance.

"I think Linnaeus might be on to something here," I said. "It would explain your awkward attempts at seduction. They come off a little like someone who is trying just a little too hard to be a smooth operator."

"I just can't help it," Shian said. "I've never been able to properly lure a man for more than the first few seconds where I know he is completely captivated. The minute I have him hooked I want to immediately force it to the next level. But it's like I have some sort of performance anxiety, and that next attempt becomes feeble."

"It's funny you should use the word *hook*," I said. "When I was younger and my dad was teaching me to fish, I kept screwing up when trying to set the hook.

"You see, when you feel the fish nibble, there's a subtle vibration on your line. Sometimes it's quite noticeable. But other times, particularly if the fish only nips the bait, it's extremely difficult to detect. You have to really pay attention. And when you do, it's important to wait for that second, or even third nibble. The one that tells you the fish isn't just tasting or playing with the bait, but actually biting into it. That's when you quickly and firmly snap the rod up into the air so you can set the hook into the top of the fish's mouth.

"But I was so excited whenever I felt that slight tug on my line that my knee-jerk reaction was to pull too fast, too hard, and too quickly."

"That's what she said!" Linnaeus blurted out, inciting a quick round of laughter from all of us before I continued.

"What I was never able to learn—much to my father's disappointment—was that if you pull the rod too quickly, before the fish has its mouth fully around the bait, the hook just pulls free. Or, if you pull too hard, the hook might tear through the fish's mouth."

Shian let out a loud gasp. I noticed that tears were freely flowing down her cheeks. "Sorry," she said. "That must be so painful for the poor fish."

"I feel that." I said, "I'm a wolf, raised by a hunter, and yet never acquired a taste for fishing and hunting. I can't imagine what the other wolves might think of someone like me.

"But I guess the point I was trying to make about setting the hook is that I was too eager. I reacted too quickly. Heck, I over-reacted. The same thing can happen when you've set the hook—which is something you're able to do so naturally, Shian—but you try to reel the fish in too quickly. My dad kept trying to teach me how to gently reel the fish in. Slowly, pausing every so often to let the fish relax and stop fighting for a bit. Because if I tried to just reel it in too fast, the tension of me pulling and the fish struggling could snap the line.

"And I think that's what is happening when you rush to those smarmy pick-up-artist lines. Maybe it's that part of you that wants to cut through the small talk and get right down to the point, the heart of the matter."

"Hmm," Shian said. "You make an excellent point. I mean, if I hadn't already met him about an hour ago, I would have asked if you were Dr. Laurier. That's really good advice, Michael."

Again, I felt her pulling me in. And she was doing it naturally, without her trying at all. I grinned at her with a closed mouth, trying not to reveal how I was clamping my jaw together hard in an attempt at restraining the desire swelling in me.

"Oh, I'm no therapist," I said. "I was just thinking about my own dating life. For the life of me, no matter what I did, I just couldn't get a date. I can only see it now, after a lot of time and space. But whenever I was interested in a woman, I didn't follow that 'gentle reel' fishing technique my dad had tried to teach me. I let my enthusiasm—and, to be honest, my desperation—get the better of me. I tried too hard. I came on way too strong. And I scared the bejesus out of any poor woman who might have been initially curious, if not interested in me."

"That makes sense," Shian said, nodding. "I appreciate you sharing that with me. It really helps."

Again, I marveled at how such a simple gesture could inspire the formidable desire that was building inside of me.

Seeming to detect the stirrings she was causing in me, Shian glanced down at my crotch, then her eyes shot back up to my own.

"But speaking of sharing, I'd be a-okay if you slipped me a little of that hearty hunk of rock-hard meat that's currently straining against your boxer briefs. I mean seriously, are *you* going to eat that? Because I could slide it between two buns and have myself a spicy sausage gobble fest, complete with mustard, ketchup, and a hell of a lot of relish."

I erupted into laughter as I felt my erection and desire subside again. Thank God Shian always took it way too far. She even started laughing when she realized the ridiculousness of what she just said.

"Oh man," she gasped. "Even I can't believe I said something so stupid."

"Hey," I said, "Don't worry about it. I've said much stupider things over the years. There are women who are likely still laughing at the goofy things I said and did in my own desperation as a single man."

"Besides," Linnaeus said, "We all have our foibles. That's what brought us to this locale, after all." He got to his feet. "Speaking of which, it's about time we return to our domicile." He offered Shian his hand to help her get up. I stood up beside them.

"Good idea," she said, getting to her feet. She looked over at me standing there in my underwear. "Oh wow, you don't just have that scratch on your face. But there are more on your arms and your chest. And there's so much bruising. I can't believe I did that to you while I was panicking in the water."

"It's okay," I assured her. "I heal rather quickly. But we need to be careful and get you back safely to the main lodge. With the amount of my DNA that's likely lodged in your fingernails, if anything were to happen to you, I'd be the prime suspect."

She smiled. "Speaking of prime . . ." she paused, winced, and shook her head. "I suspect that . . ." There was an even longer pause as she let out a long slow breath. "Wow. I was just about to try two different pick-up lines there. But I managed to control myself. Look at me, making progress."

"I'm proud of you," Linnaeus said. "As I have already expressed, that's why we're here. I suspect that if we stick together and assert our support for one another, we can all make that progress we require."

"I like the way you think, my friend," Shian said. "Okay, so my clothes are in the woods just on the other side of the river. Once I get them, Michael, I can give you back your shirt and pants."

"Sounds like a plan, Shian" I said.

Shian turned to Linnaeus. "What about you? You're just in a loin cloth. Are your Mundane clothes somewhere around here?"

"I find them exceptionally uncomfortable," he said. "They're back in my abode. I disrobed from them before coming out here to get some practice."

"Well then," she laughed, standing between us, and hooking her arms around ours as she led us up the slope and away from the river's edge. "I would be the pride of the mermaid set right now. Look at me, walking arm in arm with two burly handsome half-naked men."

All three of us laughed at that.

"Yeah," Linnaeus said. "Quite the men, indeed. A troll who just wants to please others rather than scare them away."

"And a wolf whose idea of a good morning hunt is when he's searching and pecking on the keyboard for the next words to write. You've got a couple of real manly men on your arms."

Shian snorted a laugh and then tripped over her own feet.

Because she had her arms hooked around ours, she didn't fall on her face.

We let out another chorus of laughter, this time with a bit of relief.

With her arms still hooked between ours, Shian started to hum the tune from *The Wizard of Oz*. "It does feel a bit like that, doesn't it?" she said. "Imagine someone watching us right now. Wouldn't they see us and think we're on a bold quest or adventure? Like we're off to see the wizard who is going to solve all our problems."

"It does," I grinned as we continued to walk across the bridge that led back to the main lodge of Mandrake Falls Retreat. "And that's much better than what I was thinking about."

"What's that?" she asked.

"That someone looking at us might see us as outcasts on some sort of Island of Misfit Toys."

Interlude: Therapy Session
I'm Only At Home When I'm On The Run

Excerpt from therapy session recordings of Dr. Brendon Laurier

**Tuesday, September 4, 2017
8:03 a.m.**

LAURIER: Tell me about your parents.

ANDREWS: Where to begin? [Pause.] They're everything to me. Or, at least, they were everything to me. They're both gone now. My dad died when I was in my second year of university. My mom died a few years later.

LAURIER: That's quite young.

ANDREWS: Yes. It was. My dad was fifty-four. He was on track to retire in less than a month. Freedom 55.

LAURIER: Freedom 55?

ANDREWS: Yeah. It was one of those slogans used by an advertising company that was all over television when I was growing up. The idea was to have a plan that would allow you to retire early by establishing your financial freedom by the age of fifty-five instead of the usual retirement age a decade later. It would allow a person to enjoy the fruits of their spoils of working their entire adult life before they got too old to take advantage of it.

LAURIER: That sounds nice.

ANDREWS: Yeah. My dad had been talking about it quite a bit. He loved being outdoors. Fishing and hunting. But mostly fishing. That was his much-preferred past-time. Ever since he was a little boy. Our house was filled with pictures of him posing with fish he had caught. Shots of him with his own dad and grandfather, a string of fish held between them. Photos of him as a teenager, posing with a fish and a big grin on his face. He used to get up early in the morning and hike over the hills behind his parents' house to get an hour or so of fishing in before having to come home, do his chores, then head to school. He lived for fishing. And that's what his retirement dream was. It wasn't to sleep in—you know, the natural thing that someone does when they no longer are required to get up and go in to work. It was to keep getting up early, but instead of driving in to the job, it would be driving to some secluded spot, dropping a line into the water, and enjoying the peace and calm and quiet and solitude of the lake.

LAURIER: But he never got the chance to do that, did he?

ANDREWS: No, he never did. And he was so damn close, too. It breaks my heart to think about how he spent his entire life as a slave to the paycheck that paid the mortgage and put food on the table. He was good at his job, but he never really liked it. It was something he did, a means to an end. And that end was having all the time in the world to enjoy fishing. From as early as I can remember, every day when he got home from work, he would walk through the front door and state a number in a calm and clear voice. No explanation. It was just a number. And it seemed to be a random number. 3,015, for example. My mother would smile at him then walk over and give me a quick peck of a kiss. That was their routine. I didn't realize it was an every-day thing until I was a bit older. But when I noticed that pattern, and that the number seemed to be getting smaller by daily increments of one, I asked my mom what that number was all about. She explained he was announcing the days left until he could retire. He never really complained about his job, but he was almost religious in tracking the daily countdown until he reached that golden dream. I was away at school when he must have uttered his last workday number. But I know it was twenty-one. Because he never made it back from work the next day to make his countdown proclamation. He dropped dead the next day at work. It was a stroke. Nobody saw it coming. And he never again walked through the front door of his house. He never got to announce the number "twenty" in a calm and clear voice. He never got to that "freedom" he'd longed for his whole life. He had it all mapped out. Right down to the day. I can't believe how far he'd come, and how close he was to the thing he wanted the most.

LAURIER: How old were you when he died?

ANDREWS: I was twenty.

LAURIER: How did his death impact you?

ANDREWS: Well, he died when I was in the throes of my final exams in my second year at university. So, I was really busy, and already focused and stressed out on my grades, you know. I mean, I had an exam the morning of the day before his funeral, and another one late the day after his funeral. I didn't miss either of those exams. I went back home for the funeral, but just for that. I got there at the last minute, and I left pretty much after.

LAURIER: But the institution would have allowed you some sort of special exemption, wouldn't they? To delay taking those exams?

ANDREWS: I guess they might have done that. If I'd asked.

LAURIER: You didn't ask?

ANDREWS: No.

LAURIER: Why?

ANDREWS: Because my dad taught me that I need to honor my commitments. He was very clear when I left to go to school, that my job was to focus on my education. To get a university degree and get a good job. Not to be a custodian like he was.

LAURIER: Parents often want more for their children than they had for themselves.

ANDREWS: Yes. And I mean, he sacrificed so much. He worked day in and day out at a job he didn't like to provide for his family. And he was never sick. I don't think I ever remember him calling in sick to work a single day of his life. He worked hard; he did his job. And he never shirked a commitment or a responsibility.

LAURIER: It sounds like your father exuded that same sense of responsibility you saw in your comic-book hero.

ANDREWS: I never really thought of that. Not until now. I mean, sure, I knew the type of man my father was. I respected his commitment, his resilience, his work ethic. But no, it never occurred to me. Huh.

LAURIER: Do you think you saw a little bit of your father in the character of Peter Parker?

ANDREWS: No. I always saw myself in Peter Parker. The loser. The loner. The nerd. The outcast. The orphan. I never drew that parallel to Spider-Man.

LAURIER: And yet, you did admire your father's sense of responsibility.

ANDREWS: Yes.

LAURIER: Was your father a hero to you, Michael?

ANDREWS: No. Especially not when I was young, and I felt he was too hard on me. I just never thought of him that way. I mean, don't get me wrong, I respected the man. I admired him. And I did learn things from him. I listened to him. I tried to make him proud.

LAURIER: Do you think he was proud of you?

[Long pause.]

ANDREWS: I don't know. I honestly don't know. I can't remember ever hearing him say he was proud of me.

LAURIER: Do you think he would have been proud of your commitment to your studies, especially in the face of a traumatic event, when it's natural for a person to just drop everything and mourn?

[Long pause.]

ANDREWS: Yeah.

LAURIER: You hesitated before answering.

ANDREWS: I guess I did.

LAURIER: Why?

[Long pause.]

ANDREWS: I don't know.

[Long pause.]

LAURIER: Let me ask that again. Do you think your father would have been proud of your commitment to your university exams?

[Long pause.]

ANDREWS: Maybe.

LAURIER: Maybe?

ANDREWS: Yeah, I mean, sure. He would have been proud of me, of that commitment I kept. I think. I mean, that's what he wanted from me.

LAURIER: That's what he wanted for you?

ANDREWS: Yeah. To make something of myself. To get out of that place. To escape the traps of that small town.

LAURIER: You keep coming back to what your father wanted. Are you sure it's something he wanted from you? Or is it something you wanted for you?

ANDREWS: It was what he wanted for me. He made that very clear. I was there at Carleton University to make something of myself. To get an education. I couldn't let anything get in the way of that.

LAURIER: Are you trying to convince me? Or are you trying to convince yourself?

ANDREWS: What the fuck is that supposed to mean?

LAURIER: Why did that question anger you, Michael?

ANDREWS: I'm not angry. I'm just . . . [Long silence, followed by the sound of a deep inhale of breath] *. . . what was the question again?*

LAURIER: Who are you trying to convince?

ANDREWS: You, of course. I already know myself. But I need you to see that I'm the good guy here. I didn't do anything wrong. I was just a kid. And I was hurt. My dad had died. I didn't know what to do. I didn't have any answers. And I didn't have anyone to talk to about it.

LAURIER: You couldn't talk to your mom about it?

ANDREWS: No. As far as she was concerned, I was the perfect son. When I screwed up, and my grades were slipping, my dad gave me a hard time about it. He talked to me about doing better, about honoring my commitment. But we kept it from her. He knew how much of a pedestal she put me on, and he told me that if she knew about my partying and letting my grades slip it would kill her.

LAURIER: Your father really loved your mother, didn't he?

ANDREWS: Yes. He did everything for her. I never saw him once say a single bad thing about her. Not about anything she did. He praised her cooking, he complimented her beauty, her intelligence. And when I was a teenager and I called her a bitch when we were arguing about something, he grabbed me by the arm and pulled me into my room so hard I could feel the impression of his fingers for days. He never raised a hand to me, never even spanked me. But that day, it really hurt. And when we got to my bedroom, I thought he was going to beat me. But he didn't. He closed the door and stood there. He didn't strike me, like I thought he was going to. He didn't even raise his voice. He sat me on my bed, and he sat down beside me, and in a very calm, but clear voice, he said not to ever talk to my mother that way again. Not to even think about speaking like that with her. He said that he would not stand to see me disrespect her. He told me he was disappointed in me. That he knew I could do better. That I could be a better person. And to be honest, those words hurt more than if he had smacked me around.

LAURIER: *Did you listen to him?*

ANDREWS: *Yes. Of course.*

LAURIER: *So you never disrespected your mother again?*

ANDREWS: *No, I never . . .* [Long pause] *. . . I mean . . .* [Long pause] *. . . I never did. At least . . . well . . . at least not while he was still alive.*

[Long pause. The sound of crying.]

ANDREWS: *You asked me if you think he'd have been proud of me. No. I don't think he would have been proud of me at all.*

[Another long pause. Followed by the sound of more crying.]

ANDREWS: *I mean sure, I convinced myself, for all these years that he would have admired my commitment to my studies.*

LAURIER: *But you think, now, that he would have been disappointed in you?*

ANDREWS: *Yeah. Disappointed that I wasn't there for my mother when she needed me the most. It was just the three of us. Just the three of us. Nobody else. But when I remember how deeply my dad respected and cared for my mother, I think he would have preferred that I be there with her, that I stand alongside my mother, that I honor my commitment to the family instead of my commitment to school. I think he'd be ashamed of the way I acted.*

LAURIER: *Why do you think you acted that way, then?*

ANDREWS: *I don't know. I was young. I was twenty. I was a selfish dick. I thought I knew everything about the world. And maybe I used my university commitments as an excuse. To stay away. To not have to deal with it. My school, and the fact I was attending university a six-hour drive from where I grew up, allowed me to keep quite a bit of distance. I mean, yes, like I said, I returned for the funeral, but that was between exams. I flew, taking advantage of the special bereavement fares of the airline. Instead of a six-hour drive it was a one-hour flight each way. So, I got there the day before the funeral, and I left the day after. I made it back in time for an exam I had that night. I* didn't miss that. And all this time, I continued to tell myself that my father would have been proud of me. He would have been proud that I stuck to my commitment to my studies. To get those grades, to get a degree. To work hard to get a career that was far removed from the job that he'd been stuck with.

LAURIER: *But you don't feel that way now?*

ANDREWS: *No. I wonder if I was just using that as an excuse, so I didn't have to feel. So that I didn't have to mourn my father's loss. I buried that pain under the work, the study, the goal of maintaining my grades. I mean, after all, it was the end of my second year. I was so close to finishing that year. Just a handful of exams left, and I was half-way done with that Honors degree.*

LAURIER: *So close. And you were twenty.*

ANDREWS: *Yeah, I was twenty.*

LAURIER: *You talked about the retirement countdown your father announced every day when he got home from work.*

ANDREWS: *Yes. It was his routine for years.*

LAURIER: *And what was the number he announced on that last full day of work?*

ANDREWS: *Twenty-one.*

LAURIER: And he never got to announce the count-down number the next day.

ANDREWS: No. He never got to declare: "Twenty."

LAURIER: That's an interesting number, isn't it?

ANDREWS: What do you mean?

LAURIER: How old did you say you were when your father died?

[Long pause.]

ANDREWS: Oh, wow. [Another long pause.] *Huh. Twenty.* [Laughs]

LAURIER: Yeah. Twenty.

ANDREWS: Well, no wonder I did everything I could to not think about it, to not focus on my father's death.

LAURIER: Sometimes we bury those things when they hit too close to home. Do you think that your mother was aware of the significance of those twenty days to retirement and your age at the time?

ANDREWS: She must have been.

LAURIER: Why do you think that?

ANDREWS: She never once gave me a hard time for not being there. She just accepted it.

LAURIER: Mothers can be that way, can't they?

ANDREWS: Yeah. They'll overlook the flaws, the mistakes, the faults of their own kids.

LAURIER: So, you never talked about that with her?

ANDREWS: No. To be honest, I didn't even consider the significance of my age and how many days he had left until retirement until now. But now that I think about it, I was too busy hiding, staying away, focusing on anything except my own grief to have noticed. I mean, from that point on, everything I did was about finishing my last two years, getting my degree, and finding my way.

LAURIER: Did you ever talk to your mother about your father's death?

ANDREWS: No. I mostly kept my distance. We didn't really talk about it.

LAURIER: You know, just because someone has passed doesn't mean you can't talk to them about it now?

ANDREWS: What, you mean with a Medium or something?

LAURIER: No. I mean, talking to them in your head. Sharing the things you weren't able to talk about before.

ANDREWS: That sounds a bit nuts to me.

LAURIER: It's just a thought. Something that can help. To make up for those conversations you never had.

ANDREWS: Whatever, Doc. Tell you what: I'll take it under advisement.

LAURIER: Did you see your mother much back then?

ANDREWS: I never really returned home again. I mean, sure, I visited. But I had part-time jobs in Ottawa while I was in school. I had a summer job there, too. I only returned home for quick weekend visits. I didn't like being back there. I purposely stayed away.

LAURIER: Why do you think it is that you stayed away?

ANDREWS: It was easier, I suppose. When I wasn't there in the house that I associated with my mother and my father, I didn't have to think about it. I didn't have to face the reality that he was gone. I mean, everywhere you looked there were pictures of my dad with his fish. It was a reminder of that life-long goal of his that he never got to achieve.

LAURIER: Goals are important to you, aren't they?

ANDREWS: Yes. Very much so.

LAURIER: What goals did you have for yourself at that age?

ANDREWS: I had two main goals. Two big things that drove me.

LAURIER: And they were?

ANDREWS: Well, as mentioned before, the thing I remember my father making very clear to me, particularly when I was struggling with the new-found freedom I had as a student, was that goal of learning, getting a degree, and committing myself to that pursuit. It didn't start off that way, of course. It had been my first time away from home. So it was also the first time I didn't have either of my parents looking over my shoulder, or telling me when it was time to do my homework, when it was time to eat, when it was time to go to bed. You know, things like that. But also, I was in a new place. Ottawa. And Carleton University. Somewhere that nobody knew me. But not just that, it wasn't that people didn't know me. It was that they didn't have these pre-conceived notions of who I was. There, at that school, I wasn't Michael Andrews the studious and nerdy bookworm who couldn't get a date to save his life. There, I could be whoever I wanted to be. And I'd spent my high school years keeping my head low, and just trying to avoid getting beat up, you know—particularly if I accidentally looked at one of the jocks the wrong way. But away at school it was different. In high school if someone was having a party, I'd never get invited. I mean, it wouldn't even be a fleeting thought in the minds of the other kids. But in the Carleton University dorm room, I was just one of the guys. I'd never been one of the guys before. So whenever a party was going down—which was almost every night in those early days—I was always invited. And there's no way, after years of yearning just to be invited, that I didn't jump in with both feet. So, in those first six months of being away, I suppose I let myself embrace the university student dorm life. And maybe a little too much. I was drinking, staying up until the wee hours of the morning, sleeping in past noon and skipping my morning classes. But then I'd also skip some of my afternoon or evening classes whenever someone asked me to join them at the on-campus bar for an afternoon drink.

LAURIER: *That doesn't sound much like you were committing to your studies.*

ANDREWS: *No. I wasn't. I was, admittedly, a little wild. But it felt so good, so liberating. For the first time in my life, I just enjoyed being the Michael Andrews that I'd never been allowed to be growing up in that oppressive small town where I grew up. Those first several months in Ottawa were something else.*

LAURIER: What happened to change that?

ANDREWS: My dad did. When he saw the mid-term grades that came in. That's when he sat me down and had that talk with me. I can still remember what he said, too, and how he looked at me when we were having that conversation. "Look Michael," he'd said. "I get it. I was nineteen years old once too. I remember what it was like to not have a care in the world, and to enjoy the freedom of being able to legally drink—"

LAURIER: But you were only nineteen.

ANDREWS: Oh yeah, I keep forgetting, because the legal drinking age in Ontario is different than it is in most states. It's twenty-one here in New York State, right?

LAURIER: Yes. Since the mid-1980s the minimum legal drinking age in all states is twenty-one.

ANDREWS: In Ontario it's nineteen.

LAURIER: I see. My apologies for derailing you there. So, your father was saying he knew what it was like to enjoy new-found freedom and to be able to legally obtain alcohol.

ANDREWS: Yes. He told me he remembered what it was like to be young, carefree, and admittedly, a little bit reckless. Huh. Isn't that funny?

LAURIER: What's that?

ANDREWS: I was just reminded of some Rush lyrics. There's a song called 'Dreamline.' It's on their Roll The Bones *album, which I really liked because it's a play on words, you know. There's a kid walking down the street with his hands in his pockets, and the wall behind him is made up of giant dice. Dice are where the term "roll the bones" comes from. But this kid is kicking a human skull down the street in front of him. I remember being so intrigued by that skull. I'd always had an odd fascination with skulls in books, shows, and art, you know. Like the skull of Yorick that Hamlet holds up. But the play on words there is just so magnificent. Because the theme of the album seems to be about luck, and chance, and fate, and a reminder of our mortality. That's what skulls can be, right? I mean, Hamlet is musing about mortality as he is holding the skull of the jester who used to entertain him as a child. But he's been dead for years. Where, Hamlet asks, are his jokes now? They, like everything, have been lost to the sands of time. And that, of course, is that line from the Rush song I was thinking about. It talks about these dreams of youth, and these hopeful quests of the young. I mean, dreams that most young people have, right? The song reminds us that when we're young we think we're immortal, that nothing can happen to us. But as we grow, we learn that immortality only lasts for a limited time. It's like a veil is uncovered to reveal the misconception we were under as the entire world lay before us. It was George Bernard Shaw who said that youth is one of the most precious things in life. Too bad it is wasted on the young. Faulkner was also a writer who explored mortality. And Neil Peart, the lyricist for Rush was a big reader. I wonder if he tried to assimilate writers like Shaw, Faulkner, and—*

[Sound of LAURIER clearing throat loudly.]

ANDREWS: Yeah. Right. Sorry. I got a little side-tracked there.

[Sound of something being scratched into a notepad.]

ANDREWS: I sometimes get a little carried away when it comes to exploring the meaning of song lyrics. Particularly Rush lyrics. I mean, they're so in . . .

[Long stretch of silence.]

ANDREWS: So, yeah. Where was I?

LAURIER: You said your father knew what it was like to be young and reckless.

ANDREWS: Yeah. He said he understood. "I remember what it was like," he told me, "to not have a care in the world, and to enjoy the freedom of being able to legally drink, and especially to be away from the previous boundaries and restrictions of home. I get it. But it's also something that can be taken too far. And you, son, have stretched that to the limit." He pointed out how I had shirked my responsibilities. He reminded me of what this chapter in my life was supposed to be, and how much he and my mother had scrimped and saved to have the money put aside for me to get a solid post-secondary education. "From the time you were a baby, your mother and I started putting little bits of money away for your education from every single paycheck. A few dollars here, a few dollars there. It was never a lot—because we didn't have all that much—but it was still a sacrifice for us. We had to make decisions. Did we want to go out and celebrate our anniversary together by having a nice dinner, or did we want to put that money away for your education? When my fishing rod broke and I needed a new one, did I really need to buy that rod and reel I'd seen advertised on Bob Izumi's Real Fishing *show, or could I just go back to using the worn old one I'd inherited from my father, and, instead, put that money into your college fund? We didn't want our son to have fewer choices when it came to what he wanted in life. We wanted more for you. So, we sacrificed a lot of those little things along the way. And you can be sure as hell we didn't do it so you could throw it all away by going to Ottawa and treat it like some sort of* Animal House *adventure."*

LAURIER: How did that make you feel?

ANDREWS: I was ashamed of the way I'd behaved. Of how I hadn't taken any of my studies very seriously. Of potentially wasting all those years that my parents sacrificed so that I could have money to pay for my education.

LAURIER: Any other feelings?

ANDREWS: Guilt, I suppose. I was guilty. There I was, living it up, when my parents had worked so hard to get me there, to provide me an opportunity neither of them had.

LAURIER: So what did you do with those feelings?

ANDREWS: I used them. I took that shame, that guilt, and I applied myself to the reason I was there. It was hard to abandon the Michael Andrews I had been allowed to become when I was a new person in a new place, and nobody knew anything about me. But I remembered what it took to get there, and definitely didn't want to let my parents down. So I returned to that studious academically-focused person I'd been in high school. I avoided the all-night parties and the dorm-room life by spending more time in the library. Even if it meant staying out of the dorm all night whenever things got too rowdy. I became the nerd I'd always been. I stopped drinking, too. And, admittedly, I haven't drunk all that much in my adult life. I mean, I likely consumed more booze in that six-month period than I've had in total in all those years since then.

LAURIER: So you applied yourself in order to honor and respect your parents?

ANDREWS: Yes.

LAURIER: And that goal wasn't your goal, was it?

ANDREWS: *No.*

LAURIER: *But it became your goal?*

ANDREWS: *Yes. Initially it was their goal, their desire for me to make something more of myself. But I suppose it became my goal. I didn't want all their effort and years to be wasted, so I made it my goal to make them proud of me.*

LAURIER: *You mentioned earlier that you had two main goals. So, if your education was one of them, what was the other?*

ANDREWS: *Writing. Making a living—a real living—from books and stories. That one was mine, and one I'd had from about the time I was maybe thirteen years old.*

LAURIER: *Did your parents support your personal goal in the way you supported their goal for you?*

ANDREWS: *Yes, they did. They wanted me to be happy and successful. To have the kind of life they never had. But they were also pragmatic. They supported my dreams of being a writer, but they were always very clear that the chances of actually earning a good living from writing were slim. I remember my mom telling me that it was fine if I wanted to be a writer, and that she supported it. But she said it would be a good idea if I could get a good job, something that could provide me with the means to pay for a roof over my head and food on the table. And once I had that, then I could write. Because the writing would be fun, and not something I would hate or despise, the way my father felt about work.*

LAURIER: Would you say, then, that when it came to those goals—your education, and becoming a writer—that it's a case of 'mission accomplished?'

ANDREWS: Yes. For sure. One hundred percent. I graduated with honors. And I had also sold my first story the year I'd graduated. It was only twenty-five dollars for a short story, but it was money, and it was my first published work.

LAURIER: That must feel good.

ANDREWS: It does.

LAURIER: Do you think your parents were proud of you?

ANDREWS: I don't know.

LAURIER: Why?

ANDREWS: Well, my dad died when I was in second year, and my mother died two years later the month after I graduated. But she was in a hospice, and barely conscious, or even aware of much. I don't think she even knew what was going on around her, never mind where I was. And why I wasn't there with her.

LAURIER: *You weren't with her when she died?*

ANDREWS: *No. I was working on my fourth-year thesis project when she started to get really ill. I mean, she started to get her first symptoms shortly after my father died. But it got progressively worse.*

LAURIER: *And how did you react to that?*

ANDREWS: *I stayed away.*

LAURIER: *You didn't return home?*

ANDREWS: *No. Like I said, I wasn't around much. I didn't go back home for more than a day or two.*

LAURIER: *Why do you think that is?*

ANDREWS: *I was busy studying. I was so close to getting my degree. I couldn't abandon that.*

LAURIER: *That's the second time you've used the excuse of your academics.*

ANDREWS: *It's not an excuse.*

LAURIER: *Then what is it?*

ANDREWS: It's the reality I was facing. C'mon, Doc, I was so close to graduating. I just had a bit more to do, and I was out of there.

LAURIER: Have you noticed that getting "out of there" seems to be a regular pattern?

ANDREWS: Are you accusing me of running away from things?

LAURIER: Do you think that you were running away?

ANDREWS: I didn't say that.

LAURIER: I was just repeating back to you the words that you were using.

[Long pause.]

ANDREWS: I had a thesis to work on. I had a commitment to my dad about my education that I had to complete. I couldn't let anything take my focus away from that. I was on the cusp of graduating and being able to escape.

LAURIER: Escape? From what?

ANDREWS: There you go, putting words in my mouth again.

LAURIER: What words?

ANDREWS: *Escape. Running away. Getting out of there.*

LAURIER: *Those are all things that you said.*

ANDREWS: *I did?*

LAURIER: *Yes. Why do you think you keep using those words?*

ANDREWS: *I don't know.*

[Long pause].

ANDREWS: *Okay, maybe I was running away. Maybe I couldn't handle it. Maybe I didn't want to be there, to be reminded that he was gone. So, she was on her own with that grief. While I was off focusing on myself.*

LAURIER: *Does that ever make you feel guilty?*

ANDREWS: *I sometimes wonder if that's part of the reason why she got so sick. I mean, what did she have to live for? Her husband had died, and her son was nowhere to be seen. But what could I really do? I was six hours away. If I'd made an effort to be there, what sort of difference would that have even made? I'm not a doctor. It's not like me being there would have provided some sort of cure. It wouldn't have changed anything.*

LAURIER: No. You're not a doctor. But you are her son.

ANDREWS: And I let her down, I suppose. By remaining so distant. But, like I said, what could I have done if I'd been there, anyway. It's not like I could control her disease, and what was killing her?

LAURIER: No, that's right. You couldn't control that. But focusing on your studies, and your writing goals were things you could control, right?

ANDREWS: Yes. Of course. If I applied myself, committed myself, that was something I could change. That was something I could be responsible for. That was some place where I could make a difference.

LAURIER: Do you miss them?

ANDREWS: Of course I do.

LAURIER: Did you notice that, when I asked you about your parents, you didn't tell me about them, you talked about how they died?

ANDREWS: I did?

LAURIER: Yes. Why do you think you focused not on your relationship with them but on the moments when they left you?

Chapter Seven: The Frustration of Reining Cats and Dogs

Saturday, September 2, 2017
3:11 p.m.

When I returned to the second-floor room I'd been assigned at Mandrake Lodge, I discovered most of the things I'd unpacked before I went on my exploratory hike were on the floor.

The suitcase that I'd left open on the bench in front of the mirror at the foot of my bed had been pushed off of it and flipped upside down. The book and journal I'd packed and left on the bedside table had also been knocked off it, along with the clock radio that was there when I arrived. The pillows that had been on the head of my bed were also on the floor. The keys to my apartment, which had been on the top of my dresser, had also been knocked off by something.

When I stepped into the washroom, I saw my toiletry bag was also upended from the top of the bathroom counter and its contents were scattered across the tiled floor. The towels and face cloths that had been hanging there were on either side of the toilet.

"I'm sorry," a male voice from behind me said. I turned, but there was nobody there.

Was this room haunted?

"I'm sorry," the voice said again, and I stepped out of the washroom and looked out my still-open door. "I think I'm the one who did that."

There in the doorway stood a short man with a wild thatch of messy red hair, and a similarly scrappy beard that framed his round face A wide grin that filled the entire bottom half of his face grew, and I realized that he looked like a cross between Ed Sheeran and the actor who played Ron Weasley in the Harry Potter movies.

"What do you mean you *think* you did that?" I asked.

"Hi," the man said, reaching out a hand. "I'm your neighbor. From across the hall. I'm Charles. But most of my friends call me Chester. I'd like you to do that. Please call me Chester. I'm a good person. I want you to like me. So, with your permission, can I ask? I'd like to step into your room. And clean up the mess. That I think I made."

"Uh, hello Charl—" I paused when his eyes widened and softened, as if calling him by his proper name was one of the most harmful insults I could possibly inflict upon him. He instantly shrunk back like I was about to either reprimand or perhaps even strike him. "Er, Chester. Nice to meet you. I'm Michael."

I offered my own hand toward him, and I could have sworn that he momentarily flinched before he realized I wasn't going to hit him, but shake his hand.

He took my hand and pumped it enthusiastically. His grin widened even more, which I didn't think was possible on the relatively short and squat landscape of his face.

"I'm pleased to meet you, Michael. So pleased. And so happy. That we're friends. But do I have your permission? To come in? Can I help pick those things up? Can I? I'm really good. At picking things up. And I'm sorry. That I knocked them down."

"Why do you say you *think* you knocked these things down?"

"Can I come in? Can I help?"

"Yeah. Sure. Mi casa, su casa."

"Oh good. Thanks. Watch me. Pick these things up. Watch how good I am. At it." He rushed past me and lifted the pillows from the floor, placing them onto my bed. Then he set the clock radio back on the bedside table and picked up my book and the journal.

Turning, he bumped into me as he moved to pick up the suitcase at the end of my bed. "Sorry!" he said. "I'm sorry. So sorry. I didn't mean it. Bumping into you. I'm a good person."

"Hey, Chester," I said. "Slow down. It's okay. You don't have to pick these things up. You don't need to apologize."

"Yes, I do," he said, spinning to pick up my keys and place them on the dresser. "I do. I'm a good person. A good person. I'll make this right. I'll make up for what I did."

"Chester!" I said in a firm and loud voice. "Stop!"

He froze in his spot and looked at me as if waiting for another command, or, like before, as if waiting for me to strike him.

"Please," I said in a calmer, quieter voice. "Just slow down and help me catch up here. You don't need to clean all this up. And what do you mean that you did this?"

"I'm a cat," Chester said. "I mean, I can turn into a cat. And I knock things off tables. And other surfaces. All the time. Wanna see me change?"

So he was a werecat. Interesting. I hadn't yet met any other type of were-creature.

"No," I said. "You don't need to show me. I know about that. I'm a werewolf myself."

"I knew I liked you!" Chester said, that big grin returning to his face. "I knew I liked you. I bet you're a magnificent wolf. A really good wolf. A good boy. And when I woke up. From cat form. And saw your room. I knew—"

I interrupted. "You woke up from cat form? Does that mean you don't know what you do when you're a cat?"

"No," he said, embarrassed and starting to shrink back. "I can't help it. But I don't mean to be bad. I'm a good person. That's why I want to help. To pick up your things."

"Do you get anything? I mean, do you have any memories of your time as a cat? Little snippets of things? Smells? Tastes? Sounds?"

"Uh, sometimes. I do. But not often. Just the occasional sensation, you know. Why do you ask?"

"Yeah," I said. "Oh wow. This is incredible. We have that in common."

"You and me. We have that in common," he repeated, and his face lit up in that impossibly massive grin. "We're friends, right? You and me?"

I suddenly flashed to an image of Chester the Jack Russell terrier and Spike the bulldog from that children's cartoon, and half expected him to call me Spike. At least I knew where his nickname had come from.

"Yeah," I said. "We have that in common." I was fascinated to finally meet someone who could understand what it was like for me. "Wait a minute. You asked me if I wanted to see you change into a cat. Does that mean you can control it?"

"Yeah. I can control it. The change. From human into cat. But I don't know what's happening. When I'm a cat. So I have no idea. What causes me to change back."

I thought about that. The only evidence I had about my own change back to human form was that it happened when the sun came up. I'd never even considered the possibility that my wolf self might have any control over it. Heck, I hadn't even thought about whether my wolf self even understood that I existed. What *did* he think when waking up in strange locations, like my apartment? Did my wolf self ever wonder how he got to wherever it was I happened to be when I changed?

"So, you can't control it? When you turn into a wolf?" he asked.

"No. It happens in relation to the cycles of the moon."

"Ah, like in the movies." Chester seemed to be considering that for a moment, scratching at the Brillo-pad like hair on his lower face. "But we still have that. In common, right? I mean we're still friends. Because we both change. And have no awareness. Of what we do. When in our alternative forms, right?"

"Yeah," I said. "We have that in common for sure. And we're still friends."

"That's funny," he mused. "Who ever thought that? A Felis and a Canis as friends. But here we are!"

"Yes, here we are indeed."

"So listen, Chester, I saw a chess board on a table in the lounge area down the hall. And I was thinking that, once I finish picking up my—"

"Gentlemen!" A loud and cheery voice called out. "I bring salutations and pleasant late afternoon tidings."

We both turned and saw that Linnaeus had emerged from his room, fully clothed. And he wasn't merely dressed, he was dressed to the nines. He wore a light blue suede sportscoat overtop of a black turtleneck sweater. He had one hand thrust into the pocket of a pair of white linen trousers, with the other raised in his greeting of us.

Chester immediately turned and pranced happily toward Linnaeus in a way that reminded me of a dog lopping happily to its owner. I swear if he had a tail, it would have been vigorously waving behind him.

"Oh, Linnaeus! You look. Absolutely divine. That outfit. Is the bee's knees." As he reached him, he walked around him so that he could appraise the sharp-dressed man from all angles. "You look dashing. And handsome. And ready. For the evening."

"Yeah," I said with a big grin. "An evening at Casino Royale."

"Just call me Kristiansen. Linnaeus Kristiansen," the large man quipped back. And I'll have my martini shaken, not stirred, thank you very much."

"Daniel Craig has got nothing on you," I laughed.

And at that point Chester slipped an arm around Linnaeus's the way Shian had with the two of us. "Doesn't he look great? So incredibly smart? Don't you want to? Just eat him up?"

"I don't know, I suspect he'd be way too much of a meal for me."

A hurt look crossed Linnaeus's face, and I realized that in my attempt to be funny I'd just insulted him. I wondered if I was feeling hurt and rejected myself when Chester, who'd been behaving like we were the best of friends, ended up 'dumping me' to rush over to Linnaeus. It reminded me of those times in my childhood when people I thought were my friends, were only hanging out with me until someone better came along.

I wondered if that would be something I'd be talking about with Dr. Brendon Laurier, or if my sessions with him would only have to do with the Paranormal. But I hoped he could help me, and the fact that I resorted to humor whenever I was really uncomfortable, frightened, or threatened.

And I'd lashed out at Linnaeus because it was obvious that Chester preferred him to me.

"Sorry Linnaeus," I said. "I forget that you're a little sensitive about your size. I didn't mean anything by it. And I shouldn't have said that."

"That's quite all right, Michael," the big man said, stepping closer to me and pulling me into a large bear hug. And though I had no idea what an actual hug from a bear might feel like, this experience seemed pretty on par with that. A few hours earlier when I'd put my arms around him to comfort him when he was crying, he'd just been a loose mess, sobbing onto the top of my shoulder. But now he was hugging me so tight I thought my shoes and socks might pop off.

"Hey! What about? Me?" Chester then launched himself at the two of us, and I could have sworn I heard a low rumbling purring sound coming from somewhere inside him as the three of us stood rocking in a standing embrace in the hallway.

"Well then," Dr. Laurier's voice came from behind me. "I see that the three of you are getting along quite smashingly."

We extracted ourselves from the embrace, but Chester kept one arm hooked around the forearm of his large friend.

"I'm so glad to see that," Dr. Laurier said. "It's important that we all get along here, as we each have a lot of work to do in this coming week." He turned to me. "Michael, I spotted you coming back from your walk with Linnaeus as well as Shian, who arrived shortly after you did. And now you've met Chester as well."

"Is that everyone from our assemblage?" Linnaeus asked.

"No, there are six of you in total. Our last guest is on their way. They arrive tonight. And we'll be able to begin our group sessions tomorrow afternoon. In the meantime, Chester, it's time for our daily session. But, as soon as we finish, Michael, you and I should at least have a brief one-on-one introductory session chat before the day is out. Why don't you and I get acquainted just before dinner time. Let's say 4:30? We only need about half an hour for that one."

I nodded. "That sounds good."

Chester rushed from Linnaeus's side and over to the doctor, beaming a huge smile at us. That's when I realized that impossibly huge smile on his face reminded me of the Cheshire Cat from *Alice in Wonderland*.

Most everyone's mad here, I thought to myself, as they walked away, remembering one of that character's most famous lines. *You may have noticed that I'm not all there myself.*

As we watched Dr. Laurier and Chester head down the hallway toward the stairs, I realized that I didn't particularly like Chester. I wasn't a fan of his fickle nature. And something about his quickly morphing loyalties bothered me.

"Isn't Dr. Laurier divine?" Linnaeus said. "I've already had several sessions with him, and I get the feeling that not only is he going to assist us in our ultimate enterprises, but he's going to provision us in ways we can facilitate one another's pursuits."

As Dr. Laurier and Chester disappeared down the stairs, I thought about how right Linnaeus likely was about that.

Maybe I had nothing to worry about and should just embrace this therapeutic retreat situation.

I looked up at the big man. "Do you play chess?"

Chapter Eight: The First Therapy Session. But Not One of Those Interlude Script-Style Thingies. And, Like This Chapter Title It Might Be a Little Too Brechtian, and More Meta Than Any Part of This Entire Book Series

Saturday, September 2, 2017
4:31 p.m.

"Do you mind if I record this?" Dr. Laurier said from the armchair directly across from mine. He was wearing a pair of dress pants and a thick patterned sweater that reminded me of those loud patterned ones from the 1980s that Dr. Huxtable wore. His office, like all the other interior spaces I'd seen in this building, had the warmth of light brown plank wall wood panels and a much lighter oak tongue and groove floor. There was added comfort—particularly for me—in the massive barrister style traditional mahogany bookcases that lined most of the three inner walls. His desk, off to the one side, was made of the same mahogany but was modest in size. And in the middle of the room, where we sat in our armchairs on the island of a beige and brown abstract patterned throw rug with a short, small coffee table between us.

"Is the recording a special treat for the six o'clock news?" I said, grinning. "Or maybe *The National Enquirer*?"

He looked at me with a very serious expression. I struggled with trying to pick up his scent or hear his heartbeat—anything that could help me get a fix on his emotions. But my enhanced senses were even more muted than when I'd first arrived. I not only wasn't used to that, but it reminded me too much of the disconcerting feelings I had when I was first hanging around with Lex.

"No, Michael," he said. "It's to help me with my notes. I will be writing some things down as we talk, but the recording can help to ensure I don't miss anything in our one-on-one sessions."

"I was just joking," I said. "It's fine. You can record this."

"Thank you," he said, and leaned forward to click a button on the recorder that sat on the coffee table.

"So, how does this work?" I asked.

"We talk," he said.

"Just like this? Sitting here?"

"Yes."

"What do we talk about?"

"Whatever you like."

"Yes, initially. But there'll likely come a few times where I make suggestions. It'll usually be based upon things that you've mentioned that might be worth exploring in more detail. That's where the recording and," he held up the coil-bound notebook, "this notepad come in."

"So, you won't be using that to sketch doodles or a caricature of me then?"

Dr. Laurier laughed. "No. I'm not an artist."

I glanced over at the bookshelves, admiring their aesthetic. Oh, who am I kidding? If there were a magazine called *Bookshelf Porn* I'd be the first subscriber. It was usually the first thing I looked for when entering a new room.

"You know, Doc," I said, as I completed what might have been my third visual survey of the room, "I'm a little disappointed at the setup here."

"You're not fond of the library-style setting?"

"Oh no, on the contrary, there's nothing I love more than a room lined with books. Are you familiar with that quote from Cicero? *A room without books is like a body without a soul.*"

"Yes, I am."

"Well, that's how I feel. Books bring me comfort."

"Then what is it that you find disappointing?"

"There's no couch. I thought I'd be lying on my back on the couch, staring at the ceiling and babbling on about anything and everything. But I suppose that's just the stereotype I've seen in too many cartoons."

"I could arrange to have a couch brought in if you like."

"No," I said. "That's okay. But what's the deal with the couches anyway? Was it only a stereotype, or was that actually a thing?"

"It was. And still is for some therapists. The couch services a couple of purposes. The first is that it allows the person, who is often nervous, the ability to stretch out and relax. But in addition, it removes that additional discomfort of having to make eye contact when they are relaying something that might be a bit more sensitive in nature."

"Thanks, Doc," I said. "That could be useful information I end up using in one of my novels one day."

"Do you find yourself doing that a lot?"

"Doing what a lot?"

"Making observations that get stored for use in a book."

"Yeah. It's something I can't really turn off, you know. Even if I'm not writing almost everything is fruit for some element of a story, you know. An overheard conversation in a coffee shop; attending to the unique smells of a specific location like a bakery or a dentist's office; observing the different ways that people walk down the street—and not just their gait, but their pace. Everywhere you look there's some element that you can weave into a story to bring it more life, more resonance. So, even if I'm not writing, I'm still writing, in a way."

"Do you ever take a vacation, or a break?"

"A break from what? It's not like I really *do* anything. I make stuff up for a living. And when I'm not doing that,

I'm absorbing things from the world around me that might be used in a story. It's not like it's strenuous or anything."

"Are you sure about that? Even our minds need a break, or a change of pace, or scenery. That's one of the reasons this retreat is where it is, after all."

I laughed. "I thought it was in the middle of nowhere so that people wouldn't stumble upon a bunch of disturbing monsters. I mean it's not like we could hold this little gathering at Club Med."

"Interesting," Dr. Laurier said, writing something into his notepad.

"What is?"

"That term you used."

"What? Club Med?"

"No, the other one."

"Nowhere? We are in the middle of nowhere, aren't we?"

He stared at me without saying anything and it reminded me of the frustrated look I sometimes got from my high school teachers whenever I was being a smartass.

"Yes, it's a remote location. But studies have shown the negative effects to our physical and mental health, as well as the fabric of society due to our lost contact with the natural world. Something that author Richard Louv has called 'nature deficit disorder.' I have three of his books here at the resort where he gets into detail about it."

Those books sounded interesting. I'd never heard of this Louv guy.

"What are they? Those books. They might be interesting research."

"Would this be research for a book, or to better understand the other being that is a part of who you are?"

I considered that.

"I'm not sure. Maybe both."

"The books are *Last Child in the Woods: Saving Our Children from Nature Deficit Disorder*, *The Nature Principle: Human Restoration and the End of Nature Deficit Disorder*, and *Vitamin N: The Essential Guide to a Nature-Rich Life*."

"Wow. You know the titles *and* the subtitles. Maxwell Bronte would be impressed."

He smiled. "You're referring to the main character in your antiquarian murder mysteries?"

"I am. Are you a fan, Doc?"

"I'm a reader, yes. And I have read several of the earlier titles in the series. And seen the media spin-offs."

"Are we allowed to borrow any of those books here?"

"Yes, of course. Any of the books here in this office except for the ones directly behind my desk behind that stained glass. Those are personal medical and clinical texts. All the rest of the ones here plus the ones in the extensive library and lounge at the end of this hall."

"Oh, I haven't seen that yet. With that many books I just might never leave. Say, does this library have a secret doorway that opens when you pull on a particular book on the shelf?"

"Not this one."

"Did you know that when I was a kid, I always wanted to have a library like that. You know, a special room within a room that has more books, but it's hidden from the rest of the world. My own little secret place that nobody knows about that I could escape into. Heck, who am I kidding? I'd still love one of those." I thought about it and nodded. "You know, I suppose that I'm finally at a point in my life where I could afford to have my own library, and a secret one. I could have it custom built. Well, not where I live right now, at least. The converted apartment that I have at The Algonquin Hotel is beautiful, but there's no space for a library. I'd definitely have to move if I wanted to build a library and then have a secret room built into it.

"It might have to be some place outside the city; where I could expand, you know. And, while this drive is a bit of a hike, it's nice here. Maybe it could be a second home. One to escape off to and restore my—what did you and that Louv guy call it? My nature-deficit-disorder—and maybe whenever I need to focus on getting some writing done."

I paused, considering it, while Dr. Laurier just stared silently at me.

"Do you live out here at this resort, Doc? Or do you also live in the city? Or maybe just outside the city? I mean, this place is nice, but it's massive. How many people do you have working here to help keep it running?"

"There's a staff of a four who work in the kitchen, perform cleaning and maintenance duties. They live here full-time, in a separate and smaller nearby building. There's another group of a half dozen workers who take care of the grounds and outdoor maintenance. They also live in a separate residence on the larger retreat property."

"But you don't live here full-time? You're just here for the special week-long retreats?"

"No," he said. "I'm only here with the visiting residents."

"Still, it's a beautiful place. So far, I've only seen some of the grounds and taken one of the trails through the wooded areas, but I'm looking forward to doing more exploring. Speaking of exploring, I suppose that in a couple of hours I'll be exploring this place on all fours."

Dr. Laurier looked at me without saying anything.

"You know, because at about 7:30 when the sun goes down, that's when I'll change into my wolf self."

"If you like, sure."

"What do you mean, *if I like?*"

He looked at me for a moment in silence, as if considering what he was going to say next. "Did you notice anything unusual about when you arrived here?"

"Yes," I said. "The closer I got to this building, the more my enhanced senses seem to have faded. Is that some sort of enchantment that's been placed on this resort?"

"You noticed?"

"Yes. The muting effect seems to be slightly reduced but still evident the further I go from this building. I suppose that you have this to allow us to be normal here."

"I prefer that we don't use that term, Michael. What *is* normal? In the Mundane world, perhaps, you feel separate from most of the other residents of the city. But among your kind, you are a normal Paranormal."

I laughed at that term. "Semantics are fun, aren't they?"

He grinned.

"Well, I'm not a normal werewolf. I mean, that's part of the reason I'm here, right?"

"Right. And we'll work on that together."

"So," I said, "this enchantment on the building. Does this mean that when I'm inside this building I won't change into a wolf?" I thought about what it was like when I'd been with Lex, and her own supernatural ability repressed my wolf nature. It had been so liberating to be able to not have to rush off somewhere for my nocturnal metamorphosis.

"It'll be up to you," Dr. Laurier said. "If you wish, you can go off and run through the woods and enjoy the freedom of your natural form. And I do highly recommend it. I suspect it'll be a lot more pleasant for your wolf self than even the lush and sprawling Central Park ever could be. And I think that would be a beautiful experience for you. But I would really prefer it if you could join us for our very first group dinner together tonight once our final guest arrives."

Even though I had no conscious awareness of my time in wolf form, that thought resonated with me. In human form, I found the grounds of this retreat stunning. I can't imagine how pleased my wolf self might be with it. And, remembering the negative impact that not changing into wolf form had on me—some sort of pent-up tension that led to violent aggression—I figured I should enjoy the ability to socialize in the early evening, but then head out, far from this building, and allow myself to change into Canis lupus form.

"I'm sure my four-legged-self will enjoy that. I quite loved the short hike I took this afternoon. I didn't get a chance to explore that much because I did run into two of my fellow patients here. I'm hoping to continue to explore. It has been a long time since I've had the pleasure of going on an extended hike through the natural area.

"You know, the woods were a mere two blocks from where I grew up. When I was a boy I loved—"

Dr. Laurier cleared his throat.

I stopped talking.

"Have you ever noticed, Michael, that you have a tendency to side-track things, particularly when they get uncomfortable?"

"I do that?"

"Yes."

"Hmm, I hadn't noticed. Why do you think I do that?"

"It's a not-uncommon defense mechanism. Those tangential journeys, particularly at the tensest moments, are often our mind's way of dealing with the intensity of it."

"I'm glad you get me, Doc. You see, my editor keeps reminding me, whenever I do that in my mysteries, that the reader doesn't want to be caught in the musings of my main character—that they want the story, the action, to move forward. My editor is nothing short of a genius; not to mention they have the patience of a bloody saint to put up with me. But I've always struggled with cutting those bits down, since Bronte is a book nerd, a thinker, not so much a do-er."

"Is Bronte modeled after you?"

"No. He's an antiquarian bookseller and he solves mysteries. Two things that I don't do."

"But you admitted earlier about your passion for books."

"Yes. I've always loved surrounding myself with them."

"So perhaps part of Maxwell Bronte's role is wish-fulfillment."

I considered that. "Sure, yeah, partially, I guess. I mean, I've always fantasized about working in a bookstore. No, not just working in one, but owning one. Being responsible for all of it, you know. The acquisitions and purchases. Deciding the layout of the entire place; what titles and genres get shelved. How to divide those things up. Getting into lengthy discussions with other bookish people about our favorite classics, as well as more modern titles."

"What about that other aspect of Bronte?"

"Which part?"

"Solving mysteries."

I thought about that. "Well, I've never been all that good at that deductive reasoning, but sure, who doesn't want to be the hero who solves great mysteries? I mean, growing up I used to love reading mysteries. The *Hardy Boys* ones were okay, but I latched onto this series of books by Robert Arthur Jr. called *The Three Investigators*. Although they started off as *Alfred Hitchcock and The Three Investigators*, with the Hollywood director's name in giant letters. I'd read that the author did that because he felt that using the name of and having cameos of a famous person in the book would attract attention.

"I suppose it's something I've also done as a writer. Occasionally, I'll have Bronte interact with a famous writer who comes into the store. I do it more as a bit of a treat for my readers. You know, the way that the TV show *Castle* used to have cameos from writers like Michael Connelly, Stephen J, Cannell, James Patterson, and Denis Lehane. I had a reviewer comment on that once. I think it's a lot of fun. It gives the reader one of those *I know them* moments. I really enjoy those when I'm reading something, and I recognize a place or a character from some other context. You know how Stephen King has this universe of characters and there's sometimes a cross—"

Dr. Laurier cleared his throat again.

"What?" I asked.

"Have you noticed how we just went off on another side-track?"

"We did?"

"Yes."

"Oh wow. I didn't realize how often I do that."

"I maintain my theory that your subconscious is trying to take you as far away from something that you're truly uncomfortable with."

"Interesting."

"Do you remember where this particular series of sidetracks all started?"

I laughed. "I'm not sure, Doc. I suspect we've taken a good number of trails in our Richard Louv-style exploration of the many forks on this particular forest path through my psyche. One of us should have been leaving a bit of a breadcrumb trail, don't you think?"

"Oh, I have been," he grinned.

"Okay then, where did this particular side-track start?"

"When I asked why you used the term *disturbing monsters* to describe yourself and your fellow patients here at the retreat."

Chapter Nine: In The Master Parlor They Gathered for the Feast, But Without Any Steely Knives

Saturday, September 2, 2017
8:26 p.m.

"Now that we are all here," Dr. Laurier said, standing from his place at the large round dining room table looking around at all of us, and slowly raising his wine glass up. "A toast."

I couldn't help but grin, as the way he held the glass with one finger up and glanced about the room made me think about Tim Curry in that dining room scene from *The Rocky Horror Picture Show*. I imagined for a moment that, like the interactive audience of that cult classic film, we would all respond by launching pieces of toast into the air.

Dr. Laurier's eyes landed on me, and he gave me a knowing look that suggested he knew exactly what I was thinking. "To . . . friends," he said, and then his eyes moved along. In the movie, Dr. Frank-N-Furter used the words *to absent friends*. But that pause was enough for me to confirm he must have known what I was thinking. "To newly acquainted friends. And to working together."

He went on to talk about the value and importance of mutual support, honesty, and vulnerability when it came to the group therapy we'd be engaging in this coming week. But to be honest, I wasn't paying attention to his words.

Those unspoken words from *Rocky Horror* that I'm positive he knew I was thinking about kept echoing in my mind.

A toast. To absent friends.

I know the dark humor foreshadowing meant by that line in the movie; but I couldn't help but think about what it meant to me. Because he seemed to be saying that for me.

Wasn't he?

To absent friends.

I thought about Gail, who had left for parts unknown after her mother died. And then I thought about Lex who sacrificed herself to allow me to save Gail.

To the women that I loved. And missed terribly.

I felt the darkness that had overwhelmed me when Lex died begin to creep up; and it took everything in me to fight it back and focus on what was happening right there in front of me.

". . . not to mention the camaraderie and self-confidence that I know you will gain from that combination of self-discovery combined with incorporating so many different perspectives." Dr. Laurier said. "Tonight is not about any of the in depth sharing we are going to do this week. We will continue the many one-on-one sessions we have already partaken in, and our first group therapy session will begin tomorrow evening. But tonight, we are here to feast, and to break bread together."

"I'm gluten intolerant," Vlastislav, the latest member of the group to arrive, muttered.

Dr. Laurier continued as if not hearing that statement.

"Despite the various things you are all here to address, you will see that you have more than being a Paranormal in common with one another. You will see ways that, even with your unique experiences, you are very much alike.

"And, perhaps even without realizing it, as this week unfolds, and you openly share those intimate shadows that darken your path, you will also be helping others in this group with something they have been struggling with on their own for far too long.

"Together, my friends, we are stronger. Together we shall triumph over those things that are too difficult for us to lift off ourselves in solitude."

It being clear that Dr. Laurier was finished his toast-cum-introductory-speech, we all raised our own glasses, nodding at one another, and drank the carbonated water that filled our glasses. That was one thing about this dinner, and this retreat: there were no alcoholic beverages, and no drugs allowed. Which suited me fine. I wasn't much of a drinker anyway. And since I'd arrived here, my regular enhanced senses seemed to be dulled in the way that alcohol sometimes could affect me.

As we sipped, I took in my colleagues.

To my left sat Linnaeus, who still looked like a million bucks in his blue sportscoat and black sweater. He was beaming—heck, he was practically glowing—and it was clear how much he loved being in the company of everyone here.

Beside him sat Chester, in the same beige t-shirt and jeans he'd been wearing earlier, and whose unruly hair seemed even bigger and wavier than before. I also noticed that he and his chair were tucked as close as he could get to Linnaeus without actually being on top of him. Like before, I got that "Spike and Chester" vibe off of the way he sidled up so close. And his proximity to the much larger man made him seem much smaller than he really was.

Dr. Laurier was next to Chester, wearing the same multi-colored wavy-lined sweater he'd had on during our earlier therapy session. He had a calm, welcoming way about him that was evidenced even as he sat there in silence. While Linnaeus was outgoing and welcoming to everyone, Dr. Laurier's manner was less obtrusive and far more subdued in nature. A subtle smile rested on his lips as his own eyes took all the rest of us in. He was clearly attending to the group dynamics and paying attention to each of us.

On Dr. Laurier's left was Ellie. She looked so pretty in the baby blue sundress she wore. Oh, who am I kidding?

She would look attractive wearing a paper bag. I found myself infatuated with her and had to make a conscious effort not to stare at her. It's too bad that she was seated on the opposite side of the round table from me, because it meant that, looking forward, she was always in my line of vision.

Next to Ellie was the final newcomer to our group. Vlastislav. He was holding his glass, which he hadn't yet touched to his lips, with a look on his face like it held urine rather than sparkling water. He had arrived after sunset, and I hadn't had a chance to chat with him yet. However, on our way to the dinner, Chester, the busybody that he was, mentioned to me that he was a vampire. The way he held the glass made me wonder if he might prefer it to be filled with the crimson fluid that vampires preferred. He was tall, with short-cropped dark hair, high cheekbones and a sharp jawline that made him classically handsome in a way I simultaneously admired and hated. That and the fact that, though he was wearing a similar all-black outfit of jeans, t-shirt, and sports coat, like I was, he pulled it off with far more stylish pizazz than I could ever muster. I also couldn't help feeling a tiny bit jealous of the fact he was sitting beside Ellie.

And to my right was Shian, wearing a navy pantsuit that made her look like a powerful business executive. She pulled that style off exquisitely, looking so sharp. It was quite different from when Linnaeus and I had first met her, for sure. I was kind of glad she was beside me and that I didn't have to look at her. Because if I'd found myself having a hard time not looking at Ellie, I'd likely have had an even harder time not staring at Shian. And not just because of her natural beauty, but because of those charms she exuded. She wasn't projecting any sort of siren song at this dinner; at least nothing like what I'd felt on the shores of that river.

It was interesting to me how both Shian and Linnaeus were dressed so exquisitely. They would make a lovely and complementary couple. For the third time since we all sat at our assigned spots, I considered switching chairs with her, if only to give her and Linnaeus more time to connect. But I didn't want to be rude to our host. And I imagined that Dr. Laurier might have placed us in these specific seats for a reason.

As the rest of us were setting our drinks back down on the table, Vlastislav spoke in a voice with a slight Slavic accent. "Do you mind if I ask," he said, "what is in this glass?"

"It's sparkling water," Dr. Laurier said.

"Yes, I know that. But is it naturally occurring mineral water, or artificially produced carbon dioxide injected water?"

"To be honest, I'm not entirely sure. I think it might be carbonated water."

"Club soda," Vlastislav said with such a condescending tone that the room seemed to get a couple of degrees colder.

"Let me confirm that with the staff." Dr. Laurier got up from the table and walked toward the swinging kitchen door. "I'll be right back."

"What's the big deal?" Linnaeus said. "It's all the same, isn't it?"

"It's *not* the same," Vlastislav spat back. "Proper sparkling water is derived from mineral springs and naturally occurring gases. The other type is artificially produced. And the forced carbon dioxide can set off a horrible migraine."

Linnaeus turned to me and said under his breath: "I still don't see what the big deal is."

I shot him a wry grin.

A moment later, Dr. Laurier returned bearing a small stubby bottle and a pitcher of water. "I'm sorry to say, Vlastislav, that the water is indeed a brand of club soda manufactured in New York. It's this Lemon and Lime flavored Original New York Seltzer. It is preservative-free, but I believe the carbonation is produced using a recipe rather than via natural spring water minerals."

"Flavored?" Vlastislav muttered.

"Can I pour you a glass of still water instead?" Dr. Laurier asked.

"Is it tap, or bottled?"

"It's from the kitchen tap. But our water source is a fresh water well."

"Filtered?"

"You've got to be kidding," Chester said.

Vlastislav glared at him. "Some of us care about what we ingest," he paused as he looked Chester up and down. "And also, about our external appearance."

I noticed that Ellie, and Shian, who sat on either side of the vampire looked extremely uncomfortable. Shian was slinking so low in her chair, I'm surprised she hadn't already slipped under the table.

"Now, now," Dr. Laurier said looking back and forth between Vlastislav and Chester. The faces of the two men, who were quietly scowling at one another, began to soften as they broke eye contact and looked at the therapist. Dr. Laurier then addressed Vlastislav. "I'm afraid it's not filtered. But I can arrange, tomorrow, to have a driver drop off a Brita pitcher; unless you prefer a particular brand of still bottled water."

Vlastislav looked like he was about to say something, then quickly glanced over at Chester and seemed to change his mind. "A Brita would be perfectly fine, thank you."

"So, for right now, can I offer you a tea?" Dr. Laurier asked.

Vlastislav seemed to consider the idea. "The boiling process would remove any of the impurities from the well-drawn water. Yes, that would suffice. What sorts of tea do you have to offer?"

"I know there's English Breakfast and Earl Grey," he paused, noticing that Vlastislav had started to scrunch up his face as if someone had thrust a small fresh turd directly under his nostrils, "but perhaps you could come into the kitchen with me and see what else is available."

"A most excellent idea," he said, getting up.

The two sauntered back into the kitchen.

"Well," Ellie said, "someone is a little full of himself."

"I know, right?" Chester said, nodding so vigorously in agreement with her that the mass of curly hair on his head jiggled like a plate-full of orange flavored Jell-O. "I wonder. If they're in the kitchen. Trying to find just the right-shaped teacup. For optimal drinking."

I couldn't help laughing.

"It can't be easy for him," a soft voice beside me said. It was Shian.

"What's that?" Linnaeus prompted her.

She cleared her throat as she looked at Linnaeus. "It can't be easy for him," she repeated in a louder voice. Then she cast her eyes back to the table. "He's the new one."

"You know, she has an excellent point," Linnaeus said. "We've all met one another already. Some of us have been here for a few days. And he's the new person here, arriving last. Arriving late. Is that what you meant, Ann?"

"Yes." Shian said. "It's not easy when you're the one who is different."

"Yeah, I suppose you're right. Being an outcast from other Paranormals of your class isn't easy," I said. Apparently, I wasn't the only one who that thought resonated with, as I saw everyone else nodding their agreement. This seemed to be something we all had in common.

"To top it off, Vlastislav is a vampire, which is why he had to make his entrance here after dark," Linnaeus said. "The rest of us can get about during the day without issue. That alone is likely arduous on someone like him.

And we don't even know his situation. But if he's anything like the rest of us, as Michael expressed, he's likely already feeling like an outcast. And his first interaction with the group is negative because of a sensitivity he has to a certain style of beverage."

"A certain style of beverage?" Ellie snorted. "It's a little more than that."

"Be that as it may," Linnaeus said, "how comfortable would any of us feel if the first words out of anyone's mouth were negative? And I take responsibility for initiating it. Upon reflection, I am remorseful for asking him if it was a big deal. But I honestly didn't realize until he explained it. Let's give him another opportunity, okay?"

"Agreed!" Chester chirped in.

Ellie glowered at Chester before turning her attention to Linnaeus. "Okay."

Linnaeus then raised his glass. "To fresh beginnings," he said, "for all of us."

"To fresh beginnings," the rest of us repeated in unison.

I felt myself getting a little choked up at that toast. It meant a little more to me than giving the stylish and picky new member of our group another chance. When Linnaeus mentioned that Vlastislav had to arrive after dark, because of the sensitivity that vampires have to sunlight, I remembered what day it was in the moon cycle. And the fact that, if it weren't for the special magic-repression effect of this building, I wouldn't have been able to attend this late evening dinner. I would have been—like I have since the summer of 2003—the true outcast in this group.

Interlude
Wolf Night With a Moon Memory

*T*he wolf stands on the edge of the rock outcropping, staring out over the rolling wooded moonlit hills below. The air is fresh, crisp, and clear. Full. No matter how many deep breaths he takes, he can't believe how intensely it stimulates such a deeply revitalizing sensation through his entire body.

A slight drizzling rain had moved through the forest earlier that night but had done no more than lightly mist the leaves of the trees. The soil beneath the trees is barely damp underfoot. And as the clouds drift south, it leaves the sky clearer than before. A purifying post-rainfall scent hangs in the air.

Somewhere off to the left, a warm-blooded critter scurries away in the underbrush.

Normally he would relish the hunt, the thrill of the chase, of tracking it down, and capturing it. But he knows there'll be plenty of time for that later.

He looks back up into the clear, star-filled sky at the most magnificent and bright moon he has ever seen—and the flicker of some memory of seeing the moon like this, but from some higher perch, and not alone, like he normally is, but with a *mate— brings a sense of belonging, but also of a loss he can't understand. In response, he releases a mournful howl that stirs from deep within and echoes far across those distant rolling hills.*

Though the wolf cannot possibly sense or know this, far away, the echoes of his melancholic baying are heard by some shadowy figure standing still and statuesque in the night. The only detectible movement is the curling rise of its lips to reveal white glimmering teeth that seem to sparkle in the moonlight as it grins.

Chapter Ten: A Peaceful, Easy Feeling from Cavorting on These Grounds

Sunday, September 3, 2017

"Tell me, Michael, how did it feel?"

Dr. Laurier and I were back in the armchairs across from one another, he with a notebook in hand and a recorder on the table between us. Though it was only our second session together I felt as comfortable as if we'd done this half a dozen times already and had gotten into a groove. I wondered if it had anything to do with the fact that I felt like I'd slept better last night than I had in . . . well, years if I were being honest.

"Incredible!" I responded and couldn't help but lean forward in my chair and make broad gestures with my hands. "I feel so energized, so full of life, so ready to take on the day."

"That good, is it?"

"Oh yeah. I feel like a new man. Did you put something in our food last night, Doc?"

He laughed, and it struck me as a genuine moment of surprise mirth, his eyes creasing ever so slightly and the ends of his lips turning up as he considered the question.

"No, I can assure you that the food that was prepared last night was not only drug free, but it was free of most preservatives and the toxins one would find in processed food."

I thought about the food we'd eaten the night before. It had been one of the most delicious meals I'd ever had. And, apart from some of the more awkward moments—like when Vlastislav took issue with parts of his vegan meal that weren't also gluten-free—it was also among the most delightful group meals I'd ever been a part of. Too often, either in celebration of a new contract signing, or at the beginning of one of my book tours, Mack, my agent, or one of my editors would put on a major soiree for me. I'd be showcased and often put at the center of a table of key publisher shareholders or designated media representatives. I was as uncomfortable being the center of their attention as I was figuring out the formal Martha Stewart style table settings. I mean, seriously, there were four forks alone. The only one I could ever keep straight was the little fork that was paired with the smaller spoon at the twelve o'clock position of my plate. I knew they were meant for dessert. But I could never remember the rest of it. And I always had to wait until the people on either side of me took a drink or used their bread plate to determine which one was mine. But last night's dinner brought none of the same anxiety I often felt at those formal events.

"It was quite delicious," I said. "In fact, it was the best Tuscan chicken I've ever had."

"Glad to hear it. But what about afterwards?"

"Afterwards?"

"Yes, when our dinner ended—during which I suspect there were moments when you were enjoying the moment so much that you weren't worried about changing into a wolf—and then you noticed the time."

"So, you noticed that, huh?"

Dr. Laurier nodded.

"I was nervous and anxious about it at first," I said. "Especially, just before most of us had been sitting down at the table waiting for Vlastislav when I glanced at the time and realized it was already several minutes past seven twenty-six p.m."

"Seven twenty-six p.m. being . . ."

"Sunset in this region. Based on the app I use on my phone to track these things."

"Are you usually fastidious when it comes to keeping track of the time of day?"

"Oh yeah. I'm like a drill sergeant when it comes to that."

I noticed him writing something in his pad.

"So then, what was it like to not have to worry about what time it was?"

I felt a huge grin breaking out on my face. "It was . . . liberating. For the first time in as long as I can remember it wasn't in control of me. But it was more than just that."

"How do you mean?"

"The time I was asleep. I mean, when the human consciousness part of me was asleep—the time when I was in wolf form—I felt truly rested. I can't say I've ever slept that well since the time I was first bitten by that wolf all those years ago."

He jotted something else onto his notepad. "Why do you think that is?"

"It's like," I said, leaning my head back to look at the ceiling instead of at him, "I didn't have to worry about what my wolf-self was doing while I was unaware. I didn't have to concern myself with where I'd be or if someone might discover me in the middle of the transformation back into human form. That someone might find the clothes I'd hidden while I was running around on all fours. And when I woke up this morning, I wasn't lying naked in some underbrush. I did wake up naked. But I was back in my bed. I have no idea how that transpired because I have no memory of returning to the lodge, changing back into human form, or crawling into bed. All I knew is that when I woke, I wasn't panicked about being spotted, about having to find where I'd stashed my clothes. I woke feeling peaceful, rested, revitalized. Like a normal person."

"Like a normal person?" Dr. Laurier asked.

"Yeah. Like there was nothing wrong with me."

He scratched something else down on his pad.

"Let's go back to this feeling of being rested and refreshed. Where do you think that came from?"

"Well," I said, thinking about it. "Ever since this affliction struck me back in 2003, I've been living in the big city. Manhattan. Most of the time I leverage Central Park for my changes. It's by far the largest green space in New York City. There are plenty of large fields, forested areas, perfect for a canine to run and roam, and even hunt. It has been effective, and extremely useful for me.

"Every once in a while, though, I've been in a situation where I can't leave my apartment when the change is about to happen. I end up turning into a wolf while stuck inside. Gail has been with me many of those times and has described what it was like to me so I could better understand it. That's been extremely useful, especially since I'm just not aware of much of anything when I'm a wolf, you know.

"But whenever I did that—whenever I restricted the wolf inside of me from being able to roam free—I always woke up the next day with the feeling like I hadn't quite gotten the restful sleep that I needed. It's not that I wasn't rested. But more that I hadn't rested as well as I could have.

"And, before this morning, I didn't realize that a much more fulfilling rest had even been a possibility. Because here I am, in the middle of actual wilderness. Sure, Central Park is a great sprawling space for a wolf to run around free. But it's limited. It's enclosed. There are city sounds, which, I can only imagine are disturbing for a wolf. I mean, those noises can be bad enough for a human; just imagine what it must be like for an animal who can't possibly understand what it all means. It has to be terribly overwhelming and confusing.

"But out here, in this mountainous forested area—not to mention one that is protected from the Mundane world—there is true freedom. Absolute freedom. Powerful freedom."

As I shared these thoughts, a very clear memory from last night when I was in wolf form came to me.

Like previous wolf snippet memories, it was like the memory of a dream. But this dream was far more vivid than I'd ever experienced before.

I was standing at the top of a hill basking in the fresh air, the quiet, and the feel of a soft wind gently rippling across my fur when I heard a small animal scurrying away through a bed of fallen leaves and branches. The sound, and the smell of the creature, likely a rabbit, was enticing, and a stirring inside me triggered a desire to chase after it.

But I remained rooted in my spot, choosing, instead, to look up at the bright moon and the many visible stars in the clear night sky and taking in the fresh cool night air in long, hearty breaths. That's when a moon memory came to me. The last time I'd seen the moon was from the top of The Empire State Building—and that it was Lex who gave me that moon. She gave me that New York moon for the first time in my life. And then, she gave her life so I could save Gail's.

That brought a stirring of deep grief and confusion that welled up from the center of my being; the only thing I could do was to release it in a forceful cry.

While my wolf memory often only came in teasing flashes, this one was powerful and lasted much longer. It's as if my human mind was more connected with my wolf self. And yet despite that, I also felt like I had gotten a proper and full night's sleep.

"Michael?" Dr. Laurier prompted me out of my quiet introspection.

I considered telling him about it but decided to keep that to myself; at least for now.

"I guess I was just thinking about how I haven't slept so well since acquiring this affliction. All I can say is I can't remember the last time I slept so magnificently. The charm that you put on this building; the location of this retreat. I can't believe just how much I've needed this . . . actual rest."

Dr. Laurier consulted some pages of a file folder that was sitting on his lap before responding.

"How does that feeling differ from the time when you were with Alexandria Jones?"

"What do you mean?"

"When you were with Alexandria—"

"Lex," I interrupted.

"Pardon?"

"I call her Lex."

"I know," he said. "But in the briefing notes, her name is Alexandria Jones."

"But I call her Lex."

"Why?"

"It's a pet name."

"Do you think it might perhaps be a fantasy name?"

I actually felt my head tilt the way a dog does when intensely curious. "Huh?"

He paused to write something down on his notepad before continuing.

"Let's continue the discussion we were having, instead of taking this tangent right now."

"Whatever," I mumbled.

"Right," he said. "When you were with Alexandria, she had a side-effect that dulled your senses, in a similar way that the enchantment on this building works. Did that not provide you with the same feeling of rest?

"Well, initially, when I realized that being with Lex meant I didn't have to change into a wolf during a full moon, I felt a similar sense of liberation. I could be a normal human when I was with her. For the first time since this curse took over my life, I could be myself. That was a good feeling. An amazing feeling.

"Lex gave me something I had never been able to experience. For the first time in my life, I had been able to see the full moon in New York City." I laughed at the thought of it. "Lex had given me the moon. The New York moon. Prior to her, it felt like I'd been caught between the moon and New York City." It took almost everything in me to not break into song and continue with the Christopher Cross classic theme from *Arthur*. I managed to keep the singsong tone from my voice, but I wasn't able to keep the rest of the lyrics from rolling out on my tongue. "It's no wonder that the best that I could do was to fall in love with her."

He wrote something in his notebook before responding.

"You're playing at making light of the situation. But you did have deep feelings for Alexandria, didn't you?"

"Yes," I said. "I did. I loved her."

"But you said that you love Gail."

"I did. I do. I never stopped loving Gail."

"Is it possible," Dr. Laurier asked, looking down at his notepad rather than at me as he asked, "that you didn't actually love Alexandria, but you loved what she did for you?"

Chapter Eleven: The Girl on the Bridge, and the Boy on the Page, Drifting in their Orbits, Together and Yet a World Apart

Sunday, September 3, 2017

"There's something awful grand about being out here, ya?" Ellie said, walking beside me on the forest path. The ground was still damp from the rain that had returned here earlier this morning, and the wisps of a light fog brought an almost mystical quality to the woods. Though she had asked a question, she didn't wait for a response. Instead, she continued talking, almost nervously. "Especially after a rain. There's a richness to it. Can you smell it?" She paused and laughed then smacked me lightly on the arm. "Oh, what am I saying? Of course you can smell it. You have the senses of a wolf."

I was thinking how there was something magical about Ellie. I felt so inexplicably drawn to her. And I'm not just talking about finding her very attractive or anything even remotely sexual. There was something else compelling about the way she talked, the things she shared that drew me in. I was wondering if it was an element of her faerie nature affecting me; perhaps in the same way that Shian's mermaid nature affected both Linnaeus and me. Except I seemed to be the only one Ellie had that impact on.

Maybe it was just a case of two people who enjoyed conversing with one another, and I was reading too much into it.

Ellie and I had gotten into a conversation about our mutual love of nature late that morning in the common area on the second floor after I'd finished my hour-long session with Dr. Laurier. Vlastislav was in session with the therapist, Shian was nowhere to be found, and Chester and Linnaeus were studiously engaged in a chess match on the far side of the room. In the same way that I had been compelled by the nature writings of Thoreau, Ellie shared her affinity for his contemporary, Ralph Waldo Emerson. When we noticed that the rain had stopped, she suggested that we continue our coffee conversation outside. So, we'd filled a couple of the sixteen-ounce cups—which she was pleased to note were made of brown compostable paper—and decided to head out.

I grinned at her and shook my head.

"Yeah, normally I do. And I'd not only be able to smell the richness of these woods in spectacular detail, but I'd also be able to smell if you'd added sugar or cream to your coffee. Also, I'd be able to smell a person's emotions.

It's become a bit of a lie-detector of sorts for me over the years."

"Really?" she said, quickly averting her eyes and seeming to almost blush.

"Well, normally. Since I've arrived here, things about my wolfish nature are . . . different. My senses, which, usually at this time of the month are at their strongest, are significantly muted. Almost normal human."

"Well, that's good," she said softly, her head still facing away from me.

I looked at her quizzically without saying anything. After a moment of silence, she looked back at me and said, "What I mean is I was knackered after a long day of practice yesterday, and didn't I go and sleep in. I'd have been late for my session with Dr. Laurier this morning just there if I hadn't just rolled out of bed, quickly used the jacks, grabbed my clothes, and hurried off. I'm sure the body odor smell would have been a good bit manky to your normal wolf sense."

I laughed. "Oh, I sincerely doubt *that*," I said. "I'm sure you'd still smell as sweet as you are pleasing to the eye."

She turned her head away, and this time the blushed look on her face was more pronounced. "Gwan with ya. Yer a fine 'ting yourself."

What the hell are you doing? I immediately chided myself. *Openly flirting with this much younger woman.* I thought about it.

No, another voice in my head responded. *I wasn't trying to flirt. I was trying to make her feel better. Compliment her. Let her know it's fine.*

But I still wondered at what I was doing, and why. Yes, I found her very attractive physically. It filled me with pleasure just looking at her. And she was also stimulating in a deeper way. It was so enriching to be engaged in meaningful conversation with her about Thoreau and nature, and the fact we'd both grown up near naturalized areas and continued to be drawn to them. But there's a difference between being complimentary and overtly flirting. And I'd immediately crossed that line.

"I'm sorry, Ellie," I said. "I didn't mean to embarrass you. I just meant that you are an incredibly attractive person. I'm—" I stopped myself from saying that I was *with* someone, because I wasn't technically with Gail. She was off somewhere, and definitely not with me. "I'm *attached* to someone who I love very much. I didn't mean for what I said to come off as if I were hitting on you. I just wanted to compliment you. But then again, I'm sure you must have people compliment you about your beauty all the time."

"No," she said. "I don't. I rarely ever hear that. I mean, sure, there are always those lecherous geebags who can't have a normal conversation and default to just hitting on anyone with a vagina and a pair of breasts. But there's always a demeaning insult to the catcalls. It's rare to receive a genuine compliment from someone who has taken the time to engage in a real conversation with me. So, no, I'm not used to it. But it did feel nice just there."

"I'm just calling it like I see it," I said.

"Ya, well, 'tank you. I'll take the compliment in the spirit it was intended. And not as some sort of wolf call."

We both laughed and then continued to walk in silence, enjoying being in one another's company as much as we each appreciated the picturesque and tranquil beauty that surrounded us.

As we arrived at a narrow foot bridge that crossed over a creek, without speaking we both stopped to lean over the rail and drink from our coffees, listening to the water trickling beneath us and enjoyed the way the fog seemed to dance along the top of the water.

After several minutes of basking in the splendor before us, she spoke.

"So, who's the lucky woman?"

"Her name is Gail."

"Is she a Paranormal too?"

"Yeah, she's a witch. Although we only recently learned about that ourselves."

"Go way outta that! Really?"

"Yeah. She's an occult shop owner. I met her back in 2001 when I was doing research for a novel. It's funny, she was in that trade, and quite good at what she did. But she never actually believed in magic."

"I noticed you're not wearin' a ring," she said.

"No," I thought about how Gail and I had been standing on a bridge in Central Park the fall of that first summer we'd met. It had been where we'd just witnessed a couple proposing in that stereotypical New York love bridge way, then discussed what the ideal proposal might be. That's when we first verbally declared our love for one another. Just a few months before I screwed it all up by keeping my Paranormal nature a secret from her.

"But you've been together this entire time?"

"No. Not the entire time. It's . . . complicated." I took a deep breath.

"We've got a good bit of time," she said, and playfully leaned closer and nudged her shoulder against mine.

I then explained how Gail and I had met and fallen in love. And then about her dumping me because she'd figured out that I'd been lying to her about my werewolf nature. And how she'd been out of my life for a few years before she returned. And how we had become friends and maintained that friendship for several years before re-discovering that deep love that neither one of us had ever really given up on.

Purposely, I avoided even mentioning Lex, as I was reflecting on what Dr. Laurier had asked me earlier. I hadn't answered him. Nor had I answered that question for myself. And I figured talking about my relationship with Lex might have cast me as some sort of immoral cad. And considering how I'd crossed the line with Ellie just a few minutes earlier with my shameless flirting, I just kept that part out of my story. After all, I still needed to process my entire relationship with Lex and try to understand what I had been doing.

I explained about the witch/wolf curse we had discovered earlier that summer, the artefact we destroyed, but the fact that there were more enhanced artefacts affecting the curse out there that might take years for us to find. And the fact Gail and I had to remain apart until then and how I had no idea where she even was. I ended that backstory with how I remained steadfast in my belief we would eventually overcome what kept us separated and would be together again someday.

By the time I finished recounting what felt like a never-ending saga of my long-time relationship with Gail, I'd finished my coffee. But we never moved from the spot on the bridge. We were quiet, looking out over the water and seemingly caught in a myriad of unspoken thoughts when she quietly said: "You'll get back with yer lass Gail."

"You think so?"

"Ah sure. I can feel it."

"Thank you," I whispered, trying hard not to let her see that I was crying.

We remained silent for several more minutes before I realized how selfish I had been, spending so much time talking about myself without asking anything about her.

"How about you?" I asked.

"What about me now?"

"Well, I just spent the last half hour sharing all kinds of details about my on-and-off relationship with Gail over the years. But I haven't even asked you about yourself. Is there anyone special out there?"

"No," she said. "Never."

"Never?"

This time she didn't say anything, just shook her head and looked away. She was quiet for a few moments, before lifting the coffee cup to her lips and taking a long sip. She brought the cup back down before letting out a sigh.

"What is it?" I asked.

"It's really curious to me. I know we just met. But there's this connection and trust I feel. That odd feeling hit me when we first met, ya?"

I thought about the sensation that struck me when she'd converted from looking like Dr. Laurier into her natural form. "I felt something strange too when we met outside the main lodge yesterday. Almost like a physical pull from somewhere in my chest. It was intense."

"I've started to get better at shapeshifting for brief instances," she said. "I can create the physical illusion much better than I ever have before."

"I was convinced you *were* Dr. Laurier."

"So, I'm getting good at that part. But did you notice it was when I went to introduce myself, I couldn't say it? Didn't you just notice that's when I stumbled there?"

"Yes, now why is that? You even sounded like him."

"It's because I can't lie."

"No?"

"No, that's when 'tings go a little arseways on me."

I couldn't help but grin at that.

"How much do you know about Faeries, Michael?"

"Not much, really. I'm new to the Paranormal world."

"Well, c'mere and let me explain a bit to you. Among the various abilities my people have are being playfully deceitful, a bit of a sleeveen, but we cannot tell an outright lie. I'm so new to even being able to use my abilities that I have very little practice. A well-versed, experienced Faerie wouldn't have walked into the outright lie of trying to say something like 'I'm Dr. Laurier.' Because, you see, that's a lie. A straight out feckin lie. They would have avoided that. But I stepped right into it just there, and the illusion turned into quite the holy show."

"That's when you stumbled and started to stutter!" I said, understanding what had happened. "And then I heard your real voice start to come through."

Her face scrunched up in embarrassment. "Yessir, that's when the lark I was havin' on you all fell to shite. And partly it was because I was so thrown because when our hands touched just there, that's when I first felt this deep connection.

"Anyhoo, maybe that's why I feel like it's okay for me to share with you something I've never told anyone about before. Not until I got to this resort, that is. Dr. Laurier was the first person I shared it with. But it felt good. Like a huge weight was lifted from my back." I grinned at how, every once in a while, she slipped deeper into a subtle Irish accent. She pronounced it *'me back'* rather than *'my back.'* I found that so endearing. "Dr. Laurier is such an easy person to talk to. He's already helped me so much since I got here."

"He is," I agreed. "I've only had a couple of sessions with him so far, but I know what you mean. I can already feel the positive effect that speaking with him is having on me. But listen, Ellie, whatever it is, you don't need to share it with me. Especially if it's hard."

"No. No, I want to. I think I need to. I feel safe with you, Michael." Most times when she said my name, it sounded like she was calling me 'Mike-Elle' which was another mannerism I thought was cute. "I feel like I can talk with yeh. That you somehow get me, that you understand me."

"You mean beyond our mutual love of nature, Thoreau, and Emerson, right?" I asked with a wry grin. "Or the fact that neither one of us has full control of our Paranormal abilities?"

She smiled back. "Ah, sure, that's it you know. But there's more to it. It feels like we're vibing in some deeper way. But it's not unlike the way I feel connected to this creek in front of us, the trees; even the wind that blows through the leaves. I've always felt an awful good in touch with nature, even before I was old enough for my parents to explain I was a faerie and we had to keep it hush. But most of my abilities never progressed. Especially the ability to communicate with animals. I'd always longed for that ability the most don't you know. I'm so jealous that this is something other faeries have that I don't possess.

"But here's the most fascinating thing, Michael. With you, from that first moment we met outside the main lodge yesterday, I have felt this connection. And I'm pretty sure that you feel it too. I noticed you constantly staring at me at dinner last night. And no, don't worry, I don't think it has anything to do with you being a creep. You feel drawn and connected to me, ya?"

"Yes," I said. It was this intense feeling I couldn't explain. "It's like some magnetic force."

"But it's not sexual."

"No. It's . . . natural."

"Yes," she grinned. "Yes. Natural. Like it's something that was meant to be, you know? And I have a bit of a theory on it," she pronounced *theory*, like she was saying *teary*. "I'm supposed to be able to communicate with animals. But I've never been able to do that. And yet, we both feel this underlying connection. Sure, you find me attractive, and I find you attractive. But it's beyond that, ya?"

I nodded.

"What I think is that my ability to communicate with animals, which has never worked my entire life, is, somehow, connecting with the wolf part of you. It's drawing an awful good bond between us."

"That's fascinating," I said. "Because I've never felt so connected with my wolf half as I have in the past twenty-four hours."

"Exactly," she said.

And we were quiet for a moment, the two of us content to let the trickle of the water flowing under the bridge do the speaking for a short while.

"So, c'mere to me." Ellie said, leaning and playfully nudging my left arm with her right shoulder. Then her voice got low and soft as she said the next words. "Can I confess something to you?"

I turned to see that she was looking up at me with the most adorable puppy-dog eyes.

"And," she said, "promise you won't eat the head off me when I tell you?"

"I promise," I said, placing a hand lightly on her shoulder. "You have my word."

"Okay," she said, and then turned back to look out over the water. Sensing she didn't want to make eye contact at this point, I did the same. "I have to admit something to you, boyo. I know who you are."

I wasn't sure what she meant by that.

"Uh, sure. I'm Michael Andrews. A Canadian living in New York who is more of a love-sick puppy than a wolf. I thought we established that."

"No, I do be meaning that you're *the* Michael Andrews. You know, the writer."

"Oh," I said. "Yeah. I'm that one. Does that mean you've seen my books?"

"Seen them," she said. Then her voice got even softer. "Bought them. Read them. And I mean all of them, don't you know."

"Really?" I asked, with a grin. "Even the short story collection that most people avoid like the plague?"

"Ayuh," she laughed. "Especially that one. Cause it's the first one I read. I love that the most. *Silent Screams* was the first book of yours that I read, don't you know. But after hammering it down in one sitting, I went ahead and read all your Maxwell Bronte books. Multiple times. But I've read that story collection the most. It really resonated with me."

"Wow," I said, and couldn't keep a huge goofy grin from sprouting on my face. That collection was the most meaningful of all my projects. And it was the biggest flop of my entire career. I'd pushed hard for it and managed to get my agent to convince the publisher to produce it. It was partially to buy me time between novel projects, but also quite a vanity project too. I know that Mack convinced my editor to acquire it only because we were negotiating the next several novels in my series, and because it contained a never-before-seen short story featuring Maxwell Bronte, an antiquarian bookseller who solved mysteries. It was his escapades in my *New York Times* and *USA Today* bestselling mass market paperbacks, as well as the television series and movies that were adapted from them who people seemed they couldn't get enough of. But even with that Bronte story in the collection, the sales were a huge disappointment.

"You're pissed?" she said, misinterpreting my silence.

"No, not at all. It's just that, *Silent Screams* was my most significant passion project. It's my favorite child, if you will, of all my books. After the critics panned it, and the market pretty much ignored it, I figured that there was nobody out there who liked it. So, I was a little surprised, not only that you read it, but that you liked it."

"I love it. I've been reading it so many times it's quite the state; practically falling apart."

"Wow," I said. "Ellie, you've just made my day, my week. My year."

"Gwan with ya."

"No, I'm serious. That means a lot to me. What was it about the book that spoke to you?"

"Ah, there's the thing about it just there. It practically did speak to me.

"I came across it last year in a used bookshop in Clark, New Jersey. There was a single copy, and it was thin, and my eyes passed over the title, noticing the alliteration, but the title meaning nuthin' to me and I kept walking. But as I passed it, I thought I heard a muffled cry from behind me, and I turned. There was nobody there, but that cry sounded familiar, almost like I knew it, and I saw your book again just there. And the title. *Silent Screams*. It seemed such a strange 'ting, so I picked it up.

"I looked at your name, which I didn't recognize. I flipped through it, and then didn't I come to the story "Impressions in the Snow." I so gassed I almost fell over. Because I recognized that story title just there. I'd read it when I was a teenager. It was just a story I'd read in some digest-sized magazine I'd found on a bus stop bench. Back then I did be picking up almost any reading material I could get my hands on. Short stories especially. They took me away from the absolute state my life was in just then.

"But anyhoo, when I saw the title, I remembered that story. Vividly. Even if it had been donkey years since I'd read it. I didn't remember your name, but didn't I remember how the story made me feel."

The story she was talking about was one of my favorites. It was about a teenage girl at her wit's end and about to throw herself from a bridge into the icy waters below when she spots a snowman on the one shore. She's shocked to recognize it as a distinct snowman from her childhood, and he engages her in a conversation.

"I'd read it at a time when I was, like the girl in the story, considering the same sort of ending she had been planning. But I did see myself in her ability to communicate with the snowman. Didn't it remind me that I was born with special abilities that I hadn't yet realized. And I wanted more than anything to be able to talk to animals. Reading that story when I was sixteen saved my life.

"Didn't I just stand in the bookstore and re-read the entire story just there. By the time I got to the end, tears were freely flowing down my face and onto the page. Like Karen in the story, I was born for something greater. And I could make a difference. If only I didn't give up on myself, you know.

"That's when I looked at your name. Then I saw two other books with your name on them and didn't I buy all three just there. I read them right up. And didn't I go out and get your other books, and read them too.

"I've also read hundreds of articles about you in magazines and newspapers. I watched several clips on

YouTube from your Letterman appearance in 2014 when that short story collection was released.

"And so, I already knew about Gail. I remember seeing photos of you in tabloids, and the bit where Dave teased you about the gorgeous woman who'd accompanied you to a red-carpet event; and you claimed she was just a friend."

She paused, took in and then let out a deep breath.

"So, yeah, I know you already, because I guess I'm kind of a fan."

"Wow. I don't know what to say, other than . . ." I paused, trying to gather the complex emotions that were swirling through me. And none of them had anything to do with her not previously admitting she "knew" me already. For one, it never gets old hearing how a story has touched a person. But it's more than that. To hear that my writing had such a significant positive impact on a person's life was overwhelming. "I'm not upset at all. I'm flattered. I'm honored.

"I wrote that story when I needed it. I was at a low point in my life when that story came tumbling out of me. I remember waking one morning having heard the voice of that little girl, and her snowman, in the story. I woke up from a dream, where she was explaining to me just how she couldn't take it anymore. It's how I'd been feeling when I drifted off to sleep that night. And that's when Karen, and her snowman, appeared to me. They spoke to me. I went to bed despondent, wanting to just give up writing. But I woke up and wrote the entire story in one sitting, almost exactly as you saw it published. And it helped me keep going.

"So, Ellie, I'm grateful; so grateful that those words, that character, that story, reached you when you needed it. I'm grateful that you're here. And that I got to meet you. At the time I was writing the story for me. But apparently, I was also writing that story for you. I'm so glad that we met."

We were both silent for a few moments before she again spoke.

"You believe in fate, ya?" she asked.

"Yes, I suppose that I do."

"Do you think it's fated that you and Gail would meet and be together? I mean, despite the curse and all the shite that you've had to deal with?"

I thought about that.

"Yeah," I said. "I think so. And maybe even *because* of the curse. When I first saw Gail, something struck me deep inside. And it never left."

"That's how I felt when I saw your book in that used bookshop. Stricken. And yesterday, when we met, I felt it again."

I nodded. "Yes. Some strange force that I couldn't explain."

"*There are more things —* " she began to say.

"*In heaven and earth . . .*" I interrupted.

We grinned before we harmonized the rest of that quote from Hamlet. "*. . . than are dreamt of in our philosophy.*"

As we laughed, I marveled at how we used the original phrase that Buddy had talked about the other day. There *was* something unique that seemed to connect us.

At that point she turned slightly, chewing on her bottom lip. "Can I ask you to do something just now?"

"Sure."

"Would you place your right hand against mine?" I did as she asked, and our hands pressed together softly. She then used her fingers to part mine and slowly clasped her fingers to draw our hands tighter together. "You feel that connection just there, right?"

I nodded silently.

She then pulled her thumb back and began moving it in a circular motion.

I raised my own thumb and traced matching circles around hers.

"But it's like this," she said, as our thumbs continued to swirl without touching. "Without saying a 'ting about what I was doing, you matched my movements. It's like we're together, but not completely. It's more like we're in one another's orbit. But I want us to keep doing this as I'm talking. Focus on looking at our thumbs. Please don't look at me. And please don't say anything. Just listen, ya?"

Our thumbs continued to spin slow and gentle circles around one another, and I stared at the twirling thumbs that never touched, as if mesmerized.

"Okay," I said quietly.

There was a long silence before she began.

"When I shared that I was pretty close to ending it all, I didn't say why; or how I got to that point."

She paused, and took a long, deep breath.

"My deepest trust was betrayed," she finally said, "when I was fourteen.

"It was a man who'd been like me father in a way. He was the coach of the gymnastics team. I was quite the athlete just then. Oh, you shoulda seen me. I was grand. Nimble and quick, awful good at the floor routine, the balance beam, and the uneven bars, you know. By the time I was in my freshman year of high school I had already won several medals and was as good as any of the seniors.

"Despite the good bit of gymnastic skills, and my body having formed all the fixins' of adolescent womanhood, there was still no evidence of my faerie heritage. I was, apparently, a late bloomer when it came to that.

"It was frustrating. For me and my parents. And I'd just been trying to ignore it by cracking on at gymnastics and my studies. I was a straight A student, and a grand athlete. I was up to ninety with school and with practice. I skipped grade eight, moving straight into my freshman year at high school. And that was isolating, being a little out of my element with the older kids.

"Mr. French, the school's gym teacher, took a shine to me immediately. He trained with me for hours after school. He nurtured my good bit of gymnastic talent. Mr. French made me feel like I could actually be something truly special. That I was like the grand champion he'd always looked for. So it didn't matter that I wasn't a proper faerie, you know."

She paused again, and from the corner of my eye I could tell that she was looking at me, not our twirling thumbs. But I'd promised her I wouldn't look at her, just at our clasped hands, so I kept my gaze fixed there. But I slowly nodded, letting her know that, yes, I understood.

"And it was so strange, so unexpected when it happened. Because Mr. French had been nothing other than a caring and supportive father figure. I wasn't talking to me dad back then—I wasn't communicating with either of my parents. There was a good bit of tension between us, particularly since I hadn't yet manifested any of my faerie abilities. That was bad enough. But as my body was developing, I started to have feelings for other students in the class. Not just the boyos, but also some of the lasses had caught my eye. I didn't like have any friends back then. So, I had nobody to talk to. But Mr. French listened to me. He cared and offered me advice. He told me it was natural, at my age, to have confused feelings. It was a part of growin.' That there was nothing wrong with me. And more than anything, he believed in me. He gave me confidence in myself. I trusted him completely.

"So, when that manky incident happened, I was stunned. I had no idea what was going on. And no idea how I was supposed to even react to it."

I had a sense of where this might be going, and I closed my eyes and swallowed. I couldn't believe that she was about to share something such a deeply horrifying and personal thing with me. No wonder she wanted me focusing on our thumbs. It took everything in me not to say anything in response. But I had promised her and meant to keep my word.

"It happened one Friday evening, when we were alone in the gym. It was late, there was nobody else around, just me and him. It was the night before that weekend's state championships and we were working on a part of my parallel bars routine where I was attempting to pause for five seconds in a perfectly still vertical handstand on the lower bars before swinging down and launching myself up onto the higher bar. I was great at the swing, and the launch, but I was having trouble maintaining the perfect form in the headstand.

"For weeks Mr. French had constantly been bracing me by placing his hands on my lower back, my legs, my arms, and stomach. His touch was familiar, comforting, even. And just in case yer 'tinking it, he had never, ever, been creepy in any way. Like I said, he'd been supporting, understanding, nurturing, ya?"

She was quiet for another moment, and, again I wanted to say something. But I almost wanted to stop her from saying anything more. I had a really dark feeling about where this was going, and wasn't sure if I could handle hearing about the hurt she experienced. But then it occurred to me how selfish I was being. If just thinking about it, just hearing about her trauma was going to make me that uncomfortable, imagine what it might be for her having to live with it. I swallowed—both the physiological action and my own cowardice—and kept listening.

"But that night, for some reason, when I was upside down, and he had his left hand on my lower back and his right hand on my lower pelvis—something that had always been part of the training as he was counting down from five and trying to help me maintain a straight and firm posture—that's when it happened. That's when it all changed.

"'You've done it, Li—' she paused, cleared her throat, and then started again. "'You've done it, Ellie,' Mr. French said. 'You've got perfect form. You're going to win us the championship.'

"In that moment, didn't I just bask in the pride of what I had accomplished. And how this man had come to believe in me, and help me to believe in myself.

"And then I heard these words in my head, just then. Mr. French's voice. As clear as if he had just spoken them, with his face just inches apart from mine.

"*'This Bisexual Black girl is going to win me the championship.'*

"I realized I was hearing his thoughts in my mind. My faerie ability to read a person's thoughts had manifested. Only, he didn't use the words I did just now, when he was thinking about me. I . . . . still can't bring myself to repeat them."

Ellie paused as her thumb stopped twirling around mine. I sensed her head move. She was no longer looking down at our clasped hands. The silence lengthened, and the realization of the words her coach must have actually used hit me.

I broke my promise not to look at her then, and my eyes snapped up to her face. Ellie's gaze was fixed over my shoulder, tears rimming her eyes, but she stood with her chin jutted out and her shoulders back. I dropped my eyes back to our hands and covered our clasped right hands with my left one and squeezed gently.

Her hand trembled inside mine, then she began to move her thumb in a circular motion again, so I removed my left hand and mirrored her motion once more.

She took a deep breath and continued.

"I was so shocked I couldn't react. But I kept holding that pose. Perfectly, don't you know. For another full ten seconds, not wavering in the slightest bit.

"'Okay, Ellie, now complete the swing and the dismount.' He said. And I finally unlocked from my upside-down vertical position, completed my swing and launch, to the higher bar, looped around once, twirled in the air, and dropped to the mat. It was the grandest dismount I'd ever done. But when I was standing on the mat, and he rushed over to me, I didn't know what to say to him.

"'You did great, Ellie,' he said, grabbing me by the shoulders. 'You're a master at this. The best student I've ever had. You went above and beyond. You did it! You'll be the state champion.'

"*No,* I thought, *I'll be the girl who brought YOU, a racist homophobe, the championship.* 'Thank you, Mr. French,' was all I managed to say. I couldn't even look at him. All I could do then was look down at the gym mat as I said this, before turning and slowly walking to the girl's changing room.

"I must have showered for a full hour before I left. I wanted to make sure he was gone long before I left. I also tossed my leotards into the trash in the locker room. I never wanted to see them again. I never wanted to do gymnastics again. And I never wanted to see him again. Because every time I did all I could hear was what he truly thought of me.

"I had spent years waiting for my powers and abilities to manifest; but when they did, they revealed something that disturbed me to the core. I mean, what if everyone was walking around with thoughts like that about others? If Mr. French, who had been caring and there for me, being a nurturing father figure—if *he* had thoughts like that—then what would I hear from other people?

"That's when I started to descend into quite the state. I started taking whatever medication and booze I could lift from my parents. I was so afraid of being able to read minds, and I didn't want to hear what they thought of me not manifesting my powers the way I should have been. Before she died, my nan had a sayin' that went: 'where the tongue slips, it speaks the truth.' What about when a person could hear, not the tongue, but the thoughts themselves? Their disappointment in me for being so late to bloom was already clear without me being able to read what was in their heads. So I did my best to numb it. My nan had another sayin': 'what butter and whiskey won't cure, there is no cure for.'

"I kept pissed most of the time and doubled down on my focus on my studies. And I wasn't interested in making any friends, you know. And I certainly didn't want to be getting into a relationship with anyone. Mr. French's thoughts—what he really felt about me—kept reminding me I didn't *want* to hear any of that. Didn't I just keep my nose in a book and getting straight As in school. But the fightin' and tension with my parents was a holy show. I was snapping back at anything they'd be saying to me. And they were giving out and snapping at one another, blaming one another for raising me improperly.

"I dropped out of school and ran away from home by the time I was sixteen. I couldn't be arsed with keeping going the way things were. That's when I was in a fierce state. And thinkin' it might be time to end it. I spent most of my time hiding in the woods near the back of my parents' house. Nobody ever found me. I didn't have any more drugs or alcohol, and I thought maybe I could try again with my mind-reading powers. Maybe I could talk with the animals, like my kind were supposed to. They couldn't possibly have manky thoughts like humans. But the powers never came.

"And that's when I kept finding myself to be returning to a nearby bridge and starin' at the water and wondering, you know.

"It was around that time I first discovered that story of yours, in that digest. All worn and faded from the rain and the sun. But I read it. And that story of yours spoke to me a good bit. Because it was about a girl on a bridge. It gave me a fierce sense of hope for the first time in years. So I kept on.

"I worked several part-time jobs in nearby Menlo Park after taking on a new name, forged my identity as someone who was older. After keeping off the drugs long enough didn't I just manage to activate enough of my faerie abilities to complete the new name and forgery process. And I moved into a basement apartment with a nice old lady who owned a house on a street less than a mile from where my parents lived. The back yard was connected to the conservation area that kept drawing me, and I constantly snuck into the woods and watched my parents go about their lives. I hated living with them, but I missed them a good bit. They never found out where I'd disappeared, and I've never been in contact with them at all. But the solitude of the woods suited me. No people. I'd just be enjoying the scenery and the peace. And the books. I could escape into them, you know.

"I kept trying with my powers, especially in the forest, which was the only place where I was happy out. I told myself to crack on. And I did, until I found your short story collection.

"In your story, Karen realized the importance of a friend, someone who would listen. And in your words, didn't I just feel there was a friend. Right on that page. That kept me going. But the powers were not showin' no matter what I tried. And just last week, when I was back at that bridge, listening to the water flowin beneath me, and thinking about that girl on the bridge and the snowman who talked to her, I closed my eyes, and I heard — clear as the bluest clear blue sky — the first human voices in my mind since that day in the gym those years earlier when Mr. French's thoughts had shocked me.

"The voices weren't talkin' to me, but to each other. And I've no idea who the other man was who was quoting Shakespeare, but didn't I just know the voice of the other boyo. It was you, Michael. I was hearing your voice, and realized it was the same voice that had been in my head these past coupla years when I was reading. And I knew it, because I'd heard your voice in video interviews I'd seen. And you were talking with the other fella about *this* place. This retreat.

"Then another voice spoke to me. I didn't know then, but it was Dr. Laurier. And he was like telling me where this place was. And asking me to come. Didn't he just tell me that he would be able to help me. So that's what brought me here."

She was quiet for a long time, and I continued to watch our thumbs slowly orbit one another through the blur of tears in my eyes. Finally, slowly, the two spiraling digits grazed and then rested against one another and stopped. That's when I knew for sure that she was finished sharing her story.

I glanced up from our clasped hands and saw her looking at me, tears also streaming down her face.

And despite my olfactory senses being muted I could feel not only her pain, but her desperate need to be able to trust again. But more than anything, I felt the complete solitude that encompassed her for her entire adult life.

But, burning out of that loneliness was a deeper, more meaningful connection we'd both experienced. As if we'd shared some special kinship in a past life that was manifesting in us so naturally.

"So, Ellie's not your real name?" I asked, but not aloud. I asked it in my mind.

The look on her face told me she heard the question.

"Ayuh, well it is now," she said. "But, no, Ellie's not the name I was born with. I changed it. Lindy Lea Lewis was my name. And Lindy is the actual name that Mr. French called me. That's the name he, and everyone called me by. But I couldn't stand that name any longer. I changed it to Ellie Emerson. I took the initial L and middle name and changed that to Ellie."

"And you took your last name after the writer," I grinned. "Sharp. Thank you for sharing that with me."

She smiled. "Like I said, there's this inexplicable grand connection between us."

I nodded. "Yeah, I feel it too," I said.

We stood looking at one another silently for a moment.

"Like you," I finally said, "My first name is different than the one I was born with. Edward. I didn't become Michael until I was about a year old, when I was adopted.

And I don't really know what my last name was. But I'll tell you about it some time."

"Aye, I'd like that," she said.

I smiled at her. "Ellie Emerson. I like that. It really suits you."

"Do you think so, Thoreau?"

We both laughed. I was reminded of how she had gravitated to the writing of Ralph Waldo Emerson, and I had been intrigued by that of Henry David Thoreau. They were, as I'd learned from my readings, the best of friends. And that Thoreau had been Emerson's protégé. A strange thought occurred to me then, about past lives. Perhaps Ellie and I were Thoreau and Emerson in past lives, re-connecting again as dear friends with a similar penchant for nature.

"Yeah, I do." I said. "And I like how you kept with the alliteration of your first name."

We laughed again, and then we embraced in a tight, warm, and compassionate hug. We stayed like that, holding one another in friendship and understanding, tears flowing down both of our faces until long after the rain set in, and it was difficult to tell where the tears ended and where the rain began.

Chapter Twelve: Privacy is Paramount in Peer Paranormal Palavering

Sunday, September 3, 2017

If I was at first uncomfortable with the idea of therapy, the concept of engaging in group therapy was even less appealing to me.

Our first session of group therapy happened in the evening, after Sunday dinner, which had been an "on your own" style meal. Dr. Laurier hadn't scheduled more than a few group meal sessions for us for the week. For the most part, there was always access to a host of either buffet service or limited menu items at the usual mealtimes.

The reason we couldn't do the group therapy sessions during the daylight hours, I'd learned, via the gossip that Chester enjoyed spreading, was because Vlastislav was a vampire and was sensitive to daylight.

Throughout the afternoon Chester had flitted about, sharing with each of us one-on-one that the vampire's room in the lodge wasn't on the second floor with the rest of us. He was in a special converted room in a cellar at the end of the hall opposite where the kitchen was located. There were no windows, so there was no risk of any sunlight penetrating into that space.

Chester also shared that the group therapy room had been specially set up with thick window coverings to ensure that no daylight could get in there either, so we could conduct some sessions during the day. But it was Vlastislav who insisted he take no chances and stay asleep and remain secured away in his underground room while the sun was up.

"There's just no end. To the man's very particular demands," was something I heard Chester repeat numerous times as he relayed the intel to us throughout the day.

I didn't really know all that much about actual vampire requirements. No more than the common lore that was used in popular books and movies. But I wondered how safe Vlastislav might be on a mostly overcast, cloudy, and rainy day like today. Was the effect on him related to the actual sunlight touching him—meaning the cloud cover might be protective in some way—or was it a case of all the rays that could still penetrate the cloud cover, or any sort of shading that still allowed diffuse light to reach him that would have that effect? Perhaps, like me, he was a victim of the actual presence of that orb in the day or night sky.

I hadn't had a chance to speak with him one-on-one yet but was curious about that special bond the two of us might have in common.

One thing Chester had speculated about, but hadn't been able to confirm, was whether the vampire's room had a coffin in it instead of a bed. But he was adamant that he'd find out and let us know.

This was my second night in a row of being out in human form well past my normal "sneak away to change" hours. Our session began at 8:00 p.m., and the app I'd used to track sunrise and sunset times told me that tonight's sunset had been at 7:25 p.m. And the other app I regularly consulted was that there'd be a Waxing Gibbous moon that was 91.47% full.

I didn't have to know those times and details now. But it was a well ingrained habit. But I must admit, it felt tremendously liberating not having to worry about it. A guy could get used to this way of living.

As I thought of that, I was reminded of how being with Lex had similarly prevented me from turning into a wolf at sunset. If Lex were still alive, and still here, I'd be able to enjoy this type of freedom everywhere, and not just when I was at this retreat.

Fortunately, Dr. Laurier started the session, breaking me from having to spend that much time thinking about it.

"It's good for us all to be gathered together again," he said. "I know that the idea of group discussion can be a little bit scary sometimes. We often don't know what to expect, and I'm sure that most of us are already facing challenges that ostracize us from regular Paranormal society. But I'm also confident that these similarities will assist us with understanding and empathizing with one another. And while I know we'll get used to these daily sessions throughout the week, I hope that, for tonight, we can ease into this process to make is as easy as possible for everyone."

We were in a room that, like the one I'd had my one-on-one sessions in, was decorated with bookshelves and landscape prints. Instead of being fully filled, like in his office, and the main gathering room of the lodge, this one featured some shelves with books, and others with various knick-knacks, vases, mini statues, and other similar items. Dr. Laurier was seated in front of a window that was covered with thick padding behind a set of heavy black curtains. I only knew this because, as Chester and I had entered the room, he'd rushed over to the window when we first stepped inside and brushed the curtains aside. "See," he'd said. "Fully padded, so this room can be used in broad daylight hours without the risk of a single ray of natural sunlight getting through."

Dr. Laurier's chair was one of those padded office desk chairs on wheels, with armrests and a high back support. The rest of us were seated in a combination of comfortable armchairs and a sofa that all formed a semi-circle layout.

To the therapist's left Shian, Ellie, and Vlastislav each sat in their own armchairs. I was at one end of the sofa beside the vampire, with Linnaeus on my left, and Chester cozied up close to him on the other side. Of course, we hadn't started off sitting this way. I'd originally been in the armchair beside Ellie and Vlastislav was sitting on the couch. But he made a big deal being unable to get comfortable on the couch, particularly having to sit so close to two others. Eager to put an end to his belly-aching I offered to change seats with him.

"Everything that we'll be sharing in this room is going to stay in this room," Dr. Laurier continued. "Peer confidentiality is paramount here, as we need to ensure that everyone feels equally comfortable to share.

"Does anyone have any questions about that?"

I had never done anything like this before, so I had no idea what was coming and what to ask; but a small part of me was wondering about the fact I was somewhat of a celebrity. So far, only one of the other patients here indicated that they knew I was a writer, and I had no doubt I could trust Ellie whole-heartedly with virtually any secret. But I hadn't gotten to know Vlastislav at all. And based on the way I'd seen Chester behave, I figured he was a person who couldn't hold a secret any longer than a paper bag could hold a cup of hot boiling water.

Maybe coming here was a huge mistake.

Was group therapy something I could even do?

Interlude: Therapy Session Clicking Over the Moon Under a Blood Red Sky

Excerpt from therapy session recordings of Dr. Brendon Laurier

Monday, September 4, 2017
9:23 a.m.

LAURIER: Tell me about your aversion to therapy, Michael.

ANDREWS: What makes you think I have an aversion to therapy?

LAURIER: Your discomfort was quite clear from the moment you arrived here. And last night in our first group therapy discussion, you seemed to purposely avoid participating in your own sharing.

ANDREWS: Maybe I don't trust it.

LAURIER: Why?

ANDREW: Maybe . . . maybe I had a previous experience with therapy that didn't sit well with me.

LAURIER: I saw no indication in your personal records of any prior visit to therapy.

ANDREWS: It wasn't me. It's related to my relationship with a friend in high school.

LAURIER: A friend of yours?

ANDREWS: Yes. Well, someone who was more than a friend actually. More someone that I was really into. A girl I was into.

LAURIER: Tell me about her.

ANDREWS: Her name was Melanie. She was in the same English class as me in the tenth grade. She sat in front of me. She was really pretty. And smart. And funny. And from that first day of that first class I remember noticing the scent of her hair. It was this coconut vanilla smell. And I couldn't get enough of it. I kept leaning forward when I was writing, pretending I was really concentrating on writing in my notebook. But I was really trying to get closer to breathe in the magnificent smell of her hair. I had crushes on plenty of girls before, but this was different.

LAURIER: How so?

ANDREWS: We seemed to really click, you know? Before class would start we talked about things. Mostly about the homework. But she seemed to like reading as much as I did. And she was also into writing, too. That had been the first time someone I thought was really cute was also into the same things I was. I'd always been a bit of a loner, and never really talked much to girls. I was nervous around them. I said the wrong things. Stupid things. But with Melanie, even though I always had butterflies in my stomach when speaking with her, we had a real connection.

LAURIER: That sounds wonderful.

ANDREWS: It was. As the year went by, we ended up partnering up on a few different assignments, and even studying together in the library during one of our mutual spares. We became friendly and would talk sometimes in the hallway or at lunch. And since her house wasn't all that far from mine, we would walk to and from school together. We even started to write stories together. Little round-robin style stories that we'd pass back and forth in class. I'd write a paragraph, then pass it to her. She'd write a paragraph or two, and then it was my turn again. I thought they were pretty good stories, but it was more about connecting with her in a far more intimate way. I didn't have any friends, so this was already a new experience for me.

LAURIER: That seems like it was a good experience.

ANDREWS: She started to share intimate and personal things with me in our chats. You know, things she dreamed about. What scared her. What she enjoyed more than anything. I opened up to her about stuff I'd never talked to with anyone before.

LAURIER: Is this the "therapy" part that led to your aversion?

ANDREWS: No. Or maybe partially. I trusted her by opening up. But I also felt myself falling for her. Really falling for her. I loved her. Intensely. But I kept it to myself, because I was worried about losing that important friendship we had developed. Just being around her made me feel good. I was pretty sure she felt the same way about me, but I was scared to say something. So, I wasted time not acting upon my feelings. But as we were getting toward the end of the school year, I got nervous. What if we didn't have any classes together the next year? What if I lost my convenient excuse to spend so much time with her? So I took a chance, and I told her how I felt when we were working on a project that involved watching the old black and white 1960s movie adaptation to the William Golding novel Lord of the Flies. *It was one of the most nerve-wracking things I'd ever done. I mean, what if she didn't feel the same way about me? What if that would be the end of the only friend I'd had? Melanie was the only person who I felt knew the real me, and who appreciated writing in the same way I did.*

LAURIER: So what happened when you told her?

ANDREWS: It was better than I ever could have imagined. She said she felt the same way about me. And we kissed. It was the first real kiss with a girl I'd ever had. I was on top of the world.

[There is a long pause]

LAURIER: I sense that there is a bit of an "and then" moment coming.

ANDREWS: Yeah. There is.

LAURIER: So what happened?

ANDREWS: As I said, we kissed. It was magical. This young woman I loved with all of my heart and had opened up to felt the same way about me. The kiss was magic. Beyond anything I ever could have dreamed. And I'd spent a long time dreaming about what it would be like to kiss her. I wanted us to publicly declare our love for one another. I wanted to carve our names inside a big heart on the bench in the park beside the schoolyard. I wanted to hold her hands while walking to and from school and in the hallways. But she wasn't comfortable with that. She didn't like public displays of affection. She asked if we could keep it just between the two of us.

LAURIER: That must have been disappointing for you.

ANDREWS: It was. But I was over the moon. I mean, she felt the same way about me. When we were in private, we had those intimate discussions, and we kissed. We even came up with a secret language about our love. Because it was while studying Lord of the Flies *that we first shared our feelings for one another, we used language related to the book in our private code. Referring to Piggy's glasses meant "I see what you mean." "Killing the pig" meant something we were obsessed with. Like the way I was obsessed with Spider-Man. Saying we enjoyed the book meant we were looking forward to our next make-out session. And the phrase "I've got the conch" meant I love you.*

LAURIER: Your own language based on that novel. That's very elaborate.

ANDREWS: It was. And it was so cool that we had this secret and special bond. Something only the two of us shared. It went on for that last month of school. And I wondered if she was embarrassed to be with me; to admit that to her friends. As in maybe that was why she wanted to keep it a secret. And then, before the end of the month, and when the school year ended, she told me she couldn't do what we were doing any longer.

LAURIER: What was her reasoning?

ANDREWS: She told me when we had first been sharing intimate things about ourselves that she had been seeing a therapist for years. That her therapist had been the only other person she had confided such private things to. So I knew about him. But *what I didn't know is that she was still seeing the therapist. And that she'd talked to the therapist about her feelings for me. And that her therapist was the one who told her our relationship was unhealthy and not good for her. That it wasn't good for her to be so dependent on someone else for her happiness. That she needed to be happy on her own. On her own terms. Without someone like me, whose influence was to try to force her into being codependent.*

LAURIER: *That must have been hard to hear.*

ANDREWS: *It was. Very. I was heartbroken. But I honored her wish. I thought if I gave her that space she needed, if I stepped back, I'd show her that I respected her. And then maybe, she would come back on her own. You know, after she dealt with the personal stuff. But less than a month after we had that discussion and she said we couldn't keep on the way we were, that we had to end our friendship too, that's when she started seeing this jock in our school. The school hockey team's captain.*

LAURIER: *And you blame her therapist for this?*

ANDREWS: *Of course. If it hadn't been for him, she would never have broken up with me. And ended up with him. So, yeah, ever since then I've taken issue with the meddling that therapists do in people's lives.*

Chapter Thirteen: Linnaeus and the Tale of the Trollgre

I squirmed in my chair as I looked around at the others in the room. How could I even trust these people? Sure, I'd had a chance to get to know three of them, and I really did like Linnaeus, Shian, and Ellie. But I was still leery about Chester's ability to keep a secret. And I didn't really know all that much about Vlastislav, other than the fact he was a bit of a fusspot.

Looking around the room, it seemed everyone else also seemed a little uncertain and hesitant. Beside me, I could feel Linnaeus twitch in a way that suggested he was about to say something, to try to make an opening for anyone else who wanted to ask something. But he didn't speak, which surprised me. He was, after all, the most extroverted one of the entire group.

We all seemed to be looking at one another, all speechless, before I spotted the subtle shaking of heads.

"Okay," Dr. Laurier continued. "So, the first thing that we're going to be doing is an icebreaker exercise. What does it make you think of when I say *icebreaker*?"

"Ah, the *icebreaker*," Linnaeus said, suddenly sitting straight up. "The prefatory interaction imposed upon a freshman group. An introductory activity meant to incite a base-level cordiality and to stimulate discussion."

"Yes," Dr. Laurier said. "Anyone else?"

"A way for us to get to know one another?" Shian said hesitantly. She seemed to want to say something else but wrinkled her nose and closed her eyes.

"Was there something else?" Dr. Laurier asked her.

Shian let out a breath, then opened her eyes and slowly tracked across all the males in the room. When her eyes briefly met mine, I felt that instant erotic pull she'd previously inflicted upon me. "Yes, there is. I just want to say that there's not a single guy here who I wouldn't really like to get to know in a more carnal way if you catch my drift."

After saying that, she scrunched her face up again, which was now a deep shade of red, looked down at her feet and let out a sob. "Oh, I'm so sorry," she said. "It just comes out of me. Please forgive me."

We all shifted uncomfortably in our seats as Dr. Laurier reached a hand across to her shoulder. "It's okay, Shian. There are instinctual forces that none of us control. I understand. And I'm sure that, more than anyone else out there, your colleagues here also understand."

"We do," I said. "We do understand."

"Consider yourself forgiven, Ann," Linnaeus said.

Shian looked up at him, remembering the nickname he'd come up with for her. That gesture of collegial affection seemed to put her at ease again.

Everyone else in the semi-circle nodded and offered their own verbal agreement.

"But you are right, Shian," Dr. Laurier said. "It is a way for us to get to know one another. Anyone else?"

"To get us talking and interacting in a non-threatening way?" Vlastislav said. He was looking across at Linnaeus with a tentative look on his face. The oversized man on the couch beside me nodded so vigorously that the entire couch shook. Seeing this, the vampire's worried face appeared to slightly relax. Maybe all he needed was to be accepted.

"To build trust?" Ellie asked.

"Yes. To build trust. And . . .?"

"Camaraderie?" Linnaeus asked. "Community?"

"Yes. Both of those. Anyone else?"

I decided to contribute. "To get us comfortable with talking about ourselves?" I said.

"That too."

"To establish a fellowship?" Chester asked. "A supportive pack?"

"Indeed." Dr. Laurier nodded, then looked around at each of us to see if anyone else wanted to add anything else.

"It's all the things you just said. As we spend time together this week, it's important that we ensure we know where everyone else is coming from. Yes, there'll be time outside this session and our one-on-ones, for most of you to get to know one another in a more casual way. But it's essential that we establish a solid rapport with each other in addition to your rapport with me as your guiding therapist. You will likely need to lean on one another as we explore those things that drove us to be here. So, it's important that you begin with an understanding of each other and where everyone is coming from.

"The first thing we are going to try is a fun icebreaker I like that is called 'two truths and a lie.' I want you all to think of two truths and one lie about yourself. Now the idea is that the lie you come up with about yourself is going to be something that might still possibly be true, or perhaps contains a partial truth within it. Something your fellow group members might have to really wonder when guessing which one the lie is. And we'll go around, trying to see if the others can guess which one the lie is about each person.

"Does that sound good?"

Everyone nodded in agreement.

"Okay," Dr. Laurier said. "Who wants to be brave and to start us off?"

"Absolutely," Linnaeus said. "I'll be the first to toss my hat into the proverbial ring."

"Great," Dr. Laurier said. "So, start off by saying your name, to which paranormal class you belong, and a quick summary of the issue you're dealing with, which brings you here. Even if this is something you might have already shared when getting to know one another one-on-

one so far. It's important to ensure we're all on equal footing together, here and now. And then, once you provide that information as a starting point, share the three statements about yourself where one of them is a lie."

"My name is Linnaeus Kristiansen. I'm a troll. Or at least, a half-troll, half-ogre."

"You're a trollgre," Vlastislav said with a wry grin on his face.

"Vlastislav, please don't interrupt," Dr. Laurier said.

The vampire glared at the therapist, and Linnaeus leaned forward on the couch. "No, no, that's quite all right. The point of this exercise, as you have asserted, dear Doctor, is for us to get to know one another. The nomenclature my father used was Ogroll. It's a similar derivation of the combined words of the two classes you just employed, but in reverse. And, also, the term Ogroll is often used in a derogatory fashion by those who look down upon cross-class mating. But the tradition, among trolls, is to take on one's paternal class. So, technically, I am a troll.

"But it's important to denote my half-species status, as I believe that's one of the reasons for me needing to employ the use of this facility." Linnaeus went on to briefly explain the challenge he had as an extrovert whose legacy required him to maintain an isolated existence and to chase people from his bridge.

"The first thing about me is that I am an exquisite chef—self-trained in the art of the classic Le Cordon Bleu style of French cooking. Second, I have a small tattoo of a heart on my inner right thigh. And third, I resided for several years of my youth in a Catholic orphanage."

"Wonderful, Linnaeus," Dr. Laurier said, then looked around the room at the rest of us. "Which one of those do you think is not the real one? Oh, and by the way, I'm not going to participate in guessing, since, as your therapist, I have access to your files and backgrounds, and would have an unfair advantage."

I considered all three things. I at least know that the last one was real, because he'd shared that much with me. But even though he hadn't been wearing much yesterday, the placement of the tattoo he mentioned would have been in a spot that neither Shian nor I would have seen it. So that one could be real too. The idea of a troll who was good in the kitchen seemed the least likely of the three to me.

"Ah," Vlastislav said. "I think it's the last one. You talked about your father. So, I don't think that the orphanage is real. That's the lie."

"Yes," Chester said. "Me too."

"Negative," Linnaeus said with a big toothy smile. "That one is, indeed, true."

"But your father?" Chester asked. "How can you have a father if you lived at an orphanage?"

"Therein lies my crafty deception," Linnaeus said. "I did not meet my paternal figure until I was eighteen."

"Nicely played," Vlastislav said.

"I think," I said. "That it has to be the French cooking one," I said. "I mean, yesterday, both Shian and I saw you in nothing but a loincloth. So if you'd said your tattoo was on your shoulder or ankle or something, we would have seen it. But the tattoo you mention could have been covered."

"Yeah," Chester said. "It's got to be the cooking thing."

"And I wouldn't mind one bit," Shian said. "If you drop trou right now and let where you have that heart-on."

She pronounced the last word as if it ended in a 'd' for the double-entendre. Like before, Shian's words had the effect of making me want to stand and pull my own pants down. Her power of suggestion seemed even more powerful in this closed space.

But the moment the words came out, she raised one hand to cover her mouth and turned beet red. "Sorry."

"It's quite all right," Linnaeus said. "I'm rather used to this physique having that effect on the female persuasion." He grinned, diffusing the situation with self-deprecating humor.

She smiled at him, and it wasn't one of those overtly flirtatious grins. It was one of genuine appreciation.

"Yes, we most certainly understand," Chester said. "Don't we, Linnaeus?"

"We do, my friend," Linnaeus said, patting the small thin man on the arm.

"So it's true that you do know a good bit about French cooking?" Ellie asked.

"Yes, and primarily self-educated in the culinary arts, thanks mostly to the classic two volume set of *Mastering the Art of French Cooking* by the French Chef herself, Mrs. Julia Child."

"That's most fascinating," Vlastislav said.

"So, no tattoo, then?" I asked.

"No. I am unable to obtain one. Though I have made the attempt at the shape and location I specified. But the needles are not able to pierce my skin without breaking. So that realm of subcutaneous ink art evades me."

"Thank you for sharing, Linnaeus." Dr. Laurier said. "Now who would like to go next?"

I did my best to make myself as small as possible on the couch beside Linnaeus.

Interlude: Therapy Session
Yippee Ki-Yay Mother Trigger

Excerpt from therapy session recordings of Dr. Brendon Laurier

Wednesday, September 6, 2017
7:26 p.m.

LAURIER: Do you remember a few days ago in group therapy, when Linnaeus was sharing a little about himself?

ANDREWS: Sure. I really like Linnaeus. The two of us really clicked. Of course, he's an easy guy to like.

LAURIER: Yes, he is quite personable. I've noticed quite the bond of friendship between you. But I also noticed your discomfort that day when Linnaeus started talking about the orphanage.

ANDREWS: You did?

LAURIER: Yes. You were shifting uncomfortably in your seat when he brought it up and then again when Vlastislav mentioned it. Is there something about the word orphanage that bothers you?

ANDREWS: Why would that word bother me?

LAURIER: Not the word. What is describes.

ANDREWS: And what does it describe?

LAURIER: You tell me. When you hear the word orphanage what does that make you think of?

ANDREWS: I don't know. Little kids without parents. Children without a home. An environment that is somewhat sterile. And maybe even a little sad.

LAURIER: What about your own relation to the orphanage?

ANDREWS: I would hardly think much. I wasn't in one for very long as an infant. And besides, I was far too young to even remember that time in my life.

[There is a long section of silence]

ANDREWS: Are you saying that I'm somehow scarred by the fact I was in an orphanage when I was a baby? That sounds like a whole lot of bullshit psychobabble to me.

LAURIER: I didn't say anything of the sort. I was merely exploring why whenever that word came up you became uncomfortable.

ANDREWS: It's all in your head, Doc. The word doesn't make me uncomfortable.

LAURIER: Are you sure?

ANDREWS: Yes, I'm quite sure.

LAURIER: What about something we haven't yet discussed? The fact that you were adopted?

ANDREWS: Really? You're going to bring that up? That's what I mean about all this psychobabble bullshit. Yes, I was adopted. Who cares? For most of my life whenever people found that out a look of sympathy came over their face. It was subtle, but I saw it. And I hated it. That's why I'm so glad that nobody who knows me in my new life in New York knows. Why? Because it doesn't make one iota of difference—that's why! And with my enhanced ability to pick up emotion it would annoy the hell out of me to have to smell that pity. I don't know why shrinks think that there's supposed to be some sort of trauma that adopted kids are supposed to face. I mean, c'mon, Doc. It's not like I have any memory of those first few months in my life. All I can remember, and all that I know is I was raised by two wonderful parents, and they brought me up as their own. And I had a great life growing up with them.

LAURIER: We talked about how they both died when you were in your early twenties.

ANDREWS: Yes, they did. So, I had a great childhood. A great upbringing. They set me on the right path.

LAURIER: So, when your adoptive parents—

ANDREWS: My parents!

LAURIER: Pardon?

ANDREWS: You called them my adoptive parents.

LAURIER: Well, technically, they—

ANDREWS: You want to use the word technically? Okay, let's use it. Technically, they raised me. Technically, they were my parents. And they'll always be my parents. Because, technically, they were there for me for every scraped knee, every runny nose, every childhood nightmare. Technically, they were my mom and dad. Why the hell do people try to take that away by inserting that descriptor on it? Damn, I hate that term. "Adoptive parents." And fuck you for using it. You're supposed to be helping me. And what the hell does that have to do with any of why I'm here? They were my parents, Doc. My parents. Why do people always have to put tags and needless adjectives on everything and everyone? Why try to remove what they were to me? What they still are to me! And why the hell . . . [the sound of a long deep breath is clearly audible] *. . . oh fuck it. Why the hell am I even bothering? To hell with you! And to hell with this!*

[The clatter of something falling to the floor is followed by a door slamming]

Chapter Fourteen: Chester's Cheshire Cat Deception

Sunday, September 3, 2017

"I'll go next," Chester offered. "I've got some."

"Excellent," Dr. Laurier said. "Go ahead, Chester."

"My name is Charles Vincent. But my friends call me Chester. And that's what I prefer. Only my mother ever called me Charles. When she's angry with me. I am a werecat. And proud of it. But I'm not cat-like when I'm a human. I'm more like the opposite. Like a dog. A loyal, faithful, obedient dog. That's what people say. My entire life. Which bothers me. Because I'm proud. Of being a cat. And I want to be more like a cat when I'm human. But not exactly. I don't want to be bad. Because cats are mean. They like to wreck things. And I do that when I'm a cat. But I'm really not like that. I'm a good boy. A good person. When I turn into a cat I . . . get into things. I'm destructive. I can't help myself.

"I struggle with. The things I do. When I'm a cat. I want to be good. Not wreck things. But I want that confidence. The way I feel. When I'm a cat. But not how I act. I want people to like me. To know I'm good. Not bad."

I thought about what he was saying and could see a bit of myself in Chester. Unlike me, he had full control over the change between human and cat form. But like me, he struggled with the dramatic difference in that duality.

"So, here they are. The three things. I can purr. When not in cat form. Two, I love socks. For as long as I can remember. They're fascinating. And three, I enjoy snacking on dog treats. In human form. Especially Milk-Bone® biscuits."

"That's great, Chester." Dr. Laurier said. "Really good."

"A good boy?" Chester said, clasping his hands together and rocking back and forth in his seat.

But before Dr. Laurier could even respond a distinct total fluttering sound filled the room. It was coming from Chester. I remembered wondering if he had been making a similar noise yesterday.

"I'm a good boy. Right, doctor?" Chester said, and the purring sound continued.

"Well, that proverbial cat's out of the bag," Linnaeus said with a laugh. "I'm quite certain based on the looks on everyone's faces that we can all hear that."

"Holy moly," Ellie said. "You're quite happy out."

"That's so cool!" Shian said. "I bet you could make me p—" She managed to cut herself off before finishing the sentence. "T-that, that's really cool."

"Amazing!" Vlastislav said.

Chester's face lit up. But not with embarrassment. With unabashed joy.

The soft buzzing sound he was making continued.

"I guess," Dr. Laurier said, "we're all aware that the first thing you mentioned is true. Does anyone else have any guesses about the remaining two?"

Chester flashed a glare while raising his lips to show his clenched teeth in the doctor's direction. The purr-like sound he'd been making simultaneously stopped. Apparently, he wasn't done with his time basking in the spotlight.

"I do," Vlastislav said. "I can't imagine anyone being interested in socks. They are disgusting, odorous, vile things. Worn on the feet, they spend most of their day inside of a shoe or boot, getting sweaty and smelly. I suspect that Chester is trying to trick us with this, as cats often play with or bring socks to their owners. That one must be the lie."

I thought about how Chester's human behavior seemed to fall in line with that of a dog. So perhaps he also enjoyed dog treats. "I agree with that," I said. "I'm with Vlastislav."

"Me three," Ellie said. "Vlad's right."

The vampire whipped around in his armchair, his right arm lashing out at lightning speed to grab Ellie's left forearm which had been resting on the arm of her own armchair. "Don't call me that!" he hissed. "My name is Vlastislav."

"S-sorry," Ellie said, extracting her arm from his grip and rubbing it.

"Come now, my friend," Linnaeus said to him. "One can't blame the young lass for it. After all, you are a vampire. And your name can suitably be shortened to Vlad. As in Vlad the Impaler—the man whose patronymic inspired the title character of Bram Stoker's classic literary vampire novel."

"You think I don't know that?" Vlastislav said. "Or that I haven't heard that my entire life?"

"Of course. You're quite right. I stand corrected, my friend, and certainly mean you no offense. And I'm sure the young lady here meant you no affront either."

"I meant nothin' by it," Ellie said.

"How could any of us know that it is a matter you are particularly sensitive to?" Linnaeus continued. "But now that you have stated your wishes, I shall respect your pronouncement. I'm sure this assemblage of fellow residents at this establishment will also honor your request."

There was a murmur of agreement from everyone in the room.

"Thank you," Vlastislav said. He turned to Ellie. "And I am sorry, Ellie. I should not have lashed out like that. But I suppose that nickname triggers me."

"Ah sure," Ellie said. "Think nothin' of it."

The tension in the room had been diffused, but Linnaeus, ever the peacemaker, wasn't finished trying to make the vampire feel less out of place. "Like you, I am particularly sensitive to an abbreviation of my name. When I was prepubescent, my friends called me Linus. This was before I had matured into who I am now. That was when everything and everyone in my previous life — including my dearest friend — suffered the direst extirpation. So, similar to the instinctive reaction that dominates for you, I cannot bear to hear the name I had been called before. It conjures up far too many morose feelings of loss."

I glanced at Ellie, thinking about what she had said about changing her own name. She offered me back a knowing smile.

I then looked to her left, at Dr. Laurier, who'd been sitting silent the entire time this interaction went down with a slight smile on his face. The therapist then turned his attention over to Chester. "So, Chester, which of the two is the lie and which is the truth? Is it the fascination with socks, or the consumption of dog treats?"

"I've fooled you all," Chester laughed. He then turned to Linnaeus. "Of course, you haven't said. What you think."

"That's because it would be most unfair to the rest," Linnaeus said with a smile. "Because every day since I've woken up, I have found at least one, sometimes two single socks at the foot of my bed. And I trust I have you to thank for the nocturnal treats that have greeted me each morning."

Chester grinned and began to purr again. "You're most welcome." He then turned to face the rest of the group. "I made it up. The dog biscuit thing. But have you tasted them? I found them dry. Almost like sawdust."

"Yes, I've also tried them," I said. "It felt like I was chewing on a piece of cardboard. And I couldn't get the taste out of my mouth."

"You'd think," Linnaeus said, "that a canine would have relished that kind of a snack."

I laughed. "Oh, that was years before I was bitten by a wolf and became what I am now."

A strange look crossed Vlastislav's face, and he opened his mouth, about to say something when Dr. Laurier interjected. "We are getting a little off track. We're discussing Chester's truths and lie."

"Well, on that matter, I must admit that I have also partaken in the consumption of that particular brand of dog biscuits," Linnaeus said. "With my best friend Brian. Back in the day. They were definitely not to his liking, but I didn't find the taste of them all that bad. Not much different than a thick water cracker."

"What?" Ellie said. "Are you all taking the piss, or has every man ever tried a Milk-Bone® treat?"

"Never!" Vlastislav said, making a retching sound. "I can't imagine being so stupid as to eat something so vile."

Shian said something in a low voice that I didn't hear.

"What's that, Ann?" Linnaeus said. "I didn't catch you."

"I did," she said meekly. "At a dog-themed brewery in St. Petersburg, Florida just a few months ago. They had those bone-shaped dog treats in a jar at the bar meant for the dogs who were welcome in the establishment. I ate one when I was trying to impress a guy at the bar."

"How did you find it?" Ellie asked.

"It was terrible. Dry. I choked, and couldn't swallow it, so I spit it out, right into my drink." She laughed. "Needless to say, my attempt to seduce him did not go as planned."

"What about you, Dr. Laurier?" Chester asked.

"What about me?"

"You're a man. Have you ever tried one? A dog biscuit?"

"No. I can't say I've ever been tempted. But this isn't about me. It's about you. Let's not digress."

In response, Chester huffed, crossed his arms in front of his chest and frowned, his bottom lip protruding like a Chihuahua's tongue. His visual disappointment was a bit much, acting as if someone had urinated in his bowl of corn flakes rather than the mild suggestion to keep the exercise going.

Dr. Laurier didn't seem to notice the little man's over-reaction as he turned his head to Shian. "Should we keep going in the order we are? Shian, would you like to go next?"

Shian's face turned red, and she focused her attention on a spot on the floor between where her feet were planted.

Interlude: Therapy Session
I Just Wanna Be Loved, Is That So Wahroung?

Excerpt from therapy session recordings of Dr. Brendon Laurier

Tuesday, September 5, 2017
3:04 p.m.

LAURIER: You seem to be getting along with most of the others at this retreat.

ANDREWS: Yes, I suppose I have been.

LAURIER: But your experience interacting with other Paranormals is relatively new, isn't it?

ANDREWS: [laughs] You can say that.

LAURIER: How would you describe your interactions with other Paranormal folks in general?

ANDREWS: *In general? Pretty shitty.*

LAURIER: *Why is that?*

ANDREWS: *Well, let's see. The first werewolf I met tried to kill me and the woman I loved. The next Paranormals I encountered were a neo-Nazi cult hell-bent on bringing chaos into the world. And then Gail's brother and her best friend—neither of whom liked me to begin with—show up out of nowhere and tell me I can't be with her. Because some devil-worshiping witch clan from hundreds of years ago established a curse that would prevent me from being with the woman I love. And I find myself fighting hordes of demons that seem to keep creeping out of the woodwork. So, no, I guess that most of my interactions with other Paranormals have been far from what any sane person might call positive.*

LAURIER: *The woman you love, Gail, is, herself a witch.*

ANDREWS: *Yes, but I didn't know that.*

LAURIER: *The curse aside, you've always gotten along with her?*

ANDREWS: *Yes. I've loved her from pretty much the day we first met.*

LAURIER: *And the other woman you loved, Alexandria. She was also Paranormal.*

ANDREWS: Yes, she was. But I also didn't know that when I was falling for her.

LAURIER: And your closest friend, Buddy. He also has Paranormal abilities.

ANDREWS: Yes, but again, I didn't know that until just recently. What are you getting at here, Doc?

LAURIER: I was just exploring your perception of Paranormals. And why you see it as negative when several close acquaintances are, in fact, supernatural.

ANDREWS: Sure, there are a few I get along with, and trust. But like I said, I didn't even know that about them, until after the fact. Most of my experience with the Paranormal world has not been pleasant.

LAURIER: Why do you think you're getting along so well with most of the others here?

ANDREWS: I think of it as the Linnaeus effect.

LAURIER: The Linnaeus effect?

ANDREWS: Yeah. Linnaeus is such a lynchpin, you know. He's gregarious, friendly, personable. He doesn't just welcome everyone in and does his best to try to make them laugh, but he seems to inspire other people around him to do the same. He reminds me of my friend and mentor, Buddy in many ways. Buddy has that way of just putting himself out there and making a person feel good about themselves.

LAURIER: Would you say that Linnaeus is a people pleaser?

ANDREWS: I think so. Yes.

LAURIER: How about you? Do you think of yourself as a people pleaser, Michael?

ANDREWS: I think so, yes. I mean, I'm usually not one for confrontation. I know, it's ironic when you consider how many situations I've been involved in, especially these past several years, where I've gotten into predicaments where I've needed to fight. You know, all those years in my childhood of wanting to be like Spider-Man, the one thing I could never reconcile was using my fists. It's not like I ever really punched anyone before. I'm not a violent person.

[There's a long stretch of silence with only the sound of notes being jotted onto a notepad]

LAURIER: Do you know who else here at the retreat is a people pleaser?

ANDREWS: It's definitely not the picky-pants vampire.

LAURIER: *I wasn't thinking of Vlastislav. I was thinking of Chester.*

ANDREWS: *Chester?*

LAURIER: *Yes. I think that, like you, and Linnaeus, he is eager to please others.*

ANDREWS: *[Mutters something indistinguishable]*

LAURIER: *I didn't catch that.*

ANDREWS: *Nothing. It was nothing.*

LAURIER: *You seem to be a little put-off with Chester.*

ANDREWS: *What do you mean?*

LAURIER: *Your reaction just now. And several reactions I've witnessed.*

ANDREWS: *Well, he's an annoying little twerp.*

LAURIER: *Why do you feel that way about him?*

ANDREWS: *He's like one of those pesky little mini dogs. Not even a real dog. And trying to compensate for it. He's constantly chirping, nipping at people, and he just ticks me off. I* mean, the only thing that's cat-like about him is just how fickle he is.

LAURIER: *Do you think you might be a little jealous of his relationship with Linnaeus?*

ANDREWS: *His relationship with Linnaeus? He doesn't have a relationship with him. He fawns over him. He practically throws himself at the man's feet. It's embarrassing, and pathetic. He should be ashamed of the needy way he behaves.*

LAURIER: *That's quite the strong reaction.*

ANDREWS: *Well, I'm disgusted by that kind of behavior.*

LAURIER: *Is that because it reminds you of something, or of someone?*

ANDREWS: *Maybe.*

LAURIER: *What, or who?*

ANDREWS: *My childhood. My mom. My dad always accused my mother of fawning over me. Of babying me. It made my father rather angry. He hated how my mom practically worshiped the ground I walked on and could do no wrong. So yeah, maybe that's it.*

LAURIER: *Is there anyone else?*

ANDREWS: No. Not that I can think of.

LAURIER: Did you ever wonder if you incorporated that trait of your mother's in any of your relationships?

ANDREWS: How do you mean?

LAURIER: Do you think you might place women that you know and love on a pedestal?

Chapter Fifteen: Shian Shares That There Is No Place Called Kokomo

Sunday, September3, 2017

"Uh, okay," Shian said, after a moment of silence. "I'll go next. Let me think a moment." She was quiet for some time as her eyes lifted from the spot on the floor she'd been staring at and flitted about the room. She briefly looked at each of us but without making eye contact with anyone.

I found it so interesting how she normally behaved in such a shy manner but would then go from zero to sixty with an intense and over-the-top come-on line. And when she turned those mermaid charms on, she didn't just look a person straight in the eye, she seemed to peer deep into them, and hook them by the very soul.

"Would you like us to move on and come back to you?" Dr. Laurier asked.

"No," Shian said. "It's okay. I'm just thinking."

We waited another minute in silence while she contemplated what she was about to say.

"Okay," she finally said. "I've got them." She was quiet for a while, looking at the floor. "But I'm rather nervous about sharing."

"It's all right," Dr. Laurier assured her. "This is a safe space. And you've already done quite well in sharing."

"I have?"

"Yes," Dr. Laurier said.

"You've got this," Linnaeus said. "And remember, you are among friends."

Shian looked up and made direct eye contact with Linnaeus. Unlike the previous times she'd looked one of us in the eye, there didn't seem to be any of that intense mermaid glare that charmed and seduced. It was a look of gratitude, and perhaps something a little bit deeper.

"We've got your back, Ann." Linnaeus said. "And we won't let you fall."

A huge smile spread on Shian's face. Not a seductive leer, but a grin of pure appreciation. "Thank you," she mouthed.

She closed her eyes, took a deep breath, and then opened them again, back to looking at the floor. "Okay," she said. "Here goes. My name is Shian Pederson. I'm from the Florida Keys. And I'm a mermaid. The reason I'm here is that I am extremely shy. Painfully so. I've likely spoken more in the past couple of days than I have in the previous month. I abhor small talk. Yesterday, when Linnaeus and Michael and I were chatting on the beach, I felt like I was talking with dear old friends. We were sharing openly. Like we are today. That feels good.

"But in general, my tendency towards introversion conflicts with the nature of who I am. Mermaids are supposed to be masterful at seducing men, but I expend a significant amount of energy suppressing that part of me. When I do release it, it feels somehow forced, and I go over the top, as many of you have already observed. So that is why I am here. I need to find the confidence to become who I need to be."

She paused, looked up and around the room, and this time made brief eye contact with each one of us. For the first time since I'd met her, meeting her direct gaze didn't trigger any sort of sexual reaction. I wondered if it were possible that she might actually be making progress and felt a burst of pride for her.

"Okay," she said. "For my three things. Here goes. I panic whenever I swim into deep water, especially places where I can't see the bottom. I once knocked out an alligator with a single punch to win a bar bet in Kokomo. And I am a virgin."

Linnaeus and I both knew that the first thing she'd shared was true, so we had that advantage. I thus considered the likeliness of the other two statements. It didn't seem possible that such a powerful seductress could still be a virgin. Sure, she hooked and reeled the fish in well enough, and consistently fumbled when trying to scoop them up in the net with her horrendously inappropriate pick-up lines. That pathetic finish effectively shattered the previous magic. But I knew, all too well, the intense allure she radiated, and couldn't imagine there wasn't some guy out there so desperate for female companionship that her Leisure Suit Larry come-ons would destroy his mood.

"Stunning a gator with a single blow seems a bit outrageous," Vlastislav said. "I doubt that even I could do it with only one punch."

"Ah sure," Ellie said. "I think that one could be the lie. But a mermaid being afraid of water is also a bit much."

"I don't know," I said. "I remember the might of her punch when she was flailing in the water yesterday because of her fear of the river's depth. I don't know much about the Paranormal realm, but I suspect that water gives mermaids extraordinary strength. So, I'm thinking that the third one might be the lie."

"Good point," Linnaeus said. "I witnessed your head snap back when she clocked you." He laughed. "Sorry, I thought she was going to rotate your cranium all the way around. Her punches didn't faze me, and my flesh isn't nearly as thick as an alligator's hide. So, I'm guessing that the second one is a lie."

"Yeah," Chester said, nodding in agreement with Linnaeus. "What he said."

"Nicely done, Shian," Dr. Laurier said. "You've got the room somewhat split on this. Which one is the lie?"

Shian laughed. "The alligator tale was the lie. Or, at least partially. I used Dr. Laurier's concept of making the lie something pretty close to the truth. I did stun a gator with a single blow. But it wasn't part of a bar bet. And also, there's no place called Kokomo. The Beach Boys made it up. That was a clue for anyone who knew that one."

"Do elaborate for us, please," Linnaeus said.

"I was at a waterfront bar in Key Largo—not Kokomo—when an alligator grabbed a dog by the tail and pulled him right off the pier. I jumped into the water and got to it before he could get away or harm the poor little thing. I slammed my fist so hard down on the gator that he let the dog go. While the alligator was stunned, I tossed the dog up onto the pier and swam away from there as quickly as I could. I couldn't very well hop out of the water and reveal my natural form. Especially not to my date. I never did see them again.

"But here's the thing that connects the second and third statement and would have made that third one a lie. Ironically, the date I'd been on at the time had been going remarkably well, which was a very rare thing for me. The evening was progressing nicely, and the conversation was deep and meaningful—at least until that alligator snatched the dog. Because I'm pretty sure, had things continued along the way they'd been progressing, it would have led the beautiful woman I was with that evening to my bedroom. And without any leveraging of my supernatural charm."

Interlude: Therapy Session
She's So High on A Pedestal Above Me, She's So Lovely

Excerpt from therapy session recordings of Dr. Brendon Laurier

Tuesday, September 5, 2017
3:11 p.m.

ANDREWS: You think that I place women on a pedestal?

LAURIER: No, I was asking if you thought you might do that.

ANDREWS: I respect women. I always have.

LAURIER: That's good. So tell me, what is it that you love about Gail Sommers?

ANDREWS: You mean besides the fact that she's perfect for me?

LAURIER: *Yes. What are the things about Gail that attract you to her?*

ANDREWS: *So many things. Gail is remarkable. She is drop-dead gorgeous. But what makes her a thousand times more attractive is she doesn't seem to realize or recognize it. She doesn't flaunt it around by strutting about with her nose in the air. I love that about her. If anything, she laughs about how clumsy she is. But she's not clumsy. She can be so graceful. But she laughs at herself and has the best sense of humor. A sharp, witty sense of humor, but never at the expense of someone else. She says the funniest things and makes me laugh. But again, like her beauty, she doesn't even seem to recognize that about herself. There's no conceit about her. She is spunky, and tough. Another thing is that she is so incredibly smart. She runs a small business, which isn't easy with the rent alone you have to pay for a storefront in Manhattan. There have been times when the money was tight, and I can easily afford to help her out, but never once has she accepted. She always finds a way to work things out. Because she's brilliant, and a fantastic problem-solver. Not to mention a good leader. She manages her business and staff so effectively. Everyone on staff looks up to her. But she doesn't treat them like employees. She treats them like friends, and even family. She is loyal. And trustworthy. She goes to bat for her friends. Gail is someone you can count on to be there for you. She's been there for me, and there's nobody I'd rather have watching my back. When I'm with her the world just seems brighter, and right, you know. I feel like —*

LAURIER: Okay, that's great. Now what are some of Gail's flaws?

ANDREWS: She doesn't have any.

LAURIER: Everyone has flaws, Michael. Even Gail.

ANDREWS: No. Gail is perfect. She is the perfect woman.

LAURIER: So, there's nothing you'd change about her?

ANDREWS: No. Nothing. Well, except for the fact that she's not with me right now.

LAURIER: How about an area where she could improve. Everyone has something to improve.

ANDREWS: Well, she could be a little more confident about herself. She doesn't see how amazing she is. She's humble. Maybe even too humble. So, yes, she could use a little more self-confidence.

LAURIER: Anything else?

ANDREWS: She's too giving. She is there for her friends and would do anything for them. But that often leads to her sacrificing her own needs.

LAURIER: Does she have any negative traits?

ANDREWS: Yeah. Gail is far too hard on herself. She's self-critical. That's not good. That's somewhere she could improve.

LAURIER: So, let's summarize Gail's negative traits. You say she lacks self-confidence; she sacrifices too much for others; and she's overly critical of herself.

ANDREWS: Yeah.

LAURIER: Do you realize that those aren't faults? Can you see that they are descriptions of weaknesses that paint a positive picture?

ANDREWS: They're how I see Gail. I love her.

LAURIER: And how did you see Alexandria?

ANDREWS: Oh, Lex. She was sexy, charming, and also really funny. And deep, too. I loved the long talks we had, and how much we shared. She was a loyal friend—incredibly loyal. She put herself in extreme danger trying to help a dear friend. Lex was also resilient and flexible. She gave up her life in Los Angeles to move to New York with me. She was willing to give that up. She also loved me so much that she gave up her life— her actual life—to save mine, and to save Gail's.

LAURIER: Did Alexandria have any flaws?

ANDREWS: Well, like Gail, she constantly put other people first all the time, and never once thought about herself. She was too selfless.

LAURIER: What about her association with the Proud Fighters for America? Didn't she engage in illegal activity to benefit their cause?

ANDREWS: Lex was only working with the PFA to help her friend, to save her dearest friend from their clutches. That's because she was always putting her friends and loved ones first. So that's another one of her faults. She was too brave for her own good.

LAURIER: Can you see that these negative traits you've outlined for Lex are actually positive?

ANDREWS: It's how she was, Doc.

LAURIER: Okay, let's talk about some people you just met. You and Ellie seem to get along well.

ANDREWS: Yeah. We really clicked. She's great.

LAURIER: Do you find her attractive?

ANDREWS: Oh yeah, she's adorable. Really cute. I find myself staring at her. I just can't help myself. It makes me happy to just enjoy her beauty. Not in a creepy way, of course. She's quite a bit younger than me. We're friends, and we spent a long time talking, and sharing things about ourselves. She is brilliant, and deep, and well-read, too. We talked about books and writers, especially Thoreau, Emerson, and Shakespeare.

LAURIER: *Does Ellie have any flaws?*

ANDREWS: *Well, she's also really hard on herself. And of course, there's the fact she doesn't have full control of her faerie abilities.*

LAURIER: *I see. You also had a chance to spend some time talking with Shian, right?*

ANDREWS: *Yeah. She's also stunning. I mean, even when she's not using her mermaid siren call abilities. But she's such a sweet person. And brave. And self-less too. Remember how she shared about sacrificing a positive date night to save that dog? She inspires me. She is a real sweetheart.*

LAURIER: *Would you say Shian has flaws?*

ANDREWS: *Well, she is afraid of deep water. And her pick-up lines are pretty . . . I don't know . . . outrageously corny. And raunchy. So outlandish that they break her siren spell.*

LAURIER: *Do you think that Shian might do that on purpose?*

ANDREWS: *You mean, consciously saying obviously horrible things that repel instead of attracting men?*

LAURIER: Or perhaps even subconsciously.

ANDREWS: Interesting. I never thought about that.

LAURIER: It's sometimes easier to see something in someone else that we can't see in ourselves.

ANDREWS: What do you mean?

LAURIER: Did you ever consider the fact that you do something similar in your own relationships?

ANDREWS: [Laughs] I don't think I've ever used anything close to that type of obscene pick-up line on a woman.

LAURIER: What about things that you do when you are in a relationship?

ANDREWS: I'm not one of those guys who talks dirty if that's what you're getting at.

LAURIER: No. That's not what I meant. Let's step back on this. You recognize that Shian self-sabotages her supernatural charms before a sexual relation with a man can occur.

ANDREWS: Yes.

LAURIER: Do you think that perhaps you self-sabotage relationships while you're in the middle of one?

Chapter Sixteen: Tell Me Lies, Ellie, Sweet Little Lies

Sunday, September 3, 2017

I glanced at Linnaeus when Shian seemed to indicate that she was more interested in women than the opposite sex, as I thought I'd been picking up on his growing attraction to her. Though it wasn't showing on the stone-like expression on his face, I wondered if he was disappointed. I surreptitiously placed a hand against the side of Linnaeus's right shoulder in a gesture of comfort. I was pretty sure not only that he had been taken with the mermaid, but that they had also connected on a personal level—nothing to do with her stunning appearance or the magical charm she exuded. But something genuine.

I sensed his appreciation for my attempt to offer my comfort and thought about what had just transpired between me and my new friend. Here I was without the regular extra-sensory abilities that helped me easily navigate what a person I'd been speaking with was feeling. And yet, I still managed to get by. It made me wonder if I had become too used to depending upon that enhanced sense of smell.

"We're glad that you have chosen to be with us, Shian," Dr. Laurier said.

"We all are," Ellie said, reaching her right hand to gently squeeze Shian's left forearm.

"And, as I enunciated already," Linnaeus said, "we have got your back. We are here for you, Ann."

Shian smiled at Ellie, then turned to look Linnaeus in the eyes, again—without any sign of the mystical seduction that usually accompanied her eye contact—and gave him a warm smile. "I know that," she said. "And I appreciate you. All of you. Like I said, it's rare for me to ever speak this much. I only just got here the other day and yet, this retreat has been so good for me."

Dr. Laurier nodded at Shian. "That's good to hear." He then turned to Ellie, slightly tilting his head in her direction.

"My turn?" Ellie asked. "Ah, sure." She cleared her throat. "My name is Ellie Emerson, and I'm from New Jersey. I was born here in the States, but my parents are from Ireland. My mom and I moved back to Ireland to be with my nan while she was fighting cancer, while my dad stayed in the US to work. Mom and I came back to the US when I was in fifth grade in elementary school. I'm a faerie. Or at least a part-faerie. But not a very good one. Let's see. I can't talk with animals, and I can't turn invisible. And though I am able to heal myself a good bit, I can't heal others. I have been able to shapeshift, at least for brief moments, and am getting a little better at that, especially lately. As you might know, faeries cannot tell outright lies, but we are supposed to use deceitful tactics that can fool people. Lying is not something I am able to do, which I guess is a good thing. But I cannot maintain the devious charade for long. Which makes me wonder if I'll be any good at this here game." She chuckled. "I suppose we'll see, yes?"

"Give it your best attempt, Ellie," Dr. Laurier said.

The rest of the group murmured in agreement.

"So, first, Ellie isn't the name I was born with; it's a name I gave myself. Second, I ran away from home when I was . . . fif—" she winced, "er, when I was sixteen. And third, I was," she paused, seeming to struggle again, "ah, almost, a state champion in gymnastics."

She slammed a fist against the arm of her chair. "Ah, sugar!" The pout on her face as she grimaced made her look even more adorable as she shook her head back and forth. "I tried twice to lie just there, but I couldn't. Not even trying to change the truth slightly."

"It's okay," Dr. Laurier said. "The point of the exercise is for us to get to know one another a little better. So, it appears that you tried to lie about the last two things you shared, right?"

"Ayuh."

"So tell us a little about the first one where you tried to lie."

"Ah, sure. So, as you all know. All three of them are true. Ellie is the name I gave myself. I was straight about that one. And I did run away from home when I was sixteen. But I tried that 'near truth' thing by wanting to say it was when I was fifteen. I couldn't. I just couldn't." She sighed. "And for the last one, I was a grand gymnast. I excelled at the parallel bars. And I almost did make it to the state championships. But I'd tried to lie and say that I *was* the state champion. It was close to the truth. Our team was on their way there, and they did win it. But I dropped out just before. And didn't I just stumble when I tried to say that too. It's like something is stopping me from speaking a mistruth."

"I think that's evidence of your faerie nature," Dr. Laurier said. "Which is a good thing, don't you think?"

"Yeah, but what I'm not good at is the deception part of it. Faeries can't lie, sure. But a good faerie is supposed to be able to engage in artful deception. Shrewdly leading someone to believe something that is not true."

"Subterfuge is where you falter," Linnaeus said. "I, for one, find that an admirable trait."

"I know yer being kind," Ellie said. "But do you like me praising you for being so thoughtful and friendly—when what brought you here was failing at being nasty and mean?"

"Good point," Linnaeus said. "I stand corrected. Please accept my modest apologies."

"I have an idea," Vlastislav said.

Ellie turned to look at him.

"My kind are adept at trickery. The legends of us needing to be invited into a domicile are born from truth. It's thus in our nature to cunningly convince a person to let us cross the threshold. Sure, we have the ability to charm and entice our subjects. But that comes along with practicing the art of deceit. Let's take the state championship thing, okay?"

Ellie nodded.

"You were on the team that won the state championship, correct?"

"Yes. But I dropped off the team before they won."

Vlastislav nodded, holding a single finger in the air before him. "And you did. So, you can't say that your team won the state championship." He waved his finger back and forth in the air as he said this.

"No, I can't. Because they weren't my team when they won it."

"Exactly," he said. "And that is the truth."

"It is."

As I watched him moving his finger about, I was reminded of how a hypnotist works in similar motions and wondered if he was somehow trying to charm Ellie in some way.

"But," he raised the same straight finger and pointed it at her, "I bet you are able to say something like this: *The team I was on went on to win the state championship.*"

"But—" Ellie started to say, but the vampire cut her off.

"Consider the statement!" I was shocked with how aggressively he said it. He seemed overly passionate about what he was trying to teach her.

"I see what you're getting at," Linnaeus said. "The statement is 'the team you *were* on.' Which is the truth.

You were on that team at one time. And they did go on to win the state championship. Even if you weren't on the team at the time. The operative word in that statement is *was*." Linnaeus grinned at Vlastislav. "Brilliant obfuscation."

The vampire smiled back at him, his sharp teeth glistening in the light. He then turned back to Ellie. "Try it!" he said, again in a forceful voice that I thought was a bit much for what the situation called for.

"Sure," Ellie said. "*The team I was on went on to win the state championship.*" As she completed the sentence without stumbling in any way, a beautiful smile lit up her face. "Ohmygosh," she said. "I did it! Ohmygosh! I feckin' did it! Thank you, Vlastislav!"

She then jumped out of the chair and gave the vampire a huge hug.

As they embraced, I couldn't help but feel just a tad bit jealous. And that's when I felt Linnaeus placing his hand on the side of my left shoulder to comfort me, the way I'd done just minutes earlier for him.

Interlude: Therapy Session
Just A Good Ole Boy, Never Meanin' No Harm

Excerpt from therapy session recordings of Dr. Brendon Laurier

Tuesday, September 5, 2017
3:19 p.m.

ANDREWS: You think I self-sabotage my relationships?

LAURIER: What do you think when we examine some of your behavior? [Sound of pages being flipped]. *When you were dating Lex, you secretly went to see Gail while she was back in your apartment, and you didn't tell her.*

ANDREWS: That was a last-minute thing. I didn't know I was going to see Gail. But I needed her expertise in something.

LAURIER: You didn't call Lex to let her know, did you?

ANDREWS: She was sleeping. I didn't want to wake her up.

LAURIER: So you told her about it after?

ANDREWS: There was a lot going on.

LAURIER: And when you were dating Gail, even after things got serious between the two of you, did you tell her about your werewolf nature?

ANDREWS: She wouldn't have believed me.

LAURIER: She ran an occult shop. The reason you met her in the first place was because you needed to research the paranormal for one of your books. If anyone was likely to believe you she would.

ANDREWS: Gail was a skeptic.

LAURIER: She was already sensitive about being cheated on. And you let a woman you knew that about suspect you were stepping out on her. Why didn't you just confide in her?

ANDREWS: There you go. I thought of a flaw for Gail.

LAURIER: And what is it?

ANDREWS: She has a habit of making bad relationship choices.

LAURIER: Would that include the mistake she made in choosing you?

ANDREWS: I never cheated on Gail.

LAURIER: But you did let her believe you were cheating on her.

ANDREWS: You make it sound like I'm some jerk who treats women like dirt. I don't. I treat them with honor. I respect them.

LAURIER: But do you also give them convenient excuses to leave you?

ANDREWS: I'm not a bad guy.

LAURIER: I wasn't suggesting you were.

ANDREWS: I'm a good person. A good man. A . . . oh no.

LAURIER: What is it?

ANDREWS: I just recognized one of the reasons I get so triggered by Chester. In his eagerness to please, and to be loved, he uses the phrase: I'm a good boy. I was just about to say that. And as the words were about to pass through my lips, I realized why it bothers me so much. Damn.

LAURIER: Why does it bother you, Michael?

ANDREWS: *Because that's what my mother used to say. Whenever I did something bad or wrong and my dad was mad at me, she used to say:* He's a good boy. *She insisted I was, and that she knew it. It's a mantra I repeated in my head for years. Especially when I did something bad and was feeling guilty. I'd repeat* I'm a good boy *to myself over and over.*

LAURIER: *It's okay to provide yourself with a little positive affirmation.*

ANDREWS: *Sure, I get that. But I did something really bad once that I got away with. My dad said he knew I was the one who'd done it. But my mom insisted I was innocent. And she repeated that I was a good boy. I did, too. I knew I was guilty, but I lied about it.*

LAURIER: *What was it that you did?*

ANDREWS: *I was a big fan of Spider-Man comics. I brought Issue #100 of* The Amazing Spider-Man *in to school one day for a public speaking exercise we were doing in the sixth grade. I was talking about the value of special issues of comic books. That one was estimated to be worth anywhere between $300 and $500 at the time. I had the comic with me when I was in French class. And I was reading it in class and got caught. Madame Gastonguay took it from me. I was so angry. And she refused to give it back to me. That day, after school, I hid in a broom closet and waited until she left for the day, then snuck into her classroom to steal it back. It was mine, after all.*

LAURIER: *So you broke into her classroom and took back your comic?*

ANDREWS: *I did break in, yes. But it wasn't in any of the drawers of her desk. So that evening, after it was dark, I went to her place.*

LAURIER: *How did you know where she lived?*

ANDREWS: *It was a small town; we pretty much knew where all our teachers lived. She lived on the third floor of an apartment building, and at the back was a fire escape that could easily be accessed if you were tall or could jump high. I had both advantages. I jumped, pulled myself up, and climbed it, thinking how much like Spider-Man I was being. I even had a ski mask on to hide my face.*

LAURIER: *You broke into her apartment?*

ANDREWS: *Worse than that. When I got to her apartment, I could see two of her windows from the fire escape. One was the kitchen, which is where she was, busy making dinner. The other was her bedroom window. I could see the top of her dresser which was adjacent to the window. My comic book was sitting right there on it. I pushed up at the window. It was unlocked. I slid it up, but it made a really loud wood-on-wood squeal, and it only went up a few inches. But it was enough for me to be able to reach the comic. As I was pulling my hand back out from that space of the window, with the comic in hand, Madame Gastonguay ran into the room. "Who's there?" she yelled, a wooden spoon in her hand. She came right up to the window — our faces were only a few inches apart — and she struck the window hard with the spoon. The glass rattled and cracked, and I fell back on the metal floor of the fire escape in shock as she yelled something about a Peeping Tom.*

LAURIER: *That sounds intense.*

ANDREWS: *It gets more intense. She grabbed the wooden ridge of the lowest part of the window and slammed it down. As the frame hit the bottom, the glass in it shattered, falling onto the tops of both of her forearms. She stumbled away from the window, gasping, leaned against the wall, and dropped her wooden spoon. It was lying there on the carpet at her feet beside big round drops of her blood. Then she fell sideways, onto her bed. She fainted, either from the pain or from the sight of the blood. There was a phone on the dresser beside the window. I reached through the now pane-less window, picked up the phone, dialed 9-1-1, then put the receiver down on the dresser beside the phone. I knew she needed medical attention, but that I also needed to get the hell out of there before the ambulance arrived.*

LAURIER: *You didn't stay?*

ANDREWS: *No. I rushed down the fire escape.*

LAURIER: And you didn't get caught?

ANDREWS: No. But someone in one of the other apartments reported seeing a tall male teenager scrambling down the fire escape. I had my mask on, so nobody, not even Madame Gastonguay, saw my face.

LAURIER: You said your dad accused you, right? Why did he suspect it was you?

ANDREWS: He knew I'd gone out that night. And I rarely went out. I spent most of my time in my room, reading comics, or writing. And he was missing a navy-blue ski mask. I threw it away in a trash bin behind the grocery store downtown. I threw the comic book away in there too. I figured they would both be evidence, so I got rid of them. Funny how a supposedly good boy knew the right things to do when having committed such a crime, right? When my dad searched my room, he didn't find it. He still suspected it was me, though. But my mom kept repeating that I was a good boy, and I would never do anything like that.

LAURIER: What about Madame Gastonguay?

ANDREWS: We looked at each other straight in the eye through the window. Inches apart. She couldn't see my face. It was covered by the mask. But she could see my eyes. I was convinced she knew who it was. And she must have noticed, after all the hub-bub, that the comic was missing. I mean, she had to know it was me. But she never said anything. The next day, in class, she was lecturing with both of her arms wrapped in bandages. She wore them for weeks. But she never said anything about the comic. I wondered if it was because she didn't want to rat me out. Or that maybe she'd taken the comic because she was going to sell it for its high market value. I never knew. But she never said anything.

LAURIER: The entire time your mom was convinced of your innocence?

ANDREWS: Yeah. And to the day my mom died, I never told her dad was right about what happened with Madame Gastonguay. That it had been me. And that I'd lied the whole time. I actually feel worse about lying to my mom, having her believe I was a saint, than I feel about what happened on the fire escape that night.

LAURIER: I know I've mentioned it before, but it's never too late to have those discussions with her. You can still talk to her.

ANDREWS: What good would that do her?

LAURIER: It's not meant for her, Michael. It's for you. So you can work through some of those feelings.

ANDREWS: I'll think about it.

LAURIER: Excellent. You're making progress. Last time I mentioned the idea you pretty much shot it down.

ANDREWS: Maybe these sessions have been helping.

LAURIER: I'm glad you're starting to feel that way. And that was a good revelation we just talked through. Even if we went off track a little.

ANDREWS: We went off track?

LAURIER: Yes. That's something we still need to work on. Your tendency to divert and avoid. You never answered my question from a few minutes ago. Did you notice that when I asked it you quickly changed the subject?

ANDREWS: Which question?

LAURIER: Why you never confided in Gail about being a werewolf and why you let her go on to believe you were cheating on her.

Chapter Seventeen: Nobody Knows the Struggle Vlad's Seen

Sunday, September 3, 2017

Sure, I found Ellie incredibly attractive even though my feelings for her were brotherly and more protective than anything else.

So, why, then, did seeing her in such a warm embrace with Vlad infuriate me so?

Could it be because I was jealous of her becoming close to someone else in our group? Or did it say more about the underlying feelings I had for the vampire?

Dr. Laurier waited until they finished—a hug that went on for far too long if you ask me—and both sat down before he spoke. "Excellent, Ellie. And thank you for your assistance, Vlastislav. It's now your turn if you're ready."

"I am ready to begin," Vlastislav said, with a flourish of his right hand in the air before him that ended in rolling his hand over to be palm up as his arm looped back down. I was reminded of the gesture an English gentleman's butler might make when announcing the dinner is now being served. I didn't even try to hide the roll of my eyes.

Was it just me, or did this guy seem to become a bit more animated, and perhaps a tad more exuberant the more he spoke. It was a far cry from the reserved tight ass he'd been at last night's dinner.

"I am Vlastislav Dalca the third. I am a first generation American, but my parents hail from a small village in Northwestern Romania close to the border of Hungary. Despite the most common belief about me, perhaps due to my accent, name, and heritage, I am not one of those stereotypical vampires who has lived hundreds of years in a castle in Transylvania. I have been a vampire for less than a year. I was born forty-two years ago in Pittsburgh, Pennsylvania. My father was a steel mill worker, and, up until about a year ago, I worked as a teacher at an elementary school.

"Something has always fascinated me about education, and I have always wanted to be a teacher and to inform and inspire young minds. Even when I was a child, I took great pleasure in playing as a schoolteacher with my stuffed animals, enacting full lesson plans for hours at a time.

"My mother was a teacher back in Romania, and it was a role that she loved. I suppose I've always wanted to follow in her footsteps, even though she did not do any formal teaching here in the United States after my parents arrived. I was homeschooled, and she would tell me stories about the schoolhouse she ran in her village in the building that doubled as the town's church. Throughout my life I have visited the town where my parents were from, but that building no longer stands. And yet, I still have the most majestic dreams of what it had been like for her to be in full control of the entire assemblage of students. She once told me that—"

"Pardon me, Vlastislav," Dr. Laurier interrupted. "While I'm delighted you are so comfortable with sharing this early in our process, this particular exercise isn't about that. We will be able to explore more depth such as what you are sharing in a future group session. Right now, we're sharing why you are here and the two truths and a lie."

The vampire's head snapped to the right and he glowered at Dr. Laurier for several seconds, pointing one of his long fingers at the man.

"I. Am. Getting. To. That." Vlastislav said, practically spitting each word out.

Not half a beat later, his eyebrows unknit from their previous tight-locked position in the middle of his forehead, and he made another broad hand flourish.

"As I was saying before I was so rudely interrupted," he said, casting a quick angry glance at the therapist, "I was a schoolteacher, like my mother before me. Until last year, that is, when I was the unfortunate victim of a vampiric seduction. I met the woman who turned me at a bar that several of my colleagues and I would sometimes frequent on a Friday night. She wasn't all that attractive, but, as I'm sure you all know, the allure of a vampire's charm can be quite powerful. I was captivated by her from across the room, and she—"

Dr. Laurier loudly cleared his throat.

The vampire's head whipped back in his direction and his hands came down onto the armrests of the chair. I leaned forward in reaction to this as I thought he was about to launch himself across the room at our therapist, and I realized I was steeling myself up to defend Dr. Laurier from the impending assault.

As if he knew what I'd been thinking, Dr. Laurier shot me a quick look with an almost imperceptible shake of the head as if to say *it's okay*, as Vlastislav continued to glare at him, his breath coming in a rhythmic hiss.

Dr. Laurier looked at the vampire with a serious expression that showed no traces of fear or anger. "Please, Mr. Dalca, just share what brings you here, and then the three statements about yourself in which one of them is a lie. I promise, we will get to sharing those other details in future sessions."

Vlastislav sucked in another deep hiss-like breath before he relaxed the tight grip he had on the armrests.

"I have been a vampire for less than a year. And I am here at this retreat because I am a vegan and have been my entire adult life. I have long been compassionate regarding the plight of animals who are bred and live in miserable captivity as they are inevitably prepared for the slaughterhouse. The consumption of animal flesh, or even the biproduct of animals, sickens and infuriates me.

And now, ironically, I am dependent upon the consumption of blood to survive.

"That struggle is the reason I am here. Because I can only repress the bloodlust for so long. My instincts will take over, overcome my revulsion, and I'll lose control. I'll not just drink enough blood to survive, but I'll keep drinking until I completely drain my victim dry. And then I'm stuck dealing with the guilt of violating my core principles. The worst part is that when I cry after a night of a feeding beyond my core needs, my tears are filled with blood."

He raised his right hand up as if about to carve a fresh elaborate gesture into the air and continue to say something more. But then he glanced over at Dr. Laurier and seemed to think better of it. Taking in a deep lungful of air, he spoke.

"And here are the three things about me.

"Firstly, I teach at an adult night school in upstate Pennsylvania.

"Secondly, I am perfectly fluent in the Romanian language, and that is one of the subjects I now teach.

"And thirdly, in my spare time I am a software developer and have released three open-source sand-box style video games."

He then turned toward Dr. Laurier and raised both eyebrows high into the middle of his forehead. "Is that sufficient, Doctor?"

"Yes, Vlastislav. Very much so. Thank you." He turned to the rest of us. "Is anyone willing to make a guess as to which of those three statements are the lie?"

Linnaeus was the first to speak up. "I'd be willing to place my own wager on the fact that Vlastislav is not a software developer. It doesn't fit in with his obvious passion for the teaching world, and, as I understand it, that type of work would take a tremendous amount of patience and—"

"What do you know about me?" Vlastislav barked. "I'm an extremely patient person!"

Tilting his head with eyebrows raised, as if to indicate the vampire had just made his point for him, Linnaeus finished what he was saying. ". . . and skills in collaboration and communication. While programmers are stereotypically known to work nocturnally and sleep during the light of day, which would fit a vampire's needs, I'm not sure I could see—"

"Shows what you know!" Vlastislav said. "My code is released open source. The collaborations happen in the cloud."

"Now, now," Dr. Laurier said. "Let's not reveal which ones might be true until everyone has had an opportunity to share their own guess."

He was met with a quiet and angry glare from Vlastislav.

"I'm with Linnaeus!" Chester said. "It's the programmer thing. That's the lie."

"I don't know," Ellie said, "Me, I wonder how fluent in Romanian he would be if he was raised here in America. I spent many formative years in Ireland, but I cannot speak Irish, and barely know a few phrases my mum would occasionally utter."

"One thing that I've always been extremely aware of," I said, "is the sunset and sunrise. Especially during the cycle of the full moon. Pennsylvania would be on a very similar day/night cycle to New York. Which means that night classes—which are likely to start any time between 5 and 8 p.m. would be perfectly fine for a vampire to attend during the winter months when it gets dark just before five. But that wouldn't work so well the rest of the year."

"So your assumption is that the night school thing must be the deception," Linnaeus said. "I would like to amend my supposition to concur with what Michael is suggesting."

"Me too!" Chester said.

"That makes sense to me," Shian said.

"Go on with you all," Ellie said. "I'm going to stick with my theory. I'm pretty sure that he can't speak Romanian."

Turning in his seat to face Ellie directly, Vlastislav said: "Vorbesc perfect romaneste cu toate ca am crescut departe de tara."

"And I stand corrected," Ellie said with a huge grin. "That was quite beautiful. What was it you just said there?"

Vlastislav did one of those hand-gestures, this time with his left hand. "I speak perfect Romanian despite not having grown up in my homeland."

"So, you *are* a game programmer, then?" Linnaeus asked.

"I am indeed," the vampire beamed. "It is a pastime I've been engaged in for many years. But your friend is correct about the night school misconception. I do still teach, but in a strictly virtual and online environment. And Romanian is one of the courses that I teach. Computer programming is another.

"In manufacturing that deception, I followed similar advice to what I offered to Ellie. Only I am not bound by the inability to lie. But sticking as close to the truth as possible makes a lie far easier to get away with."

When he said this, he pointedly looked at me with a most intriguing look on his face. As if he were implying something.

"Excellent work, Vlastislav." Dr. Laurier said. He then glanced in my direction. "And now, it's your turn to share, Michael."

Interlude: Therapy Session
Fangs for the Memories

Excerpt from therapy session recordings of Dr. Brendon Laurier

Tuesday, September 5, 2017
3:21 p.m.

LAURIER: What is it about Vlastislav that bothers you so much?

ANDREWS: You mean besides the fact that he's one of the most pretentious and annoying fussbuckets I've ever met?

LAURIER: I don't think you're being either fair or open-minded.

ANDREWS: Open-minded? Me? He's the one who isn't willing to compromise on practically anything. Nothing is to his liking. The food, the drink, the chairs. Goldilocks was less picky when she was making her way through the bear cottage.

LAURIER: *Where do you suppose your intolerance for him originates?*

ANDREWS: *Intolerant? Yeah, that's a good word that describes him, not me.*

LAURIER: *That's quite an elevated level of hostility you have. Is there something specific that he did to offend you?*

ANDREWS: *Something specific? No. How about everything he's done since he arrived.*

LAURIER: *Would that include the way he and Ellie embraced after he assisted her with a significant challenge she has been facing?*

ANDREWS: *What about it?*

LAURIER: *I noticed two things about it, which I'd like to share if that's okay.*

ANDREWS: *Okay. Shoot.*

LAURIER: *While everyone else in the room seemed positive about Ellie's achievement in that moment, you were wearing a rather noticeable scowl on your face.*

ANDREWS: *No, I wasn't. I was happy for Ellie.*

LAURIER: I wasn't the only one who noticed. I saw Linnaeus attempting to comfort you.

ANDREWS: Huh, you don't seem to miss a thing, do you?

LAURIER: A good part of my role is to observe, and to listen, and ask questions that allow you to better understand the source of your physical debilities and emotional malaise.

ANDREWS: I've always thought that malaise sounds like something you spread on a piece of bread or toast. I think it's because the word reminds me of a few different words, like mayonnaise and marmalade.

LAURIER: Would you like to know something else I've observed?

ANDREWS: What's that?

LAURIER: How adept you've become at dodging a topic by taking tangents.

ANDREWS: My werewolf powers have dramatically improved my agility.

LAURIER: Do you think that you use humor as a mechanism for avoidance?

ANDREWS: You know what they say: always leave 'em laughing. But I guess I recognize that I sometimes use humor when I'm in tense situations; particularly when I'm fighting.

LAURIER: Do you think that you're fearful of confrontation?

ANDREWS: Perhaps. I've never been good at it, that's for sure.

LAURIER: As we've discussed before, you can be a bit of a people pleaser, correct?

ANDREWS: Yes. I find it's easier to compromise and to back off, than to push for something. I wouldn't be where I am today if I didn't have a literary agent who was ruthless and who fights for me.

LAURIER: It's interesting that your agent fights for you. Do you think that you, in turn, fight for other people?

ANDREWS: I guess I do. It's that Spider-Man "with great power" mantra, after all. If I have these special abilities, why not use them to stand up for those who aren't able to stand up for themselves?

LAURIER: Do you think it's possible that one of the reasons you stand up for other people is one way of compensating for not ever really standing up for yourself?

ANDREWS: I've never thought about that.

LAURIER: It's worth considering. Sometimes it's easier to recognize external needs while ignoring those internal ones.

ANDREWS: I suppose so.

LAURIER: Would you say that you have recognized the needs of the friends you've made at this retreat?

ANDREWS: I think so.

LAURIER: Have you reflected on the possibility that many of the things you've seen in them are similar issues to what you struggle with?

ANDREWS: Now that you mention it, yeah, that thought has occurred to me these past few days.

LAURIER: When it comes to Ellie, you say you connected with her, right?

ANDREWS: Yes, in a deep and powerful way.

LAURIER: So let's consider your reaction to when Vlastislav and Ellie embraced.

ANDREWS: You're back to that again?

LAURIER: *I let you take us away from that topic, but I think it's worth returning and exploring.*

ANDREWS: *If you insist.*

LAURIER: *Would you say you were jealous of what happened between Vlastislav and Ellie?*

ANDREWS: *No way. Like I said, Doc, Ellie and I connected. But as friends. Nothing more. I'm not jealous.*

LAURIER: *I wasn't talking about their embrace. I was talking about how Vlastislav helped her.*

ANDREWS: *You mean teaching her how to creatively lie without actually lying?*

LAURIER: *Yes. Were you jealous of that?*

ANDREWS: *No. Don't be ridiculous. I'm glad that he helped Ellie.*

LAURIER: *But is it true that you would rather have been the one to help her in such a way?*

ANDREWS: *No. That would be selfish. That's stupid.*

[There is a long moment of silence]

ANDREWS: Okay, maybe I was a little bit jealous of that. Maybe I felt like I'd already invested quite a bit of time with Ellie. That we trusted one another. That there was a connection between us. A real connection, you know? Maybe I wanted to be the one who was helping her to overcome her challenges. But instead, the one person who keeps getting under my skin more than anyone else here had to be the one who did it. Why couldn't it have been Linnaeus or Shian. Or, heck, even Chester. Why did it have to be him?

LAURIER: Your hostility seems deeply rooted. Are you sure there's not something else making you feel this way about Vlastislav?

ANDREWS: He did pretty much inspire that reaction from the moment he first opened his mouth.

LAURIER: Could there be something from your own past that has influenced your perception of him in some way? Were you afraid of vampire movies growing up, for example?

ANDREWS: No, they were just another type of monster I'd seen in movies and read about and—oh my.

LAURIER: What is it?

ANDREWS: I just thought of it now. Remember the story of that one hundredth issue of Spider-Man? And how I lied to my parents about what I did when trying to get it back? That issue is about Peter Parker deciding he has to end his life as the crime-fighting wallcrawler. So he devises a special formula that he believes will cure him of his spider powers. He takes it and passes out, only to wake up and find he has grown four additional arms. He is a monster.

LAURIER: *I can see how that relates to your own discomfort with your abilities. But how does this relate to Vlastislav?*

ANDREWS: *In the very next issue, he meets and fights a man called Michael Morbius. A vampire. They are instantly mortal enemies. It comes to pass that something in Morbius's own blood is what Peter needs to cure himself of the monstrous growth. The vampire ends up solving the problem he caused himself. A vampire introduced a solution that he was unable to come up with himself. It took away his power.*

LAURIER: *Do you think that Vlastislav triggers your feelings of inadequacy and powerlessness?*

ANDREWS: *I guess so. But I also just remembered another time I felt powerless. It was when Gail, Lex and I were fighting this motley crew of super-powered neo-Nazi bad guys. One of them was a flying bat-creature with fangs. He grabbed Lex and lifted her up in the air, and I was completely powerless to help her as he sunk his fangs into her neck. That was the only other vampire I'd ever encountered. So no wonder I have this bad taste in my mouth—so to speak—when it comes to vampires.*

Chapter Eighteen: Two Mistruths and a Lie Followed by Two Partial Truths

Sunday, September 3, 2017

"Oh, well, would you look at that," I said, pointing at the clock on the opposite wall. It's almost nine thirty. I really should be going off now to engage in my nocturnal scampering about these most majestic woods."

Dr. Laurier beamed a huge smile. "You still have plenty of time," he said. "Besides, this won't take more than just a few more minutes. And I'm sure everyone here is interested in what you have to share."

"That we are," Ellie said.

"Indubitably," Linnaeus said.

"That's right." Chester quickly replied.

Shian and Vlastislav were both nodding quietly, and then the vampire swept his left hand out from the center of his body in a flourishing wave in my direction. "The floor, as they say, is now yours."

"Well," I said. "I'm not sure where to begin."

"Perhaps you should start, like the rest of us, with your name," Linnaeus said.

"Sure," I said, rubbing my hands together as a way to buy time.

I had already spoken to Linnaeus, Shian, Ellie, and Dr. Laurier about myself. And at relatively great length. The only two people I hadn't connected with yet in any meaningful way were Chester and Vlastislav. And it's not like I hadn't become used to speaking in front of groups of people. I had to do it at public readings and events on book tours. So, I wasn't sure why I was so uncomfortable in the moment. All I knew is something was bothering me that I couldn't quite put my finger on.

"My name is Michael Andrews. And I'm a werewolf. From Ontario, Canada. But I now live in New York."

"Hey!" Linnaeus laughed. "You're a Canadian werewolf in New York! I just thought of that."

"Yeah, I suppose I am," I said, smiling at Linnaeus. I was sure I hadn't heard it before, but it did seem somewhat familiar. I appreciated how much effort he put into trying to break the ice and make other people feel a bit more comfortable. "Anyway, I came to New York in 2003. And I was hitch-hiking through upstate New York when I was bitten by a wolf."

"You mean, like a vampire?" Vlastislav said. "I didn't know that was actually a thing for werewolf transition. I thought that was just an urban legend. Werewolves aren't turned with a single bite. Neither are vampires. It's not merely the bite that turns someone into a vampire, there is a specific ritual that involves the exchange of blood which must be conducted. In the matter of my own evolution into this form, my seductress and I were required to engage in—"

"Vlastislav!" Dr. Laurier barked, glaring at him.

The vampire shot a glare back at the therapist and there was a moment of tension between the two.

"What I believe Dr. Laurier was getting at," Linnaeus said, "is that it's time for us all to listen to what Michael is about to share. And I must apologize, as I was the one who started this with my play-on-word interjection which broke the flow of Michael's relaying of his story."

"No," I said to Vlastislav. "That's how it happened to me. I was bitten by a wolf. Or at least nipped by one, before a car arrived and frightened it off."

Vlastislav opened his mouth as if he was about to say something else, but then looked over at Dr. Laurier and abandoned the previous look of defiance.

"I've been living with this werewolf curse for fourteen years now, but unlike other werewolves I've encountered, I'm not able to control the change. Or at least, I haven't been until I arrived here. And also, unlike others of my kind, I have no conscious awareness of my time in wolf form. Again, that's changed a little already since I got to this retreat.

"And also, I've been struggling with the duality of my nature. And my lack of control. Like Vlastislav, when this one time I tried to deny the wolf part of me, I ended up acting out in an extremely violent nature. And recently, in a blacked-out state of human consciousness, that wolf nature must have gotten the better of me, because I killed a man with my bare hands. So, I've been dealing with that guilt. And, to top it all off, as if the werewolf curse wasn't bad enough, I learned that the woman I've loved more than anyone else in my life and I cannot be together because of an ancient curse that was placed on her family. But, in addition, I have some guilt about this other woman who—"

Dr. Laurier cleared his throat, interrupting me.

"Yeah, right," I said. "I'm side-tracking again."

He smiled at me, nodding.

"So anyway, that's why I'm here. So now on to those three things.

"The first one is that I've always dreamed of being a super-powered hero with wolf-enhanced powers living in New York City ever since reading *Wolverine* comic books when I was a kid. Number two: I wrote my very first novel at the age of thirteen on a dusty old Underwood typewriter I found in the back of my mother's closet. And three, I am one of only a handful of authors to have appeared on David Letterman's show in his more than thirty-year late-night career."

Ellie winked at me when I finished. I figured, given how much she claimed to have read about me, she'd know it was the first one that was the lie. Or at least a mistruth. Sure, I was a New York Times bestselling author, but it's not like I was a household name. Most people aren't readers, and apart from a handful of writers like Stephen King, James Patterson, Toni Morrison, or J.K. Rowling, whose names are known by readers and nonreaders alike, the majority of the world's top selling writers are able to avoid the limelight. I was curious to see what the others might know about me.

"So here's the thing," Ellie said. "I have to recuse myself from this one. I have an unfair advantage over the rest of ya."

"You do?" Dr. Laurier asked.

"Ayuh," she said. "I've read all of his books, and articles about him. I've heard him mention some of what he just shared in interviews, or even in the authors notes that he puts at the end of his books."

"Very well," Dr. Laurier said. "What do the rest of you think?"

"Intriguing," Vlastislav said. "I think it's obvious that the third one is the lie. It's hard to believe that you would have been a guest on David Letterman."

"Yeah," Chester said. "Hard to believe."

"I don't know," Shian said. "Is he really old enough to have written on an actual typewriter? And c'mon, how likely is it that he could write a full novel when he was only thirteen? I think that one is the lie."

"She's right," Chester said. "He's too young."

Beside me, Linnaeus was scratching his chin. "While I have never been a purveyor of comic books, I have partaken in the watching of several of the Marvel movies; including the *X-Men* ones. I don't think that Wolverine lived in New York City. Professor Xavier's School for Gifted Youngsters was in a more rural location on some huge estate far from the city. And if I'm not mistaken,

Wolverine hails from Canada, not New York. I speculate that our Canadian acquaintance here is trying to deceive us with the wolf-like reference. Especially because though the moniker of the two words—wolf and wolverine—sound somewhat similar, the wolverine itself is a member of the Mustelidae family, along with the weasel, the badger, and the otter. And not related to the Canis lupus."

"Yeah," Chester said. "Not related."

"So, Ellie," Dr. Laurier said, turning to look at her. "You're the expert who recused herself from this. Tell us: Which one is it?"

"Linnaeus is right," Ellie said. "It's the first one that was the lie. But he did make it close to the truth. Michael grew up reading comics and dreaming of what it might be like to live in New York and have super-powers, that's for sure. But they were Spider-Man comics he was reading."

I let out a laugh. "Indeed." I smiled at Linnaeus. "You did well. That's definitely the one. Of course, I realized that I also included a couple of mistruths in the other statements."

"How so?" Dr. Laurier asked.

"Technically, the typewriter I wrote on wasn't dusty. It had been under a dustcover when I found it. The cover was dusty, but the typewriter was in perfect working order. And the book I wrote at that age wasn't a full-length novel. It was only about twenty-five thousand words and would have more accurately been classified as a novella.

"And I was a guest on Letterman's show back in 2014, the year before he retired. Though I made up the part about being one of only a few writers on the show. But I had been making an educated guess. I mean, how many writers have you seen on late-night talk shows over the years? It couldn't have been more than a handful."

"He should be disqualified!" Vlastislav said.

"Yeah," Chester said. "Disqualified."

"This isn't a competition, Vlastislav," Dr. Laurier said. "And we aren't keeping score."

The vampire scowled at the therapist, not for the first time during this session, I had noticed.

"This exercise has been about getting a few personal items out in front of a group to develop a sense of trust. And perhaps to find a few things you might have in common with one another. I must say that you've all done quite well with this."

"Speaking of which," I said, "I was really nervous about sharing.

"So was I," Shian said."

"There you are," Dr. Laurier said. "I hope that you, and everyone else here has seen that it's not so bad once we are willing to share. Often, the things we keep inside and are afraid to discuss openly have much more power on us than when they can be placed out there and explored."

He was right about that. I'm not sure why I'd been so nervous sharing in this group, or even about therapy in general. I'd only been here for a day and a half but already I was starting to feel a little better. Sure, I had a long way to go still, but it felt good to be taking this first step.

I looked around the room at the faces of the others, who were all grinning with pride. We had, after all, just gone through a pretty important step for all of us. As I was looking at the group, just for a moment, as his eyes met mine, I thought I caught a glimmer of red from Vlastislav as he was smiling at me; and for a moment my mind flashed back to the same look that flying vampire with bat wings gave me when he had grabbed Lex, not long before she died.

A chill that originated from deep inside me rose to the surface, making me visibly shudder. Which seemed to make Vlastislav's grin a little wider, further exposing his fanged teeth.

Interlude: Wolf Night
The Boy Inside the Wolf

Overnight
Wednesday Sept 6, 2017 / Thursday Sept 7, 2017

The wolf stood on the same hill with the rock outcropping that he returned to the previous four nights. He felt drawn to it, as if something more than its proximity to the moon above compelled him to be there. Was it the familiarity of the spot or perhaps just the fact this had been the place where, for the first time since he could remember, he felt free. Truly free, and not at all trapped in an artificial and limited space environment.

There was something else, too.

The wolf felt more of a connection with the human it knew lived somewhere inside itself. The human whose memories occasionally invaded its conscious thought.

Speaking of thought, the wolf had started to better understand some of the non-natural elements of the environment where he spent most of his adult life. Terms like city, building, park, street, *and* car. *These things—words, he realized—and the understanding of them came from the human's own knowledge and understanding.*

He also became aware that he and the human have always been connected. And that there had been a time, when they were both very young, that they didn't just communicate with one another, but they were almost as one. But this came in the form of a memory that was old, decades old.

Another word came to him. A name.

Edward.

It sounded familiar, but the wolf wasn't sure from where. Then another name replaced it.

Michael.

That name he remembered clearly. It was what the woman he shared a bond with had called him. What was her name?

Gail.

Yes, Gail was her name. And she had repeatedly referred to him as Michael. Was that his name when in human form? The wolf knew he had spent many occasions with Gail and that she had always been a comfort to him. He also remembered the last time he had seen Gail. It had not been comfortable. It had been tense. They had been fighting together. Alongside several other people, some of whom had a familial resemblance in their scent to Gail. Together they had taken down many of the demons that threatened not only the wolf and its adopted pack. But at least one or more of the allies fighting alongside them had died. And that caused a sudden and intense explosion of grief in Gail.

The wolf wondered where Gail was now, for her scent was nowhere near the place he was now in. As he reached back into the depths of his consciousness, he understood that she was no longer near; and that the human inside of him had a deep and powerful longing for her.

The bitter taste when he thought of the human's longing was one the wolf was not familiar with. But the human mind filtered in, and allowed the wolf to define it.

Jealous. The closest the wolf could understand about this more foreign human was that of rivalry.

His speculation about the woman that both the human and the wolf had a deep passion for, was interrupted by an odd fluttering sound and a high-pitched shriek from above.

The wolf looked up and saw a dark shape briefly pass in front of the moon, moving in a very sporadic fashion.

He locked onto the scent and the sound of it, and took chase, tracking it as it flew far above the trees.

He followed the small rodent-like bird for half a mile before the name for what the human part of him knew the creature was came to his mind.

A bat.

He was following a bat. But the human in him also suspected that it wasn't just a bat. It was someone the human thought he knew.

As the wolf loped through the underbrush, a rabbit that had been hiding there burst off to the left in a terrified flight.

In response the wolf instinctively took chase after the rabbit for several steps, before the human part of its mind urged it to stop the natural inclination to hunt and to continue tracking the bat.

By the time the human voice in his head coaxed him back on his previous trail, the bat had gotten a significant lead. He heard its wings and screeching muffle as the little airborne creature descended into the trees at least a hundred yards ahead.

The wolf picked up speed as it raced in that direction.

And as he was breaking into a small natural clearing, it stopped, startled by what was there.

A tall thin dark figure was standing in the forest where the wolf thought the bat had come down. But it wasn't just some stranger. It smelled familiar. The human, Michael, knew this other man, and with that understanding, a hot, burning anger welled within filling the wolf with rage.

The rage, and a name, came to the wolf.

Vlad.

A disgust and unjustified rage that was completely foreign to the wolf, an emotion obviously coming from the human filled him, and he bolted in the direction of the man at full speed, intent on attack.

The wolf did not understand. The other human had not been a physical threat; and it definitely was not encroaching on the wooded area that the wolf had temporarily adopted as his territory. But it also understood that humans acted upon numerous irrational acts. Apart from Gail and a few other allies he could trust, the wolf had known enough to stay well away from humans for this very reason.

What bothered the wolf most was that there was no escaping this particular human who lived in his own mind.

As he raced across the field to where the stranger that Michael hated stood, something happened that confused the wolf enough to stop running.

The human was no longer standing upright on two feet the way humans do. It was, instead, down on all fours. And though it smelled the same as before it had taken the shape of a black wolf.

In the wolf's confusion, Michael's consciousness slipped further in, beginning to take concrete shape.

The wolf was suddenly both wolf and human in thinking, as the duality of perception and thought processes came into perfect alignment with one another.

Suddenly Michael was the wolf, and the wolf was Michael.

He stood looking at the black wolf across the field and understood what was happening.

The legends about vampires being able to transform into other creatures, like a bat and a wolf were true. And Michael got the feeling that Vlastislav was out here and up to something nefarious.

Michael embraced the wolf's natural form of communication as he felt his fur standing in the way to make himself appear larger, and he let out a fierce challenging growl.

Vlastislav, now in full wolf form, shot off through the woods.

Michael let the uncontrollable anger flow through him as he gave chase. He was going to stop Vlastislav from whatever evil he was up to.

He caught up to Vlastislav almost immediately. He shouldn't have been surprised about that. After all, he'd had plenty of experience in wolf form, but the vampire had mentioned he was new to his own Paranormal life. How much time could he really have spent as a wolf?

Leaping through the air at the other wolf, Michael landed on top of him, grabbing him by the side of the throat with his teeth. He bit down only hard enough to take a firm hold, not to tear or kill.

The two wolves rolled several times down the side of an incline, and as they reached the bottom, Michael let go of Vlastislav, twisting him in the direction of a nearby tree.

The other wolf howled in pain as he struck the tree, then collapsed onto the ground and immediately shifted into human form. He wasn't naked but dressed in the same black t-shirt and jeans he'd been wearing all week.

Michael growled and slowly advanced.

Chapter Nineteen: This Is the Chapter That Returns to the Scene You Read in the Prologue and Have Been Waiting For

Thursday, September 7, 2017
5:53 a.m.

I yawned as I got up from the table in the common kitchen area and went to refill my coffee cup. I was exhausted from the activities of the night before. This had been the first time my human consciousness had been fully present in the werewolf body, and for a full couple of hours I remembered everything clearly from the first second I'd spotted Vlastislav in bat form flying above me to the moment I finally caught him, and what went down between us. That's when my human consciousness faded back into the darkness.

Sure, over the years I'd caught glimpses of what it had been like when I was a wolf. But never had I been fully in the moment. Never had I felt like I'd been in such control of it. At least for a few hours.

Normally after a night in wolf form, I woke up fully rested as a human.

But not now.

Is it possible that the merged consciousness prevented the human part of me from getting a full night's rest? Did that mean I would start to need to sleep as a wolf or as a human to get the appropriate amount of sleep so I could effectively function?

At times like these, I really wish there was another werewolf around I could talk to about this. But the only two wolves I'd known were dead. The shock rock star sociopath known as Knell had been the first werewolf I'd encountered after years of believing I was the only Paranormal in the city had full conscious awareness in either human or wolf form. We never talked, except in anger and threats, and fought to the death over a territorial dispute. And a few years later, I encountered and befriended Irwin Herschell. Like Knell, he had full control over the change from human to wolf and retained his human consciousness and memory. But we weren't friends long enough for me to learn much from him about being a werewolf.

Checking my watch for what seemed like the hundredth time in the past half hour, I noted it was ten to six in the morning. Dr. Laurier's first morning one-on-one sessions started at six, and today's schedule had Ellie slotted into the first one-on-one therapy appointment this morning. My own slot was for seven o'clock. But I couldn't sleep, despite being so tired. I was too wound up. I was eager to speak with Dr. Laurier about what had happened to me the night before. Not just about my own personal connection with my wolf self, but my surprising encounter with Vlastislav, and the startling revelation that resulted.

In addition, I realized that, where I had become accustomed to instinctively knowing exactly what time of the day it was, being here had changed that. Ensconced in the enchantment of this retreat that prevented me from automatically changing into a wolf at sunset meant I'd quickly gotten used to not being overly concerned with the exact time of day. That was an incredibly liberating experience.

As I was just about to pour fresh coffee into my cup a horrific shriek sounded from the direction of Dr. Laurier's office.

It was Ellie.

Even without my enhanced wolf hearing it came through crisp and clear.

I dropped both the carafe and the cup to the floor and rushed in the direction of her scream.

Linnaeus and Shian were in the hallway outside the kitchen, and the three of us ran together. Chester was already standing in front of the open doorway, gaping at what he saw through it. As we got to the office, I saw Vlastislav and Ellie both already inside.

And on the floor between them was Dr. Laurier's prone body.

As I stepped into the room I stared at the therapist's dead body, still not able to believe what I was seeing.

How could my therapist be dead?

When did it happen? And who was responsible?

Somewhere after my encounter with Vlastislav I'd blacked out again, but it had been just as I'd been feeling the overwhelming urge to rush back to the main lodge to get to Dr. Laurier.

The next thing I could remember was waking up naked in my bed at five, confused as to why I was awake before sunrise. But also, burning with a combination of excitement and confusion about what had happened the previous night. Everything between standing in the field and feeling that urge and waking up was a complete blank.

Could I be responsible for what had happened to him?

I looked up from Dr. Laurier's lifeless body, slowly panning the faces of my companions. They looked as shocked as I likely also appeared to them. How was it possible that I'd found myself in the middle of something like this?

My mom's voice came to me then.

It was from one of the exercises Dr. Laurier had suggested I practice.

A practice I had initially felt was a waste of time. And yet, in the height of the tension of what was in front of me, I started having a back-and-forth dialogue explaining to my mother what my recent life had become.

I shook the voices off, thinking just how ironic it had been that Dr. Laurier was no longer around to appreciate I'd embraced that therapeutic practice.

But this was definitely *not* the time for such naval-gazing introspection.

Though my senses were still mostly muted, I was able to pick up the most intense of emotions. But there was no scent of guilt coming from any of the others who now formed a complete circle around the dead body of Dr. Brendon Laurier.

The main emotive smell I was picking up, which layered the air around us, was shock, tinged with a layer of confusion.

But how could that be? Certainly, one of us had to be the guilty one.

I looked around the room one-by-one at the other monsters in the building.

At Ellie, whose brow was scrunched up as she, too seemed to be deeply analyzing this situation.

At Shian, whose eyes were wide with shock and fear, reminding me of the first time we'd met.

At Linnaeus, whose hands kept gesturing in the air in front of him, as if he were trying to keep the entire group calm, but without knowing exactly how to do that.

At Chester, whose own body subconsciously followed Linnaeus's every move while absently reaching out to touch the fabric of his sweater, as if wanting to be picked up by the giant of a man.

At the thin, emaciated face of Vlastislav, whose silent tears were thick and cloudy with what looked like bloody tears.

One of us had to be guilty of whatever lead to the death of the therapist who was supposed to help us learn to become better functioning Paranormals.

"Ellie," I said. "What happened?"

She was breathing so fast she was practically hyperventilating. "This isn't happening!" she said in a shrill voice.

I stepped over to her and put my arms around her, noticing Vlastislav glaring at me as I did so. As I stared back at him, I noticed that the dark cloudiness in his eyes were blood tears. I remembered him mentioning that after a feeding his tears would be filled with blood.

As I pulled Ellie in closer to me, I glanced back down at Dr. Laurier's body and noticed something I hadn't seen before. Two small round puncture wounds about an inch apart from one another on the side of his exposed neck. They looked fresh.

Both Ellie and Vlastislav were in the room when the rest of us arrived. Had Ellie walked in to find the vampire feasting on our therapist?

"It's okay, Ellie," I whispered into Ellie's ear. "Tell me what you saw. I'll protect you."

"Dr. Laurier was alone in the room when I came in," she said.

"Are you sure?" I asked.

"Yes. He was alone when I arrived."

"And I was just down the hall when I heard her scream," Vlastislav said.

I glanced over at the window, which was opened a few inches. I was fully aware of at least two of the forms the vampire could shape-shift into. He could have killed Dr. Laurier and then escaped out the window as a bat and made his way back into the hallway. And if I wasn't mistaken, he looked far less pale than he had before. As if he, perhaps, had recently feasted on someone.

"It looks like someone broke his neck," Chester said. He was kneeling near the head of the man's body. As I looked down, I noticed that the reason I'd been able to see the bite marks so clearly was because the side of his neck was almost fully facing the front—because his head was twisted all the way to the side.

"Back off!" Linnaeus said. "Don't touch the body!"

Chester turned to look up at the large man.

"I mean, we shouldn't. It'll disturb the evidence."

Linnaeus was acting rather nervous, which caught me by surprise. I figured he'd be the one taking charge in this situation and trying to comfort everyone else. But he seemed rather panicked. I'd never heard him snap the way he just had at Chester.

Could he be involved in this?

While I was certain that a vampire had the strength to twist a man's neck around, I was also aware that Linnaeus would be capable of such a feat. Sure, he was my friend, and I trusted him. But how much did I really know about him? And maybe he was in on it with the vampire. Or maybe he was protecting Shian. We all knew she was certainly capable of such an incredible feat of strength.

"L-look at his arm," Shian said, almost as if sensing I'd been considering her role in this. "At the scratches."

The underside of Dr. Laurier's right forearm, which lay along the side of his body was covered in thick long scratches. The kind a cat might make.

Vlastislav reached down and turned the therapist's other arm, which was resting across his stomach, over. It too was bloody with huge scratch wounds.

"Those appear to be defensive wounds," Linnaeus said. "As if the good doctor had raised his arms up in a vain attempt to ward off an attack."

I looked at Vlastislav. Vampires had sharp nails, didn't they?

But just then, Chester stood and backed away, as if trying to put further distance between himself and the fresh evidence we'd just noticed.

I pointed at him.

"They're cat scratches!" I yelled.

This was getting more confusing by the second. Had Vlastislav, Linnaeus, and Chester all ganged up on Dr. Laurier?

"No," Chester said. "No. No. No. Not me. It wasn't me." He couldn't look any of us in the eye. Instead, he was looking down at the doctor as if there might be an answer coming from the group's now dead therapist.

But then Chester raised his right hand and pointed at the body.

"Hey," he said. "Look at that. Dr. Laurier has a boner."

What the hell was he saying? And why would he point something like that out?

"We all know," Chester said, his head bobbing in a panicked fashion as his sentence came out all chopped between big breaths. "Which one here. Has that effect. On men."

"The mermaid!" Vlastislav said, pointing at Shian. "She seduced him with her siren charm."

"Shian would never do such a thing!" Linnaeus snapped.

But could Shian have been involved in this as well? Could she have seduced Dr. Laurier to distract him? So that the others could kill him? No, Vlad was right. I just couldn't see it. It didn't make any sense.

But if my understanding of vampire lore was correct, vampires also had the ability to charm people.

"Vampires can also seduce people," I said, pointing my finger at Vlastislav. He took a step back and opened his mouth to respond. But Linnaeus spoke first.

"Postmortem priapism," he said.

"What?" Chester asked.

"Rigor erectus. That's likely what happened to him," Linnaeus said. "Sometimes, in death, especially a sudden death, blood rushes to the penis, causing a post-mortem erection. You see, it couldn't have been Shian."

"But what about the rest of it?" Vlastislav said. "You know what type of creature could leave all those marks, and do the thing we see evidence of here? A wolf. Or, more accurately, a werewolf."

"You're out of your mind," I hissed at the vampire. "It wasn't me."

But I couldn't be sure of what I was saying. I had blacked out. And it was just before I'd decided to head back to the lodge with a burning desire to see Dr. Laurier.

"I witnessed overnight that you're fully capable of controlling the change between human and wolf," Vlastislav said. "And the way you man-handled me last night, I know just how strong you are. Enough to easily break a man's neck. And those scratches could be wolf claws. The bite wounds on his neck could even be wolf fangs for all we know."

"I heard you yelling. At Dr. Laurier. Yesterday." Chester said. "And then you stormed. Out of his office."

"That's right," Linnaeus said. "Chester and I were engaged in a hearty chess match down the hall when we heard you yelling angrily and then slamming the door."

"It wasn't me," I said in a weak voice. "It couldn't have been me that killed him."

Shian, Linnaeus, Chester, and Vlastislav were all looking at me with matching wide eyes and round opened mouths. If I hadn't been mortified by what was being suggested I'm sure I would have found it amusing how similar they all looked.

I tightened my grip around Ellie's shoulder.

"They all think it's me," I said to her. "But you believe me, don't you?"

Ellie slipped out of my embrace and backed away. She looked more sad than horrified. "Oh, Michael, I'm so sorry," she said.

I stood looking at the others, a gut-wrenching fear welling up inside.

Interlude: Wolf Night
The Bugs Inside the Bat

Overnight
Wednesday Sept 6, 2017 / Thursday Sept 7, 2017

Growling, Michael advanced toward Vlastislav who had scrambled into a sitting position with his back against the tree trunk.

The vampire's eyes were wide, and the fear emanating off him was palpable. That fueled the wolf.

"Michael," Vlastislav called out. "Please stop. Do not hurt me."

Michael stopped and glared at the vampire wanting to say something in response. *Why should I listen to you?* was what he wanted to say. But his wolf lips and tongue would not produce more than a strange grunt.

He thought how it would be easier for Vlastislav to understand him if he could change into his human form.

That's when he felt a trembling and heard an odd popping and cracking sound. A pain tore through his head and back, and he arched his neck up and let out a howl. A burning sensation rushed through his veins, and he felt an uncontrollable spasm *take over his limbs. The pain continued as he felt his limbs and torso elongate.*

Within a few seconds, I was lying on the ground, completely naked, and human.

Two thoughts flowed almost simultaneously through my mind.

That wasn't nearly as painful as I thought it would be. And: Why is it that I'm naked, but he still has clothes?

I shoved that meek voice aside, finding it annoying and I growled again—an animal growl issuing from my human throat—as I stood, glaring down at the thin vampire who cowered in front of me.

There were two things I knew. I had the power. And he was without any.

Not even trying to cover my nakedness, I stood tall, fierce, and proud. Not ashamed of my nakedness, but proud of it. So unlike the way I remember feeling most of my life.

The complete unadulterated confidence I'd always suspected an alpha wolf possessed flowed through me. It was incredibly powerful. A guy could get used to this.

Despite this newfound confidence, that long-term part of me that still lingered deep inside forced me to briefly glance down at my manhood, worried I'd be shriveled and shrunk in response to the damp and cool night air. But I was pleased to see the evening chill had not had the negative side-effect on me.

"What are you up to out here, Vlad?"

The vampire was so frightened that he didn't even object to the nickname that had riled him up.

"Nothing," he said.

"Don't give me that. You were up to something, and I want to know what it is."

"It's none of your business."

"You're in my woods. It's my business," I said. It was quite an odd feeling being so forceful, so dominant. while standing over him, completely naked, and unfazed about that. It made me wonder how he was fully clothed, despite having transitioned between bat, man, and wolf, then back to man.

"Why is it you always have clothes when you change form?"

"I don't know," he said. "That's just how it is. I'm always in this same outfit when I turn back into my human form. It's not like anyone provided me with a handbook."

I couldn't argue with that. He had a good point. It had been something I'd long thought about. But finding something to agree with him about angered me.

"That's enough bullshit!" I said, stepping closer, grabbing him with one hand by the shoulder, and lifting him off his ass and into the air.

I raised my other arm with a tightened fist and felt a part of me wrestling for control, fighting the overwhelming urge to punch him. Giving up that struggle, I let go of his shoulder, watched him collapse back down to the ground like a rag doll, and shot my fist into the tree a foot above his head. The tree shook from the blow.

"Tell me what the hell you're doing out here!"

"Okay, okay!" He raised his hands in that universal 'I give up' gesture. "I'll tell you. I didn't want to say because I was embarrassed that you found me."

"Why?" I asked.

"I was getting sustenance out here."

I considered that. "You're consuming the blood from wild animals? Would that even work for a vampire?"

"No! Never! That's disgusting. But it could work. Vampires can live off the blood of other mammals, so that would sustain a vampire. But as I shared with the group the other night, I am a vegan. I swore off deriving nourishment from any animals."

This was utterly confusing to me.

"Then what were you out here eating? Leaves? Twigs?"

"No. I was eating bugs."

"Bugs?"

"Yes. Flies mostly."

I stared at him with what must have been a completely blank look on my face before I realized what he was saying. "As a bat, you mean?"

"Yes," he laughed. "As a bat."

"Why?"

"Dr. Laurier gave me the idea. I was getting weaker and losing weight, and most of my energy."

I remembered seeing him eating the night of our first group banquet, and a few other times. He was picky as hell but had consumed quite a huge portion of the food. "What about the food that you eat?" I asked.

"It's not enough," he said. "It can keep me going, but it barely brings any value other than some caloric intake. I suppose my body processes that type of food too quickly. Even if I ate non-stop, all night long, at a giant buffet, it wouldn't sustain me the way that a single pint of blood would."

"That's just so weird," I said.

"You're telling me!" He grinned, showing his sharp incisors, which I still found disturbing. "Try living like this. It's not easy getting used to. I mean, of all the reasons why me being a vampire is humiliating, I have this fresh hell to contend with."

"The food you've been eating at the lodge hasn't been helping?"

"Not nearly enough. I need blood to survive. It has been almost a month since I'd consumed blood. But it wasn't even fresh blood. It was the blood that had seeped out of a hunk of steak in one of those Styrofoam trays they come in. It was disgusting and it took everything in me to choke it down without throwing up. But I knew I had to, because otherwise I would have lost control and killed someone else.

"I've been getting progressively weaker since I got here, and in our evening session, Dr. Laurier suggested that I try converting into a bat and eating flies. His theory was that the nutrients I could get from eating several hundred insects might be enough to power me in that more compact format."

"Bugs have blood?"

"A type of blood, yes. Hemolymph. It's a combination of blood and other intestinal fluids. But contains the nutrients to sustain life. And if I happened to consume a mosquito carrying mammal blood it consumed, there'd be a much more powerful infusion of life energy. But Dr. Laurier's theory was that it would fulfill that hunger in bat format, and when I changed back to human, all things being equal, it would have been like I'd consumed a larger quantity of blood."

I had no idea how this worked. Science was far from my strong suit, and this odd combination of science with Paranormal biology was even further beyond my ability to comprehend.

"Do you think it's working, then?" I asked.

"Yes. I think so. It feels like it's working. Or at least it did before I was forced to change form so many times. While I'm not a fan of harming any creatures, I'm far more tolerant of the indignities being inflicted upon insects. This could be a viable solution. But, of course, you so rudely interrupted me."

"You interrupted me!" I yelled. "You're the one who flew right over me."

He looked embarrassed. "I was trying to distract you."

"Distract me?"

"Yes. As I was flying, I spotted you. But I also sensed, off to your right, a pack of young rabbits. I was worried that you were going to attack and eat them, so I swooped closer to you attempting to draw you away from them."

I hadn't even been aware of the nearby rabbits. At the time I was so consumed with the fact my human and wolf consciousness had overlapped I hadn't been attending to much else. But I wasn't about to admit that to him. Something about him still bothered me.

"Listen," he said. "It's going to be light out in just a few hours. And the chase combined with changing from bat to human, and then to wolf seems to have removed most of the regenerative properties of the bugs I've eaten."

"I still don't understand how that works," I said.

"You've been a Paranormal longer than I have," he sneered. "How is it possible for you to be so utterly stupid and know so little."

He then morphed into a bat, seemingly without the same metamorphosis pain that I went through and squeaked off into the night.

I thought about what he'd said. The little bastard had the gall to insult me just before he flittered off. Which I suppose is good for him, because if he was still in front of me, I'd likely have punched him. But he was right. I've been a werewolf for well over a decade and still knew so damn little.

Also, I still wasn't sure I trusted him and what he had told me.

But I did have a lot of new information to consider and process about myself.

For the first time I'd merged human and wolf consciousness. And I'd been able to control the change out here, far from the enchantment of the main lodge. Something good was happening to me. At least I thought it was good.

I was eager to get back to the lodge, see if I could wake Dr. Laurier and talk to him about it. I could also confirm the story Vlastislav had shared about the bug eating. See if he had been lying to me about that.

Turning, I started to run in the direction of the main lodge.

As I ran, the previous manhood I'd been proud of became an inconvenience. It bounced and slapped against the sides of my upper thighs like an annoying restless toddler who wouldn't stop asking 'are we there yet?'

This was stupid, and embarrassing. Not that there was anyone out here to see me.

Other than Vlastislav, of course, if he was paying attention.

I started to feel my old less confident self begin to take hold again, as I pictured what I looked like naked running full tilt through the woods.

And at that thought, I realized I'd be able to cover ground a lot more quickly in wolf form.

So, I stopped running, dropped to my hands and knees, and thought about turning into a wolf.

A similar rumbling pain to the one I'd felt in the opposite transition began. Then I heard what sounded like bones cracking, and I gasped in pain. This was twice as painful as the wolf to man metamorphosis I'd recently experienced.

As the burning sensation intensified, I blacked out completely.

Chapter Twenty: An Answer, a Resolution, And a Revelation

Thursday, September 7, 2017
6:07 a.m.

Was it possible that I had done this?

I looked back down at Dr. Laurier's body. At the broken neck, the bite marks, the scratches, and I reached into the depths of the darkness that had consumed my consciousness when I morphed back into a wolf to run back here. Why couldn't I remember anything?

I concentrated hard, trying to come up with anything from the hours before I remember waking naked in my bed. And something did come to me. A brief flash.

Dr. Laurier's face. Looking at me. Saying something.

It was too fuzzy. Too clouded. And his words were mumbled. I closed my eyes and pictured it again.

We were standing here, in his office. He was looking at me. Straight at me. That meant I was a human, not a wolf. So why the hell couldn't I remember what was happening? Had my wolf consciousness taken over?

Among the last things I remembered from earlier today was how uncharacteristically dominant and alpha I'd been in my confrontation with Vlastislav. I'd come close to hurting him. But had something happened between Dr. Laurier and me that resulted in me doing *this* to him?

I tried to think about the look on his face in that brief flash of memory.

His lips were pursed. And he looked concerned. Or was it fear? I couldn't be sure.

I thought about the sound of his voice from that flash of memory.

There were three words. The first one was short, one syllable and said with urgency.

Stop.

There were other words, but too indistinguishable in the memory cloud. But another word suddenly stuck out from the haze.

Killing.

Were the words said together?

Stop killing?

No, that didn't make sense. The words weren't uttered one after another. There were other words in between. Then the auditory memory of another word, a single syllable like the previous one, punched through. He'd said it loud and forcefully.

No!

What had Dr. Laurier been saying to me in that memory? And before that.

Stop.

Killing.

No!

What had we been discussing?

And what had I done to him?

I looked up from Dr. Laurier's body and at the others who were silently staring at me, horrified looks on their faces. Well, all but one. Like before, Ellie was still looking at me not with fear, but sorrow.

And what had she said?

Oh, Michael, I'm so sorry.

Why was she sorry? What had she done?

Was she sorry because she was the one who killed Dr. Laurier? And maybe used her growing faerie abilities to frame me with all the visual evidence? Is that why she was sorry and not fearful?

I remembered the long talks we had these past several days. The bonding. Was it possible she'd been getting to know me, to learn more about me, to gain my trust? She already admitted having practically stalked me in the media and reading all my books. Was it all part of her plot to set me up? Had our intimate conversations been real, or had they been a ruse of some sort?

It just didn't seem possible that she could have been lying to me the entire time we were talking. I felt this real connection with her. And even though my enhanced senses that acted like a built-in lie-detector were taken away from me, I still felt like she'd been genuine and that she truly cared about me.

If this lodge wasn't held under some enchanting spell, I'd be able to know for sure if she was lying. Or who else here was lying.

I thought about trying to get us all as far away from the main lodge as possible. If we could all re-locate, somewhere far from the enchantment on this building and these main grounds that prevented magic, I'd be able to—

Wait a minute. I've been such an idiot. If this lodge is enchanted to prevent the paranormal in the same way that Lex's presence prevented it, why did Vlastislav need to hide in a coffin when the sun came up? Wouldn't the very same charm that allowed me to not have to turn into a wolf work in a similar way with him? On my first day here, Chester changed into a cat inside the building before he tossed all the items in my room.

Speaking of which, if magic is being repressed how could Ellie have created the illusion that she was Dr. Laurier right outside the main entrance? And how could I have felt Shian's alluring siren song compelling me at our first dinner and in our first group therapy session?

Dr. Laurier had never actually told me that the enchantment that had been placed on this retreat nullified the paranormal. He'd merely asked me if I noticed the effect on my senses, which I had. But I'd been thinking about Lex and assumed whatever spell had been cast here was removing all magic.

But he never actually said that. He let me believe it.

That's because it wasn't a magic-cancelling spell at all. It was one that specifically targeted enhanced senses. Including my ability to detect a lie.

And speaking of lies, Ellie couldn't lie. Faeries are unable to. I learned that this week. The two times I'd seen her try she faltered. Once when she was pretending to be Dr. Laurier but got flustered because she'd tried to say the words 'I'm Dr. Laurier." The other time when we were playing our truth and lies game and she had to get some assistance from Vlastislav to craftily deceive.

That's exactly what was going on here. She was playing at deceit. Letting me—no, letting us all—make assumptions based on what we were seeing.

"Why are you sorry, Ellie?"

"Eh, what's that now?" she said, taking another step back, looking extremely uneasy.

"What is it that you're sorry about, Ellie?"

"Er," she looked down at Dr. Laurier, then back up at me. "The . . . I mean . . . you know . . ."

"You can't lie. Can you?" I said, then turned to the others. "She can't lie. Faeries can't lie. We've all seen that." I faced Ellie again and walked toward her.

Linnaeus started to take a step, but I put out a hand. "I'm not going to hurt her. I didn't hurt anyone here today. I just want to ask her a few things."

I stepped up to Ellie and looked her straight in the eyes. "Do you believe that I killed Dr. Laurier, Ellie?"

"No, I don't," she said.

"Did I kill Dr. Laurier?"

"No."

"And you didn't kill him either, did you?"

"No. I could never."

"Is Dr. Laurier even dead?"

"Er, well he looks dead, doesn't he?"

I leaned right in close to her, face to face.

"Is Dr. Laurier dead, Ellie?"

"No! He's not!" she blurted, then winced. "Ah sugar!" She swung a clenched fist in the air, upset with herself for not being able to control her response. "Sugar and shite!"

I stepped back and Ellie grinned at me. "You figured me out," she said, laughing. And her laugh lifted my heart from the dark place it had been just moments earlier. She smiled at me, and then turned to look at the others. "But you have to admit I had you all goin' there for a good bit."

"That's okay," Dr. Laurier's voice came from the floor. The entire group—well, everyone except Ellie—let out a collective gasp to see him sit up, his neck no longer twisted around, and no visible bite marks on his throat or scratches down his arms. "You did an excellent job, Ellie." He stood and looked around at us all. "And you, my friends, also did extremely well. I'm proud of you. And you should be proud of yourselves."

"I don't understand," Vlastislav said.

"Why the dramatic subterfuge?"

"Yeah," Chester said.

"What just happened?" Shian asked.

"I'm sorry for the dramatic manner by which I had to fool you all, but I felt an urgent need to do it, for Michael's sake. And the reason most of you have been brought together was for Michael's sake. But also, of course, for your own needs. For there is a strong overlap in each of your issues, as I'm sure you've discovered these past several days. I'll get to that in a moment.

"First, Ellie, I'm sure you'll agree with me that your week here has been entirely successful. It's good you could arrive several days early and spend some time practicing with me to help with the elaborate and extended illusion.

"Thank you, Doctor," Ellie said. "Working together on it with you and talking through why I'd been repressing my powers helped me to embrace my full potential."

"You still have a lot of work to do with expressing things in ways that lead people to believe something without outright lying." He smiled at her. "But that's more of a Mundane trait than a Paranormal one; and it'll get better with practice. Until the moment that Michael started to directly grill you, I thought you handled the deception masterfully. And I believe that you've achieved what you set out for with your stay here. Your treatment and therapy are complete."

Ellie blushed and I smiled at her.

"Vlastislav," Dr. Laurier said, turning to the vampire. "You're looking so much healthier this morning."

"I feel great," the tall thin man said. "Better than I ever have since I've been in this state. Your idea about the bugs worked wonders."

"I am confident that, with a solution that does not violate your moral compass, you can continue on with a long and prosperous existence. As far as I'm concerned, you can take your leave. Your therapy here has been successfully completed."

"Thank you," Vlastislav said.

"Linnaeus," Dr. Laurier said. "You have also done extremely well. But I think we have a long way to go in finding a solution that is going to work for you. I don't think you'll ever be able to terrorize people from a bridge in the traditional sense. But I believe, if we continue to work together, we can find a way for you to fulfill your role, but also maintain your compassion for other people. In fact, I've seen evidence that you would make a most empathetic therapist."

Linnaeus scratched his head. "I'd love that. But that's not within the parameters of my troll heritage."

"One of the things I've been doing is research into that. Troll is only half of your lineage. You're also Ogre."

"But it's the father's lineage—"

"In a truly patriarchal society, maybe. But it only stays that way if we allow it to. I'd like to see if there's a way we can use your half-Ogre nature to enact change upon that heritage. And I think, working together, we'll find a way to make that happen. If you think you're up to it."

"I would appreciate the opportunity to cultivate that," Linnaeus grinned. "I'm willing to effectuate a substantive change if it means I can continue in my solicitive nature."

Dr. Laurier then addressed Shian. "You've come out of your shell, particularly with your meaningful friendship with Linnaeus. I believe that you two are good for one another in the way you offer mutual support. And we have only begun the process of understanding the conflict between your siren calling and your natural inclinations."

"Yes," Shian nodded. "I've started to realize things about myself that I'd never bothered to consider. Being here helps. Making actual friends with men has allowed me to see why I get along so well with them but don't actually want to seduce them. I may actually feel more like a man in here." She placed a hand over her chest, and then moved that same hand to the side of her head. "And in here."

"I believe that staying here for a while longer, and continuing to talk through these things, and exploring options, we can take our time and find a path that's right for you. A path that might seem to be a little unorthodox to some. But one that could allow you to embrace the Shian that you really are inside. Just because tradition has mermaids seducing men, doesn't mean they, too, can't evolve."

"I would like to explore the possibilities and options to feel more of the real me." Shian nodded, a tear rolling down the side of her cheek. "I would really like that. But I'm sure it won't be easy."

"We'll do it together," Dr. Laurier said. "You won't be alone."

"No, you won't be alone." Linnaeus took Shian's hand in his. "I'll be with you for every step of this process," Linnaeus said. "Through thick and thin, I'll have your back."

The two beamed smiles at one another that filled my heart with joy. Like Ellie and I, the two had bonded in a completely platonic yet deep and meaningful way. They were good for one another this week, and would continue to be as they grew and evolved.

"Chester," Dr. Laurier said. "Similarly, our work together has only just begun. You have made some progress gaining self-confidence, but there's still much work to do in terms of accepting your own duality. That you can be a cat and have canine traits. And learn to love yourself the way you so easily love others. And, like Shian, you also have become friends with Linnaeus."

"Oh yeah. We're pals!" Chester said, looking up at the troll. "Right, Linnaeus. We're buds, right?"

Continuing to hold Shian's hand with his own left one, Linnaeus reached his right hand to take Chester's. "Indubitably, my compadre," he said.

Dr. Laurier then turned to me. "And finally, Michael," he said. "You have come a long way in a short time. You have overcome a number of important elements. Especially the ones that you have in common with each of the others here. Taking part in a group therapy has worked well, despite your hesitancy about it. Your mistrust of the Paranormal world has reduced dramatically since you've gotten here. You have formed positive and healthy relationships with most of the others. Both your initial aversion to therapy and your thinking of Paranormals as abnormal or even monsters has improved wonderfully. And you've begun to embrace that in yourself by making incredible breakthroughs in accepting the wolf-part of your being. Even without your enhanced senses, or being able to read others' emotions, you were able to listen and attend to others better, and even start to intuit things about the Paranormal realm, instead of blocking them, too."

"Speaking of blocking," I asked. "I know that the enchantment blocked my senses, and it prevented me from automatically changing into a wolf. At least when I was inside the lodge. Or was that some other enchantment? Because why didn't it affect anyone else in a similar way? And why do I have this vague memory of talking to you early this morning but that whole section of time is a complete blank?"

"First things first, Michael.

"With respect to the enchantment you mentioned, there was never anything preventing you from automatically changing into wolf form at sunset, Michael."

"Wait? What the hell? But you said . . ."

"What did I say, exactly?" He smiled at me, and I tried to go back to the exact words he'd used. "Think about what happened in the early morning hours between you and Vlastislav. What you were so eager to talk to me about earlier this morning."

"Yeah, but I thought that me changing like that was a side-effect of whatever enchantment gave me control when I was here."

"All you needed was a little guidance to try controlling the change on your own. All werewolves have that ability. But yours has been blocked for some reason and has been for most of your life. Likely due to some childhood trauma."

"But before I got here, I couldn't control it. You said that—"

"I said that it was up to you. Nothing other than your own will."

"There was never any magic assisting me with that control? I've had the ability to control it all along?" I was still confused. "Wait a minute. You're saying that the enchantment on this place was just on my senses?"

"Yes," Dr. Laurier said. "But not just your enhanced senses. The enchantment is on all extra-sensory powers. Your prominent sense of hearing, smell, and taste. But also on the mind-reading acuity of faerie-kind."

"Oh," I said. "So, Ellie also can't read minds when here."

Ellie shook her head. "I can't. I mean, I can feel the ability is there, and I tried but can't do it. Not here, just now, at least."

"Nor can I," Dr. Laurier said.

I turned back to look at him. "*You're* a Paranormal too?"

He grinned. "Like Ellie, I am also a faerie. But these grounds are covered with a powerful enchantment to prevent us from being detected by Mundane perception. You likely recall the illusion that masks the entrance to the road that leads here. That's part of my ongoing charm spell. But that same spell has the effect, once a Paranormal is inside of its area, of reducing those enhanced perceptions. And while therapy would be a lot easier if I could read my patient's mind, I much prefer to employ the route of helping those I work with take their own path of self-discovery by asking probing questions.

"But now that Ellie has come into her own with her powers, and why she blocked them—especially the ability to read minds—in the first place, I'm confident that she'll have that ability restored once she leaves this locale."

"That's great!" I said to Ellie. "We can both leave."

"I didn't say your therapy was done, Michael," Dr. Laurier said, "only that you have made excellent progress. You're still struggling with some issues related to your up-bringing, and your relationship with your mother, as you and I discussed this morning. And there's the whole matter of your parental lineage, which we also discussed."

"When?"

"This morning. Here. In this office. But that's what you blocked out, isn't it? You can't remember any of that?"

I scanned back through the fleeting memories I had of facing Dr. Laurier in both human and wolf form. Of the words he'd uttered. *Stop. Killing. No!* But nothing else came. "No! I don't!"

"Well, then that's something else we need to spend a lot of time working on."

I lept at him and grabbed him by the collar. "What did you tell me? I need to know!"

Like before, Linnaeus stepped forward, prepared to prevent me from hurting the therapist. Dr. Laurier raised a hand to let Linnaeus know that he was fine and to stand down.

"I'm afraid that what I told you this morning is what led to you blocking your memory. You refuse to believe it so much you wiped it out. Likely in the same way you wiped out that early childhood trauma and a significant part of you. We really should take our time and explore it carefully."

"I. Want. To. Know. Now." I hissed, my spittle visibly landing on his face.

He sighed. "Okay. Very well. It's not like I haven't already shared this with you."

"What did you share?"

"I told you that Vlastislav was right. The other night, when he said that a human can't be turned into a werewolf with a simple scratch, or bite. There is a long and complicated process involving the exchange of blood."

"Told ya!" Vlastislav said with a sardonic smile.

I glared at him before looking back at Dr. Laurier. "But that bite. On the highway. Up north."

"I suspect that bite triggered something in you that was always there. Something you had repressed."

I didn't understand. "Something that was always there?"

"You were born a werewolf, Michael."

"What?" I couldn't believe what he was telling me. How could that be? I remember the night I got bitten. The feelings after. That first change during the next cycle of the moon.

"You've always been a werewolf."

"No!" I said, thinking I'd lived my life up to that point as a human. "I don't believe you. That can't be."

"It is. Your birth parents must have been werewolves. When I investigated the records, I found some that align with when you were adopted. And I suspect your birth parents are not only from Canada, but that they're both still alive."

Chapter Twenty-One: The Uncharacteristically Abbreviated and Not at All Over-explained Denouement with a Not So Long Goodbye

Friday, September 8, 2017
11:41 a.m.

"I really wish you would re-consider, Michael," Dr. Laurier said, warmly shaking my hand as we stood in the doorway of the main lodge. "We were making such good progress. You're so close. And I do worry about the conflict that still exists between your split consciousnesses."

"Thank you, Dr. Laurier. You, and . . ." I turned to look at Ellie who was standing beside me on the front step, "everyone else here have helped me so much. I am starting to understand a lot more about myself, and about the Paranormal aspects of our world. But I really have to do this. Besides, I'll have your protégé by my side. Our friendship and our numerous marathon chinwags this week have been a significant part of my healing."

Ellie and I had already shared our goodbyes to Shian, Linnaeus, and Chester, who were back inside and upstairs, already working on a group exercise the good doctor had set them up with. I was pretty sure that I'd see Linnaeus and Shian again. Linnaeus made me promise to stay in touch. I knew I would. I really liked him. And I'm sure his friendship with Shian would allow me to stay in touch with her.

As for Chester, well, if I were to be entirely honest with myself, I couldn't see being more than an acquaintance with him. And it's not that I didn't like cats. I got along quite marvelously with the house cat at the Algonquin Hotel in Manhattan where I lived. It's just that Chester and I didn't need to be close friends, and that's okay.

I didn't think that Vlastislav—who had left after sunset last night—and I would be staying in touch, either. Sure, I'd started to tolerate him, but it didn't mean I'd become besties with a vampire any time soon. Even if he could turn into a wolf, we just didn't mix well.

After a long discussion that we weren't done exploring whatever imperceptible bond seemed to knit us together, Ellie and I formulated a plan on continuing with our mystical dance of fingers, as we jokingly came to call it. Like that first afternoon when we'd been standing on the bridge, we'd gotten into the habit of joining hands in that same fashion for further deeply intimate and personal talks. The connection continued to feel almost electrical, and we were wondering if, once she vacated the enchantment of the retreat, her telepathic ability and my enhanced senses would help us unravel why we were so connected to one another, and the reasoning behind why we felt it was important to take the next step on our personal healing journeys together.

Part of me was a little bothered by the way we'd met and gotten close so quickly, and then decided on our course of action—returning to my home in New York together—paralleled the way Lex and I connected and flew back home together from Los Angeles. But that was different. Lex and I had been lovers.

What Ellie and I shared was far deeper than that sexual intimacy. It seemed as powerful as my connection to Gail, but without the messy romantic notions that so easily slapped a confusing filter on things.

Dr. Laurier smiled at me with his lips pressed tightly together. "Knowing that Ellie will be with you does bring me some comfort. But I know your mind is made up."

"Sure, go on," Ellie said. "I'll keep an eye on him. Two, even."

We all laughed, then looked at one another for a quiet moment as the same car that had dropped me off almost a week ago came around the corner and pulled up at the nearby curb.

"Thanks, Doc."

"Don't forget, Michael, you can always return," he said. "Whenever you like."

"I won't forget, Doc," I said. "And thanks again."

Holding hands, Ellie and I walked down the front steps and toward the car that was waiting to bring us to New York City.

Epilogue: That Information Michael So Conveniently Blocked

Excerpt from therapy session recordings of Dr. Brendon Laurier

Tuesday, September 7, 2017
5:28 a.m.

LAURIER: That's because you've always been a werewolf, Michael. You were born a werewolf.

ANDREWS: No, that's impossible. I've only been a werewolf since I got bitten by that wolf on the side of that highway at midnight.

LAURIER: I believe that event is what broke through whatever it was that you'd been repressing your entire life. That bite didn't turn you into a werewolf. It allowed you to begin to accept who and what you truly are. But the trauma that caused you to repress it so deeply is likely the same trauma that continues to keep your wolf and human mind separate. It has only been the past several nights that you've been able to remember more about your alternative form's nightly actions. Since you've been here, right?

ANDREWS: Yes. Every night, it's gotten clearer.

LAURIER: And your two minds, for a brief time at least, they merged into one, didn't they?

ANDREWS: Yes. I had human consciousness in wolf form. And in human form, I could feel that wolf part of me filling me with a confidence I've never experienced before.

LAURIER: We need to keep working on this. It's dangerous for you to merge those divided minds too quickly. We also need to work on your sensitivity to your adoptive parents.

ANDREWS: Again, with that bullshit. Leave my parents out of this. Didn't I make it clear to you last night that they're my real parents? So shut your—

LAURIER: Stop!

ANDREWS: What?

LAURIER: Michael, you need to come to terms with the fact that your real parents—your birth parents—are werewolves, like you.

ANDREWS: Shut up! I don't want to hear it. They're not my real parents. If they were, why would they abandon me? How could they do such a thing?

LAURIER: Oh, Michael. I suspect that's where this trauma comes from. That's the deeply rooted intensity to deny whatever it was that happened. At whatever caused this. We have much more therapy to get through before you're ready to face that aspect. Before you're ready to meet with them.

ANDREWS: Meet with them?

LAURIER: Yes. I believe, based on the records I've looked into, that they are still alive.

ANDREWS: You know who my parents are? Who are they? Where are they?

LAURIER: Michael, slow down. You're not ready to deal with this yet. Not even close.

ANDREWS: Don't tell me what I'm close to. I'll decide that.

LAURIER: If you keep on this path, it's dangerous. Can't you see that is what is ultimately killing you?

ANDREWS: What's killing me is not knowing. I need to go, Doc. I need to find them. I need to find out who I am. What I am. Why I'm like this.

LAURIER: Go? No, Michael, you need to think about this. We need to continue our therapy, work through the issues slowly.

[Sounds of a skirmish]

ANDREWS: You need to stop telling me what to do

LAURIER: No! [Long pause] That's it. I knew you didn't want to hit me. Okay, Micheal, please put me down. Can't you see, you're still not in control of your duality. It's going to take some practice, some time.

ANDREWS: Time! Time! It's always about time! Waiting for Gail to love me! Waiting for the curse to let go of its hold on us! Well I'm done waiting. I'm taking action. And I'm going to start with finding my parents. I'm so tired of waiting. I'm so . . . damn . . . tired.

LAURIER: Okay, okay. And I can see that you're not just tired, you're exhausted. You're behaving irrationally. Listen, I'll tell you what I know about where I believe they are in Canada. But not now. Later. Please, Michael. Right now, I need to get ready for Ellie's session, which starts shortly, and you need to try to get some rest. Okay?

[There is a long pause followed by the sound of movement]

LAURIER: Thank you. Okay, please, go back to your room and try to get a little bit of sleep. We'll talk at seven, in our scheduled appointment.

ANDREWS: Okay.

LAURIER: You get some rest. I'm going to get myself a coffee.

[Footsteps are heard, then the sound of a door opening, and the muffled voices of LAURIER and ANDREWS as the door closes and they are outside the office. The tape continues to record for another full minute of silence before the sound of the window sliding open, followed by a shuffling noise, then footsteps.]

UNKNOWN MALE: I'll see you in London, Michael. Where we'll have our little reunion. [There is a pause] *Oh, this thing is still running.* [A rustling sound is heard as the tape recorder is picked up] *I'll just —*

Coming Next

A Canadian Werewolf in London, Ontario

To unravel the mystery of his werewolf roots, Michael Andrews returns to his old stomping grounds of Canada and traces a bizarre path of destruction that lead him and his faerie companion on the trail of the father he barely knew.

Get notified about this next book's release:

markleslie.ca/london/

Authors' Notes

I won't lie. This one took a long time. I hell of a lot of time in my head, and then, as often happens, a mad scramble as I raced to the finish line.

I suppose that comes when all I have is a vague idea, a fun title, and no idea of any of the details.

Of course, in the year I was mulling over the story, I came up with numerous thoughts of who the murderer might be, or how the characters were going to find a way to collaborate to solve it together.

But then I realized something important: I wasn't trying to write a proper mystery novel. I was writing a Michael Andrews Canadian Werewolf humorous adventure.

I had a grand time (as Ellie might say) introducing a cast of new characters and trying to make them as unique and interesting as possible. It was also important for me that I tried to flip some tropes on their head. Not to mention the heads—or minds—of those characters themselves.

I mean, in such a messed-up world as ours, why should Michael Andrews be the only Paranormal that doesn't fit in, who doesn't live up to the "expectations" of what he is supposed to be? Wouldn't there be others our there who needed some help?

I purposely did a few things as I was crafting this tale and the characters. I tried to ensure that there was at least one specific trait—if not more—in each of the other patients, that Michael might see in himself.

Like Ellie, some traumatic event occurred inciting the blockage of his Paranormal abilities. Also like her, he grew up a nerdy loner.

Like Linnaeus, Michael was an orphan, and wasn't "raised" as a Paranormal, which altered who he grew up to become.

Like Shian, Michael subconsciously sabotaged the efforts of establishing a relationship.

Like Chester, Michael has no conscious memory of time in animal form and struggles with the duality of being so different than the other mammal who lived within.

Like Vlastislav, Michael felt bound by the rhythm of celestial movements that limited him and also lost control when he tried to repress his true nature for too long.

There are other commonalities. But it was important for Michael to be able to see those things in the others before recognizing them in himself.

Isn't that part of the work of therapy—or even speculative fiction? A mirror held up to reality?

But back to what this novel is, and what it isn't.

It's set up to be much like a mystery. And, of course, the title is a play on words of a popular comedic mystery streaming series starring Steve Martin, Selena Gomez, and Martin Short. But the mystery in this novel isn't so much about the "dead body" that appears in the prologue. The real mystery is the round-about discovery of the underlying things Michael has lied to himself about, that he has denied, and that he has repressed.

In several of the books in the series, I got into some deep and traumatic moments. I put Michael through a significant amount of hell.

And this therapy that he begrudgingly undergoes ends up forcing him to face some of those moments as well as some of the things he's spent a lifetime craftily avoiding.

I needed to explore that darkness while maintaining the fun and humor I've always wanted to be a part of the Canadian Werewolf series. After all, no matter what is happening, whenever Michael starts to take himself too seriously, that's when it's game over.

A lot of those aforementioned dark areas are partially parallel and partially tangential to my own life. In the same way that Michael and I have a few things in common, so too are some of the elements that I drew upon for the trauma.

But despite many similarities, most of the details employed in this novel are fiction.

For example, while I am a writer and I did grow up with a fascination for Spider-Man, I've never turned into a wolf, nor spent more than a week at a time in New York City. I've also not yet been a New York Times bestselling author, nor yet had a movie or television series adapted from one of my books or stories.

Like Michael I was adopted. But unlike Michael, it hasn't been a struggle for me. I've read a lot on the subject over the years and did feel like a bit of an outcast because I hadn't felt like I'd been dealt a poor hand. For many, there is trauma associated with that. Feelings of rejection, abandonment, loss, grief, identity, self-confidence, guilt, shame, and intimacy. Adoptees are often at a higher risk for mental health issues that include anxiety, depression, bipolar disorder, ADHD, PTSD, and ODD. The risk of substance abuse is also prevalent.

For the most part, I haven't struggled much with those issues. Or, to put it another way—just to be safe—I either haven't struggled with them or I've repressed it all so deeply that it hasn't yet surfaced in my 54 years.

But when you look at that list of psychological effects, do they sound a little bit like anyone's favorite Canadian lycanthrope who lives in New York City?

I mean, seriously, how could I possibly resist?

I was lucky enough to know and love both my parents and my birth parents. I'm fortunate, and extremely lucky to have had an incredible life, and to have been loved by two sets of parents.

All four of them are wonderful people I am so grateful for. I love them dearly. They are who I dedicated this book to.

Gene and Jean were the father and mother who raised me. I love them and miss them dearly. They are both now deceased, but I did have the privilege of knowing them as an adult and appreciating them not just as parents, but as people. Most of my joys, my sorrows, my pain, my happiness, my fears, my pleasures, they were there for; and I have such powerful memories of the love they had for me as well as for one another. Unlike Michael, I was there when they both passed.

I drove home to be with my father the day before and the day of a serious operation that went south and resulted in his unexpected and tragic loss on the operating room table. I'm so grateful that I overcame the typical toxic masculinity trait of not showing my feelings, and that, in my final moments with him I kissed him and told him I loved him as he walked through those hospital room doors from which he never returned.

Most of the last month of my mother's life was spent sitting by her hospital bedside and either talking for hours, doing work on my laptop while she rested, or slipping out to my car to take calls and engage in video meetings.

I was there, in mind, body, and spirit, when I lost them both. And yet I still feel the guilt that I did not do enough. How could I possibly ever do enough for all they'd done for me? I suppose that's where I pay it forward and attempt to do right by them with my own kid and step-kids.

I met Eddy and Lorraine, my birth parents, when I was in my twenties, so we started off our relationship where they never treated me like a child. We skipped those painful teenage rebellion years and got right on to knowing one another in face-to-face discussions. Sitting down with them as mutual adults was such a remarkable experience I shall always treasure. They accepted me, and loved me, and I was so happy to get to meet them and learn about their unique love story. Not to mention how cool it was that, though I was raised an only child, I not only had a full sister a year younger than me, but six other half siblings. I truly got the best of both possible worlds.

And I'm so lucky I met them before Eddy got sick and eventually passed away. Spending time with him and my siblings throughout the ordeal of his illness, allowed me an opportunity to get to know them all in a more intimate way.

It's funny that I see so much of myself in both Eddy, my birth father, and Gene, the father who raised me. I think they both would have been so proud of the stupid dad jokes I love to share. The two of them relished in making other people laugh. And if that laugh could be accompanied by a solid roll of the eyes, all the better.

I'm also lucky that Lorraine, my birth mother, is still alive and is only a phone call away at any time. She gave me life, and she gave me a life, at a difficult time for her when it would have been so much easy for her to have chosen otherwise. She is sweet, and compassionate, and has an energy and spirit that, if I retain even a small portion of when I'm approaching her age, I'll be thrilled. I love her smile and I love her laugh. In fact, I can clearly remember the sound of the laughs of all four of my parents. Their smiles, and their laughter is music to both my heart and my ears.

All this about them is to say that, unlike Michael, I harbor none of those hard feelings and bitter anger that he continues to struggle with. I feel like I absorbed all the best from all four when it comes to both nature and nurture.

I had some fun inserting meta and self-referential nuggets for long time readers and super fans who are familiar with my other work. There are too many of them to cover, but here are a few you might find interesting.

The story "Impressions in the Snow" is a tale I wrote about a suicidal teenager. It was in a YA anthology edited by Rebecca Moesta called *Sparks* published by WMG Publishing in 2016. That anthology is still available, but the story will also appear in my October 2024 20th Anniversary of the first book I published: *One Hand Screaming*.

Speaking of which, Michael's short story collection *Silent Screams* is a cheeky nod to that collection. It's derived from the introduction of my horror collection *One Hand Screaming* where I wrote: "Silent screams bounce around my head like an impending storm, brewing into a force that will escape in a wild dance of chaos if I don't stop to write them down." That book is also where I first began my practice of sharing behind the scenes author notes specifically for readers. (Something I admired in authors like Piers Anthony and Stephen King).

There are, of course, many other sneaky little details planted in the book that are drawn from the real world and fictionalized. But those are things we might discuss on another day.

As always, writing a book is an intensely solo effort. But it's not without the support and council of so many different people who have helped me along the way—and yes, even if they had nothing to do with this specific manuscript. Here are just a few thank yous. Just know that I'm sure I easily missed a dozen.

To Jan, John, Paul, and many others over the years who have reached out—thank you for always asking for more. And yes, I know, Bridge is one of those characters you want to see return. So do I. She'll be back.

To Scott—thank you for giving Michael such a perfect voice. Your talent as a narrator is matched only by your skill as a science fiction writer and your generosity as a supportive writer friend. I appreciate the extra layer of proofreading you do when I think all those rounds are done.

To Alina—thanks for the random and scattered chats about writing horror and dark fiction, the writer's life in general, the smiles and laughs, and for the assistance with Vlastislav's Romanian roots and language.

To Julie—thanks for talking me off a few ledges while I was stuck on this project and for listening to me, so patiently, when I flailed about. Your honestly, friendship, advice, and reminders of the importance of not stopping at the low-hanging-fruit in my tales or settling on the easy tropes are appreciated more than I can ever effectively express. The work we did together on *Lover's Moon* and *Hex in the City* continues to inspire me to reach deeper and harder and to be both a better writer and a better person. Also, I am bursting at the seams for you to share what Gail Sommers is getting up to on her solo adventures.

To Jeff—your books, podcast, and several of our one-on-one discussions have helped me to up my game when it comes to dialogue. I had a particularly fun time employing several of your strategies in this book. Thanks, Doc.

To Sean—thank you for inspiring me by asking me the questions that make me question myself and the bits of writing that either need more polishing or need to just be put out of their misery and end up on the cutting room floor. I wouldn't even have this series if it wasn't for that first question you asked that pushed me to find something I didn't even know was there.

And finally, to Liz—what can I say? When I began to write Gail as that fictional "ideal woman" years before we even met, I had no idea she would walk into my life. But as Gail continued to develop, and we began our journey together, I realized that you were my own real-life version of that perfect "fated for me" partner. When I'm in the throes of a writing project you not only understand and accept my oddity, but you also patiently listen to my endless and incoherent babbling and become a critical soundboard for that creative energy. And more than anyone you understand the power and intense motivation that comes from true power of a *Last Minute Production*. After all, we are the power couple when it comes to putting PRO in procrastination. We were, like Michael and Gail, destined to meet. Some things, like our love, are just fated to be.

And now, it's time for me to finally put this project to bed. Thanks for letting me bend your ear. I hope you enjoyed reading it as much as I enjoyed writing it.

And thank you for being a reader.

Yours in writing,
Mark Leslie
April 2024

About the Author

Like Michael Andrews, **Mark Leslie** considers himself a beta human. However, unlike his fictional character, Leslie doesn't have an alpha-wolf persona, despite hair growing on his aging body in all the wrong places.

Mark lives in Southern Ontario and can most likely be found behind the keyboard, with his nose stuck in a book, enjoying and tracking craft beer, sharing musical ear-worms and dad jokes, and wandering, awestruck, through bookstores and libraries.

You can learn more about him at **www.markleslie.ca**.

The Canadian Werewolf Series

In Order

This Time Around (Short Story)

A Canadian Werewolf in New York

There Ain't No Cure for the Winter Wolf Blues
(Short Story)

Stowe Away (Novella)

Fear and Longing in Los Angeles

Fright Nights, Big City

Lover's Moon (*with Julie Strauss*)

Hex and the City (*with Julie Strauss*)

Only Monsters in the Building

A Canadian Werewolf in London, Ontario
(Forthcoming)

Selected Other Books by Mark Leslie

Non-Fiction Paranormal
Haunted Hamilton
Spooky Sudbury (with Jenny Jelen)
Tomes of Terror
Creepy Capital
Haunted Hospitals (with Rhonda Parrish)
Macabre Montreal (with Shanya Krishnasamy)

Non-Fiction Trivia/Comedy
The Canadian Mounted: *A Trivia Guide to Planes, Trains and Automobiles*
Yipee Ki-Yay Motherf*cker: *A Trivia Guide to Die Hard*

All books by Mark Leslie:
books2read.com/markleslie